"Jennifer Slattery writes about topics [...] ble, if not taboo. However, divorce, add[...] ns, and perpetual victimhood are very r[...] ip-ples of these life ruiners affect all of [...] do you know who are touched by addic[...]

God alone is the reason I've managed to remain married for nearly 35 years. My hus-band's addiction to alcohol and my issue of self-righteousness drove us to the brink of divorce more than once. Sin is ugly and Satan sets out to steal, kill, and destroy. I'm convinced he doesn't care which one of those derails us. What he doesn't want is truth and light. Slattery, though writing about broken families and difficult subjects, tells the truth. Jesus is the only hope for a hurting world. Healing is available. Lives are saved every day in His economy.

Breaking Free gives glimpses into a marriage bogged down with lies, addictions, and fear. Spanning several months, the reader is given a taste of the horrors of lost control. As Alice's and Trent's lives implode, the story seems hopeless. Deeper and deeper they climb into deception until they both hit bottom. The story ends with hopeful steps. God, in His mercy, doesn't always erase natural consequences. However, sometimes that is the one of the best gifts He gives. In growing and struggling, we are changed into people He can use to teach and help others along the way. God reveals that religion and a whitewashed surface are not the antidotes to death, a real relationship with Jesus Christ is.

There are so many people who could benefit from the reality behind the stories Slattery has woven together."

—KELLY KLEPFER , book reviewer, Novel Reviews

"Slattery reminds us that giving it all to Jesus doesn't magically fix the messiness of this life but leaning on Him gives us peace in the midst of chaos."

—SHANNON TAYLOR VANNATTER, award-winning author

"Jennifer Slattery's book *Breaking Free* will no doubt be an important read to countless many. Today, our 'solid families' deal with private issues—infidelity, alcoholism and drug abuse, wayward children, and gambling disorders. Jennifer's book attacks the latter head-on, with-out pretense or soft shoes. This is what life is all about and this is how God can redeem what seems completely unsalvageable."

—EVA MARIE EVERSON, best-selling, award-winning author of *Five Brides*

"This story is well written and filled with a great message of hope, forgiveness, and renewal. You can feel yourself glued to the story as the characters try to restore what the enemy tried to destroy."

—DEANA DICK, NetGalley Reviewer

"Jennifer Slattery tells an everyday story, throws in a little suspense and faith, and the result is a gripping book with characters taken from real life that has a message: there's always hope in Christ."

—BARBARA TSIPOURAS, NetGalley Reviewer

"*Breaking Free* will seize you by the heart and refuse to let go. Author Jennifer Slattery handles the themes of addiction and marriage—and how the two concepts struggle to coex-ist—with realism and emotion but offers grace and hope for readers who might find it hit-ting close to home."

—CARRIE SCHMIDT, NetGalley Reviewer

Other New Hope books
by Jennifer Slattery

Beyond I Do

Intertwined

When Dawn Breaks

BREAKING FREE

JENNIFER SLATTERY

NEW HOPE® PUBLISHERS
Gospel-Centered. Missions-Driven.

BIRMINGHAM, ALABAMA

New Hope® Publishers
PO Box 12065
Birmingham, AL 35202-2065
NewHopePublishers.com
New Hope Publishers is a division of WMU®.

Library of Congress Cataloging-in-Publication Data

Names: Slattery, Jennifer, 1974- author.
Title: Breaking free : a contemporary romance novel / Jennifer Slattery.
Description: Birmingham, AL : New Hope Publishers, [2016]
Identifiers: LCCN 2015038355 | ISBN 9781596694682 (softcover)
Subjects: LCSH: Married people--Fiction. | GSAFD: Christian fiction. |
Love stories.
Classification: LCC PS3619.L3755 B74 2016 | DDC 813/.6--dc23 LC record
available at http://lccn.loc.gov/2015038355

ISBN-10: 1-59669-468-8
ISBN-13: 978-1-59669-468-2

N164108 · 0416 · 2M1

DEDICATION

To my sweet husband, STEVE SLATTERY,
and our princess, ASHLEY,
I appreciate your continual
encouragement and support.

ACKNOWLEDGMENTS

Every gift, opportunity, or blessing we receive comes from Christ, to be used by Him as He wills and for His glory. I'm so incredibly grateful that He has allowed me to do that which I love—write—to point people to Him and, hopefully, inspire them to find their place in His kingdom work.

I want to thank my husband and mother-in-law for reading through this novel to offer suggestions and feedback. I also want to thank my critique partners, especially Tanya Eavanson, without whom this story wouldn't be nearly as strong. I also want to thank the talented and incredibly patient staff at New Hope Publishers, not only for bringing my novels to print but also for helping me to make them as strong as possible.

CHAPTER 1

This place, these friends—her life—was exhausting. What Alice wouldn't give to hide away . . . indefinitely. And yet here she sat in an upscale Seattle restaurant with her upscale Seattle friends, playing the part, while her latest keynote cycled through her brain again and again. *Authenticity. Transparency. That's the key to the Christian life.*

Right.

Breathing deeply, she glanced around. The quaint little bistro was busier than normal. Wait staff, dressed in white double-breasted shirts, flitted around brightly colored tables, heavily laden trays in their hands. Bottles of wine lined the far wall, their red and green labels adding a splash of color to the exposed brick. Alice raised her fork and nibbled on a piece of chicken, careful not to smudge her lipstick. As she chewed, she studied her friends.

Friends? What a comical word choice. Beth was the only one Alice trusted, and yet she spent countless hours with the others, listening to them go on and on about their passionate marriages and honor roll kids. Either they all lived picture-perfect lives or they were Academy Award winners. Like Alice—always carefully groomed, full of smiles, and positive words. The boys? They were great. Trent, her husband, he was great. Everything was great. Just perfect.

Not.

And the fear that one of them would find out just how imperfect her life was consumed her like a rapidly growing cancer.

Misty, a redhead with glitter-blue eye shadow, grabbed a slice of zucchini bread from the center basket. "We need to meet for lunch more often."

"Speaking of getting together . . ." Beth, a petite blonde with sparkling blue eyes and skin too smooth for a woman in her forties, flashed a smile. "Who's hosting the next women's game night?" She glanced from one face to the next.

Avoiding eye contact, Alice swallowed and tucked her hair behind her ears. Her house was off limits.

Beth's gaze zeroed in on Misty.

She waved her hands in the air. "No way. Not me. I'm still trying to clean the chocolate stains out of my carpet from last time." She threw her hair over her shoulders, exposing large gold hoop earrings.

"Yeah, but you were the one that started flinging the cake around in the first place." Beth dabbed her mouth with a napkin and looked at Alice. "Looks like it's on you."

Alice raised a hand and opened her mouth to protest when someone touched her shoulder. She glanced at the waiter standing over her.

He leaned closer and whispered, "There seems to be a problem with your credit card, ma'am."

Her cheeks burned as everyone looked at her. "What do you mean by problem?"

The kid shifted, eyes darting from face to face. Turning back to Alice, he spoke quieter. "Your credit card company declined the charges." He placed the card on the table.

Alice's stomach dropped. They had a $10,000 limit. She'd done some minor shopping last week, bought a new dress and matching shoes, but nothing big. Unless Trent went on a Saks Fifth

Avenue shopping spree, there should still be plenty of credit left on their account. Certainly enough to pay for a chicken-and-watercress salad.

She pulled her wallet from her purse, flipped it open, and stared at the empty pocket. Where had her $20 gone? Maybe her boys had grabbed it without telling her. So she'd pay with debit.

"Here." She handed her bankcard to the waiter then turned back to her friends with a forced smile. "OK, OK, I'll do it. I'll host the next game night." Anything to get the focus off her and her finances.

Misty's eyebrows raised and Alice could only imagine all the nasty thoughts swirling through her mind, thoughts that would spew out as soon as Alice left the table. Oh, well, let her talk. Let them all talk. Nothing major, probably just a computer error. But when the waiter returned less than five minutes later and said her debit card had been denied as well, Alice felt sick.

"Are you sure?" She pressed her sweaty hands flat on her thighs. "Maybe if you tried it again?"

"I'm sorry, ma'am. Would you like to contact your bank yourself? Perhaps it's a security issue."

She nodded and searched for her phone. "Yes, I am sure that's what it is." She flipped the card lying on the table over and dialed the customer service number on the back. Feeling as if everyone's eyes were boring holes into her forehead, she excused herself from the table with a nod.

After an eternity of elevator music, a man with a deep voice picked up. "Good afternoon. How can I help you today?"

"I'm having trouble with my debit card."

Alice gave the representative her information.

"Hello, Mrs. Goddard. What can I help you with?"

"Yes, there seems to be a problem with my account. Le Petit Bistro informed me that my debit card was denied, and I know that can't be possible. Is there a security concern?"

"Ah, I see. Yes, ma'am, I can help you with this. The charge was denied because you've reached your limit."

"That can't be possible. Could you please tell me the last five transactions?"

"Yes, ma'am. I can help you with this. On March 12 there was a cash withdrawal—"

"Cash withdrawal? What do you mean?"

"Using an ATM."

"For how much?" Alice rubbed the back of her neck as a dull ache crept up her spine.

"Ah, yes. There was a cash withdrawal for $400 made on March 12."

The man continued to list a series of debits made over the past month.

"I don't understand." She gripped the phone tighter. "There must be a mistake. When did these withdrawals first start?"

Computer keys clicked on the other end. The man's voice returned a moment later, and she strained to make out each word. "Two withdrawals were made in February, both for $400, the maximum amount allowed per transaction." There was more clicking. "Three were made in January, again, for the maximum amount." He paused. "How far back would you like me to check?"

She blinked. "You mean there are more than three months worth of withdrawals? That can't be possible." Why hadn't she paid more attention to their accounts?

"Ah, yes. I see. Are you saying that these transactions are fraudulent?"

Of course! It made perfect sense. Alice exhaled, the tension draining from her neck. "They must be."

After a brief lesson on how to file a claim with the fraudulent charges department, she felt much better. Until she remembered her credit card had been declined as well. Grabbing her phone once again, she called the credit card company. Five minutes later, she returned to the table with a sinking feeling in her gut.

"Everything all right?" Misty's plastic smile failed to hide the scorn in her eyes.

"Everything's fine." She set her purse on her lap under the table-cloth so her friends couldn't see her desperate search for cash. Like she would find $15 in spare change. A few bills were tucked beneath a tube of lipstick and 80 cents lay scattered across the bottom among crumpled gum wrappers. Not enough.

Now what? Sure, everything would be straightened out eventually, once she filled out the fraud claims and they found whoever had drained their accounts, but what about now? How would she get out of this mess without humiliating herself further? And how long did she have before the waiter returned?

"I need to use the restroom." She surveyed the restaurant to make sure the waiter wouldn't intercept her. Good, he was five tables down busy with a party of 12.

Beth jumped to her feet. "I'll join you." She reached under her seat and pulled out a massive brown leather purse.

Alice lifted her chin as she made her way around brightly colored wicker chairs.

Once in the bathroom, Beth faced her with wide eyes. "Is everything OK? Do you think someone stole your identity?"

"They had to."

The door swung open and a plump lady with auburn hair and freckles that covered nearly every inch of her face walked in. She smiled, glanced at herself in the mirror, then disappeared behind a stall.

Alice lowered her voice. "That's the only thing that makes any sense." She swallowed, heat crawling up her neck. "You think you could—?"

Beth raised a hand. "Not a problem." She reached into her purse, pulled out a crisp 20-dollar bill and handed it over.

Alice smiled. "Thanks. I'll pay you back."

"Don't worry about it. It's my treat."

She followed her friend back to the table in a daze. The thought of having her identity stolen, of a stranger rummaging through her things, sent a chill through her. She needed to call Trent. Hopefully he had purchased the credit card protection plan.

"I have to get going." She placed the money Beth gave her next to her plate then turned to her friends with a tight-lipped smile.

Misty glanced at her watch. "Me too. I need to stop by Broadmoor Golf Club to pick up my clubs. I had them regripped for the ladies spring tournament this weekend."

Everyone gathered their things and moments later, they stood in the parking lot shielding their eyes from the bright, midafternoon sun.

A cool, spring breeze swept over Alice, making her shiver. She faced the ladies. "This was great. Thanks."

"See you at the gym tomorrow?" Misty pulled a tube of lipstick from her purse.

"Sure. Of course." Alice tried to sound cheerful, but her voice came out flat.

After saying a few hurried good-byes, she walked briskly to her minivan, glanced at her "friends" one last time, then slid into the driver's seat. From the rearview mirror, she watched Misty's pinched expression. No doubt she was just waiting to call up all her gym buddies—to share her latest nugget of gossip.

"Are Alice and Trent having financial problems?"

"Maybe Trent lost his job."

Beth caught Alice's gaze and held it. Looking away, Alice frowned and headed east on Harrison toward Mercer Street. With trembling hands, she phoned her husband. His voice mail picked up.

"Call me. It's important." She rang off and massaged her temples. It didn't make sense. Had someone gone through her purse? She thought of her trashcan tucked beside the house. Her dad always told her to shred everything, but she never listened. Besides, Trent handled the finances, not her.

She worked and reworked a million scenarios as she drove home. Traffic was backed up on the Evergreen Point Floating Bridge, and Alice found herself sandwiched between two semis.

What if whoever had hacked into her and Trent's accounts had gotten hold of the college funds? Did their bank have insurance for this kind of thing? With both boys in high school, Tim in his junior year and Danny a year behind, there wasn't enough time to earn the money back. Then there was Trent's retirement. How many accounts had been stripped? Her pulse quickened as one depressing thought spun into another. By the time she reached home, the flutters in her stomach had turned into full-out cramps.

She checked the time—1:30. Trent rarely returned her calls, not anymore. Maybe he'd shoot her a quick email, one of those one-liners, but that was about it. And trying to talk to him once he got home wouldn't be any easier.

She headed straight to the basement. The scent of old, musty socks wafted from the 12-year-old carpet.

She paused, her hand on the doorframe, to steady her breathing. An empty beer bottle sat on the desk and three more filled the trash.

An image flashed through her mind of Trent's father staggering into Danny's eighth grade graduation so drunk he could barely stand.

She closed her eyes and rubbed her face. *Focus. And drop the pity party.* So Trent drank. A lot of men did. He had a stressful job and two boys about to enter college. This was nothing more than a hiccup. They'd been married for 19 years, had weathered ten moves, three job changes, and the death of Trent's mom. They'd get through this.

Leaving the "cave" as Trent liked to call it, she walked down a short, narrow hallway and into the office. Papers cluttered the heavy antique desk and spilled onto the beige carpet.

She settled into the desk chair. As it was in the "cave," empty beer bottles filled the trash, evidence of Trent's increased drinking.

When did drinking go from a stress reliever to an addiction?

Forcing the question out of her mind, she turned her attention to the computer, typing their bank's name into the browser. Then she paused, trying to remember their login information. *A&TGoddard. No. Seahawks4. No.* After a few more failed attempts, she gave up. She took in a deep breath, released it slowly. *Relax. There has to be an explanation.*

Maybe Trent had recorded their usernames and passwords somewhere. She closed the Internet browser and began rummaging through the desk. A bottle of vodka lay in the top drawer shoved behind a box of envelopes.

Reaching for the bottle, she knocked a picture frame over. It landed on the ground, shattering into pieces. She picked it up and studied the image of her and Trent taken on their wedding day. An easy grin spread across his face, and his dark eyes sparkled as he looked at her. Her heart squeezed as memories of their former love came rushing back. How long had it been since he'd looked at her that way?

How pathetic. The woman who taught others how to build their marriages couldn't hold on to her own.

Her phone rang. She checked the screen and exhaled. "Trent. I've been trying to reach you. Someone must have gone through our trash, or maybe they used one of those card readers or something." The word tumbled out. "I don't know. I can't figure—"

"I took care of it."

She paused and took in a deep breath. "What do you mean?"

"I took care of it. Look, I've got to go. Things are crazy today. I'll see you tonight."

The line went dead. Blinking, she set her phone on the desk and leaned back in the chair. She should feel relieved, right? So why did her nerves still feel charged with electrodes?

Because stolen accounts or not, their life—their marriage—was still a mess.

Cigar smoke burned Trent's eyes and throat. A single lightbulb dangled from the ceiling, casting dark shadows across the hardened faces hovered around the small, circular table.

"What you got, old man?" Henry, a pale kid with bony shoulders that poked through his black T-shirt, studied Trent. He picked up a stack of chips and let them fall to the table one by one.

Trent gulped the last of his Scotch. They'd called his bluff, and now he would pay. Bile soured his mouth as he dropped his cards on the table. "Spot me another hand?" He needed one win, just one.

The tendons in Henry's jaw flexed.

Trent's pulse pounded in his ears, drowning out the steel drums and electric guitar that reverberated through the thin walls. His gaze darted to the metal door separating the back room from the bar. Swallowing hard, perspiration beading on his forehead, he considered making a run for it.

They'd kill him.

Jay, a short, pot-bellied, bushy-browed man with clumps of hair growing out of his ears, dipped his head and Bruce, a man with arms the size of tree trunks, pushed up from the table. His eyes narrowed. Pricks of electricity shot up Trent's spine.

"You saying you ain't got the cash to pay for your losses, man?"

Trent's mind raced. He was broke. Flat broke, so far in the hole he wouldn't be able to claw out no matter how hard he tried. Unless they let him play another hand. Just one more—that was all he needed.

"Pay up." Jay stood. His beady eyes narrowed. "We aint got all day."

Trent rose on shaky legs and shoved his hands deep into his front pockets. Nothing. He wrestled his wallet from his back pocket and flipped it open. Empty. Staring down at the worn leather, his eyes latched onto the shiny gold band encircling his ring finger. How much was that worth? A couple hundred at most. Nowhere near the $2,000 these thugs expected. But at least it'd buy him some time.

He jerked off his ring, and then froze. What was he doing? His wedding ring? The thought sickened him, but what else could he do? Besides, it was only temporary. He'd get a new one soon. Before Alice even noticed it was gone. Releasing his grip on the smooth gold, he tossed it onto the table with a flick of his wrist.

Jay gave a high-pitched cackle, making him sound insane, and maybe he was. He grabbed the band. "What? This like a good-faith offer? Because unless you've got a lot more where this came from, you're gonna be eating your teeth."

Bruce watched his boss, Jay, closely, hands fisted at his sides. Trent's lungs constricted, his breathing quick and shallow. With the slightest nod from Jay, Bruce would unload his 250 pounds worth of muscles into Trent's face.

"There is, I swear." He spoke fast. Where was he going to get the money? How much time would they give him? He'd already blown through his and Alice's savings, and telling them his paycheck was coming wouldn't help.

Jay scowled. "You've got two weeks, with interest."

Bruce uncoiled his hands and stepped aside to allow Trent to pass. Trent took three tentative steps, then spun around and bolted across the room and out into the crowded bar. His eyes fought to focus amidst the throng of gyrating bodies. In his haste, he nearly collided with a waitress carrying a loaded drink tray.

"Sorry."

Once in his car, he slammed then locked the doors, trying to catch his breath. To slow his pulse. He needed a drink. With a trembling hand, he pulled the liquor bottle from the glove box. His taste buds swelled as the cool glass touched his dry lips. The warm liquid bit at his gums and warmed his throat. After taking two more gulps, he tossed it back into the glove box, turned the key in the ignition, and gripped the wheel with clammy hands. This was it. This was the last time he was going to throw away nearly half a month's wages in one night. He was done—for good.

CHAPTER 2

Alice's husband sauntered in well after dark, a dopey smile on his face. The smell of sour whiskey mixed with smoke assaulted Alice's nose, eliciting a gag reflex. As a third-generation drunk, he was becoming just like his father. She tensed as she thought about Tim and Danny. How long would it take before alcoholism got hold of them?

Meeting him in the foyer, she crossed her arms. "Where have you been?"

"What's got you going tonight?" He stared at her for a long moment, and she stared back. "I watched the game with some guys from work." He continued into the living room.

She followed. "This is the third night you've gone out this week. I don't like how much you're drinking."

"So I had a few beers and lost track of time. Who are you, the curfew police?"

"A few beers? You're drunk, Trent."

"Buzzed, Alice. I'm buzzed. Seriously, you need to chill it." He stormed into the kitchen.

She chased after him. "No, I won't *chill it*. We need to talk."

He whirled around, blotches of red coloring his neck. "I said lay off!"

She sucked in a sharp breath and, blinking, froze, acutely aware of his size and strength. These angry outbursts were becoming more frequent. What if he—

No. He'd never hurt her or the kids.

Trent opened the fridge, grabbed a beer, and then slammed the door shut. When he turned around, he nearly ran into her standing a few feet behind him. Pressing his lips into a tight line, he pushed past her and trudged into the living room.

Alice started to follow, then noticed the kitchen window hung open. How far had Trent's voice carried? She shut and locked the window.

Getting emotional would only make things worse. Lifting her chin, she strode into the living room.

Trent lounged in the recliner with his legs extended. He flicked on the television. Alice perched on the edge of the loveseat. She checked the digital clock on the DVD player. Almost nine. The boys would be home soon. Trent was tired. So was she. Talking about his drinking, their failing marriage—about anything—would only lead to an argument.

She huffed and sank into the corner of the couch.

He took a long gulp of beer. Watching her, he stood. "Hey now." He drew closer and held out his hands. When she remained seated, he took hers in his, and lifted her to her feet. "Come on. Don't be mad." He pulled her to him, gentle but insistent, until she finally gave in. "I should've called. Forgive me."

He gripped her waist and peered into her eyes, his breath hot on her mouth. "You know I'd be lost without you, right?" He brushed his lips against her cheek, then her neck, and began to serenade her. "Oh, woman, what you do to me. You've made me such a lovesick guy. Oh, woman what you do to me. Darling, if I were to lose you, you know I'd simply die." His voice turned husky. "I love you way too much, Alice Goddard."

Tears stinging her eyes, she leaned against his strong chest. She stiffened. Was that perfume she smelled?

Now she was being paranoid.

The front door clicked open, signaling her boys' arrival.

"We need to talk. When you're sober." And the boys weren't in earshot. She took a deep breath, which did little to calm her nerves. Walking to the entryway, she met Tim and Danny with a very wide, very forced smile. Tim stood in the hall with his duffel bag draped over his shoulder. Danny tossed his backpack on the ground. They were both covered in dirt and sweat.

Alice surveyed their mud-smeared cloths. "Leave any dirt on the field?" She laughed. "Looks like you had a rough day at practice. Didn't break anything, I hope." She shot Danny a wink.

"Tried not to." A crooked grin spread across Danny's face as he wiped his forehead with his sleeve.

"And you boys studied, right? Like you said you would?"

Mumbling, Tim gave Alice a sideways glance before disappearing around the corner.

Alice followed her boys into the living room where they plopped on the couch. "I'm serious, Tim. Remember our deal. Bring up the grades or no soccer."

Tim rolled his eyes. "We studied."

"Good. Thank you."

Trent flicked Tim's arm. "So, how was practice?"

"Like you care." He stretched his feet in front of him.

Trent frowned. "Drop the attitude, buddy."

"Whatever."

Rubbing her temples, Alice retreated to the kitchen. She gripped the counter with both hands. Fatigue crept up her back and seeped into the base of her skull. When would this blanket of gloom lift?

Late the next morning, Trent scanned the living room, glanced at the front door, then down the hall. The ticking of the clock punctuated the silence. A car approached. He froze, his heart hammering. The vehicle passed and the house went quiet again. He slipped into the bedroom and closed the door. His lungs tightened, his breath coming in raspy spurts.

Alice could return home any minute, or she could be gone for hours. Her schedule was incredibly unpredictable. Best to get in, do what he needed to do, and get out before she returned and started asking a million questions, questions he had no intention of answering.

He closed in on his wife's dresser, and the shiny wooden jewelry box sitting like a neatly wrapped gem on top. He ran his hand across the smooth, glossy wood, his fingers tracing the delicate vines etched into the stained mahogany.

What kind of husband stole his wife's jewelry? The kind who had thugs breathing down his neck, that's who. He had to do this. He had no choice. Not if he wanted to keep both kneecaps.

Swallowing hard, he threw open the box and sifted through Alice's trinkets. Rhinestone earrings lay next to pearl necklaces. The bracelet Tim and Danny gave her for Mother's Day two years ago shimmered in the dim light. Trent fingered the delicate charms dangling from golden links then set it aside. He was desperate but not that desperate. He'd take what he needed and leave the rest alone.

Most of it was costume jewelry worth a few dollars at best, but a few pieces, like the gold bracelet Alice inherited from her great-great-grandmother and the sapphire medallion set in white gold, would get him a pretty price. Enough to buy him a few days, or even better, a few hands of poker. All he needed was one good hand to fix everything.

He squeezed his eyes shut. No more! He was done gambling. It was time he settled his debts and got out. For good.

He selected a handful of jewelry pieces, those that could earn a decent sum without alerting too much attention, and dropped them into a zip-lock bag. After stuffing the bag in his front pocket, he hurried out of the room and to his car. He stowed them in the glove box beneath the car manual until he could find a pawnshop. One that wouldn't rob him blind.

He made it back to work in time for his boss's afternoon "catch-the-vision" pep talk.

Mr. Lowe met Trent in the hallway with a grin. "And in walks our star player." He gripped Trent's shoulder with his powerful hand.

Trent widened his stance and forced a smile.

"Got a whole list of new clients waiting to be dazzled by your creative genius, my man. I'd love it if you'd share what you're doing with the Peak Performance Food project."

Trent blinked. He needed to come up with something . . . anything. No, not just anything. Mr. Lowe expected the best. Normally Trent could deliver no problem, but now . . . His creative juices had evaporated to the point of famine. How could he be expected to create anything, let alone design the biggest campaign of his career, with the threat of severe bodily harm looming over him? But if he didn't get his act together soon, broken kneecaps wouldn't be his only worry.

Alice studied her reflection in the locker-room mirror. When had she become so pale? And contrary to the stylist's promises, her new bob cut didn't take years off her appearance. If anything, it accentuated the wrinkles fanning from her eyes. Next stop? The makeup counter at Macy's for a large container of wrinkle cream. Except that required money.

She glanced at the clock on the locker-room wall. She was late. Tucking her hair behind her ears, she ran up the fitness center stairs to her BOSU class. Whoever invented that plastic half ball and thought it should be used in an aerobics classes suffered from insanity. As did Alice for coming.

She paused at the double doors leading to the gym to watch the other ladies. Most of them were half her age and nearly half her size. The instructor, a young blonde with tight abs and about 18 percent body fat, stood in the center of the room. According to the schedule posted to the wall, this was her third class today, yet the woman didn't have a drop of sweat on her.

Alice glanced at her stomach and tugged at the hem of her T-shirt. Sucking in a deep breath, she threw the doors open and quickstepped to the far corner of the gym. With her rear end to the wall, she could stretch and jump and kick and basically fly all over the place without sending the entire class into fits of laughter.

"Hey, Alice. Over here." Misty stood in the front row waving like an over-caffeinated teenager. She wore a color-coordinated—most likely size six—aerobics suit.

Alice's cheeks warmed as heads swiveled in her direction. *Call attention to the fat, old lady in the baggy exercise clothes. Thanks, Misty.*

She shuffled to the front of the room. A brunette to her right leaned forward and pressed her palms to the ground. She glanced at Alice through her legs and offered a smile.

Misty smacked on a wad of gum. "I left you a message about the women's retreat. Beth keeps nagging me to go. Is it too late to sign up?"

Alice shook her head. "There's still room."

"Cool. I'll talk to the hubs. So, you find out what happened to your accounts?"

Alice set her water bottle on the ground. "Trent took care of it."

Misty's mouth parted like she wanted to say something else when Beth bounded up to them and tossed a large blue duffel bag on the floor. "So, you ready to die a slow, painful death?" She poked Alice in the arm.

Alice grimaced. "Is that a warning or a promise?"

As a BOSU newbie, Alice had yet to make it through an entire class. Usually she floundered after 20 minutes and spent the rest of the time huddled in a corner, gasping. She still felt the effects of the last session. Stairs were a bear. Her obliques were so sore, yawning hurt.

Was it worth all this just to be thin?

"All right, everyone. Let's get warmed up. Jack it out!"

Arms and legs flapped throughout the room like a hip-hop frenzy. Alice felt like a bouncing inflata-ball.

"Three, two, one! High knees—got 16 here!"

She stared at the half ball in front of her. The flat bottom rested on the ground, leaving a smooth mound of rubber on top. She eyed the other women balanced on top of their mounds and shook her head. High knee jumps on a ball? Really? Her arms flailed up and down while her feet sprung from one side of her BOSU ball to the other. Every third bounce, she jumped too far and went flying.

"On the floor for suicides. Let's go! Harder! Faster!" Ms. Bunny Rabbit slid across the gym in wide, sideways steps. "Two minutes here, then squat kicks for two."

Alice shuffled from side to side, bottom out, torso angled to the ground. She crashed into a perky little 20 something to her right. Misty stifled a laugh, her hawk eyes devouring every unfeminine drop of sweat that plastered Alice's hair to the sides of her face like thick strands of cooked spaghetti.

Beth, on the other hand, offered a gentle smile. "You're doing great. Keep it up."

Easy for you to say. You're not the one acting like a human cannonball.

An hour later, Alice sat on the locker-room bench, hot, sticky, and gasping for air. Meanwhile, Beth and Misty looked like a couple of beauty queens.

Beth took a swig of water. "So, you guys wanna come over for lunch today? I've got some amazing leftovers waiting."

"I wish I could." Misty dabbed her neck with a towel. "You know how I love your soggy, day-old tuna sandwiches." She laughed. "Seriously, though, I've got some shopping to do for our trip next week." She cupped her knees with her hands. "You'll never believe where Drew's taking me."

"Where?" Beth asked.

"He's going to wine and dine me at the Le Taha'a Island Resort and Spa. The place is amazing. Did you see the pics I posted on Facebook?"

Alice suppressed a sigh. When was the last time she and Trent had gone somewhere nice? Or anywhere. At this point, even a trip to the hardware store together would seem romantic. If they spoke. To each other. Without fighting.

"Oh, that's right." Beth smiled. "You and Drew are taking a little romantic getaway, aren't you?"

"And would you believe he planned it all? Told me all I need to do is pack my bags and get in the car. He's taking care of everything else."

Beth and Misty jumped into a conversation about steamy date nights, but Alice tuned them out.

"So, what about you, Alice?" Beth took a swig of water. "Want to come over for a bit? We could nail down the schedule for the retreat. Are you giving your 'Set the Tone For Your Home' speech? Because I've got an excellent tie-in."

Alice used her towel to wipe the sweat from her forehead. "I don't know. I really should . . ." What? Do the laundry? Dust the floorboards? Eat another container of cookie dough?

"Oh, come on. Whatever you've got to do, it can wait."

"Yeah, you're right."

Trent pulled up beside a red truck with a dented door and stared at the flashing neon sign in the pawnshop window. The rectangular shed-like building looked ready to fall over. Scanning his surroundings, he glanced at a lady sitting in the truck beside him. Her sallow cheeks caved in as she sucked on a cigarette, eyes locked on the pawnshop door.

Trent tensed and looked away. *I'm nothing like her.* She pawned junk for drugs or booze. He was here for survival. For his family . . . and his kneecaps.

He grabbed the small bag of jewelry from the glove box and headed toward the shop. As he opened the glass door, the stench of mildew and rusted metal flooded his nostrils. A lone florescent bulb flickered from the ceiling and a thick layer of dust covered the small glass window cut into the wall. He paused to give his eyes time to adjust to the dim light.

The pawnbroker, a thick-necked man with a long beard, stood behind the counter inspecting a stainless steel Movado watch. Across from him, a short, squat man in a checked dress shirt watched him closely.

The pawnbroker placed the watch on the counter and folded his arms. "As I said, most I can give you for this thing is $20."

The other man shifted. He glanced outside, frowned, and looked back at the watch. With a loud sigh, he gave the timepiece a shove. "Cash is cash."

The pawnbroker scribbled on a notepad, tore off the top sheet, and handed it to the man along with a crisp $20 bill. "Read the fine print." He placed the watch in a drawer behind him and turned to Trent. "You here to buy, sell, or trade?"

Trent clutched his bag of jewelry tighter. Twenty bucks for a designer watch? How much would this guy give him for his wife's jewelry? Fifty? Seventy-five at most? Not even half of what it was worth. Didn't matter. This was only a hiccup. Once he got paid, he'd settle his debts with Jay for good. The bonus he'd get for the Peak Performance account would take care of everything.

"I'm here to sell." Trent poured the contents of his bag on the counter. The pawnbroker rummaged through Alice's most prized possessions, some of which had been in her family for over three generations.

"How much you asking?" The guy inspected a Victorian bracelet given to Alice by her great-grandmother.

"Three hundred?"

The man snorted. "I'll give you $35. Two hundred for all of it."

Trent shifted and pressed his palms against the smooth glass. Two hundred dollars for high-class, antique jewelry? But what choice did he have? Besides, he'd get it back, soon, before Alice noticed it was gone. He'd even pick her up a little something, like maybe one of those topaz rings or pendant necklaces displayed beneath an adjacent glass counter.

He took a deep breath and looked the man in the eye. "All right."

"You planning on buying it back?"

"Yeah."

The guy shoved a pawn ticket and pen at him. "Read and sign."

Trent strained to read the fine print. Buy back price was double, with a 40 percent interest rate tagged on and a $20 monthly "storage" fee. He grabbed the pen and scribbled his name across the bottom.

"If you're not back in 60 days, it gets sold."

CHAPTER 3

Trent's eyes blurred as he stared at his blank computer screen. The ticking of the office clock set him on edge, reminding him of his upcoming deadline.

Laughter floated down the hall, stealing his concentration. He jumped up, slammed the door shut, then fell against the chair. What was wrong with him? He'd been with Innovative Media Solutions for going on 20 years and had accumulated numerous awards, so many, his co-workers had begun to call him *the man with the golden keyboard*.

Leaning back, he eyed the plaques lining the far wall. In 2001 he won the Palmer Awards for Creative Web Design. In 2002 his record-setting productivity earned him the title of Innovative Media Solutions's Graphic Designer of the Year. In 2003, 2004, and 2005, the American Graphic Design Association nominated him for the Golden Keyboard. Years' worth of accolades, and all he had to show for it was a bottomed-out bank account and a pile of expectations cluttering his desk.

He needed a drink. He pulled open his desk drawer and fished around the envelopes and Post-it notes until he felt the smooth glass of the vodka bottle. With a glance to the door, he pulled it out, and took two esophagus-burning swigs. The tingle of his taste buds mirrored the electric cravings that shot through his nervous system. Fighting against an urge to down the entire bottle, he shoved it behind a box of paper clips and shut the drawer.

The phone rang, a welcomed distraction.

"Trent, my man." Arnold, an old college friend and poker buddy. "What are you doing tonight?"

"I don't know. Why?"

"The crew's getting together at Matthew's for one last hand before Nathan leaves for Thailand."

The "crew" was comprised of a bunch of friends from the University of Washington. They used to meet in each other's dorm rooms every Friday night for penny poker. Over time, the stakes got higher, especially when liquor was involved.

Trent thought of Alice waiting for him at home. "I can't make it. Not tonight." He squeezed his eyes shut and pinched the bridge of his nose.

"Whatever you've got going on, blow it off. Stay for a few beers, play a couple of hands."

His pulse quickened as memories of big wins filled his mind. He flipped open his wallet and pulled out a photo of him and Alice. "I told you, I'm not coming." He cradled the phone in his neck to type a response to a recent email sent by Mr. Lowe outlining a new expense account policy. Starting May 1, every claim over $10 needed a receipt. So much for padding the reports. Maybe playing a few hands of poker wasn't such a bad idea after all.

"Mr. Deal-'em-and-cash-'em's gonna turn down a sure win?" Arnold laughed. "Don't you remember all the green you left with last time?"

Yeah, he did remember, every win. Unfortunately, memories of his countless losses weren't nearly so vivid.

"Seriously, bro. This may be our last chance to get together, all of us. I have a feeling Nathan's three-year gig might turn permanent."

"So I'll send him a postcard." Trent gripped the phone tighter. *Just one more hand. One more win.* He gritted his teeth in an effort to increase his self-control. *No! No more!* Beads of sweat broke out on his forehead.

"Oh, I get it. Wife's got you on a ball and chain, huh? Little Trenty-poo can't get away."

"Ha ha ha. Very funny." He rubbed his face. One game wouldn't hurt. Besides, what if this was it? The one time he hit it big. The law of averages said his win was coming. "All right. All right. But just for an hour."

"That's my man. See you tonight."

Trent hung up and massaged his temples. This was his last game, period.

The rest of the afternoon crawled by. He pecked at his keyboard and sifted through various ads and photos scattered across the desk hoping for a spark of inspiration. Nothing helped. His brain was blank. By five, he was more than ready to head to Matthew's. A few beers and some time with the boys would do him good.

He started to gather his things when the phone rang. He glanced at the number displayed on the screen. Alice.

"Hi. Whatcha' got?" He checked the clock again.

"What time do you think you'll be home? I wanted to know when to start dinner."

"I'm running a little behind."

"Oh." She paused. "So, how long will it take you to catch up?"

"I don't know. Maybe eight o'clock." That'd give him time for a few hands.

She sighed. "Great, if you stick to it."

Slumping, he rubbed his forehead. "I'll be there."

After answering three more emails, he snapped his laptop shut and shoved it into its carrying case. Rounding his desk, he paused. Mr. Lowe's voice drifted down the hall. Trent froze and held his breath. When the door swung open a moment later, he picked up a magazine from a nearby end table and flipped through the pages. He watched his boss out of the corner of his eye.

Mr. Lowe eyed Trent's computer bag. "You heading out already? I thought you'd be burning the midnight oil, all things considered."

Trent closed the magazine. "I need to stop by Centinell to pick up some files."

Mr. Lowe nodded. "I forgot all about the Centinell brochures." He looked at Trent's desk. "You juggling everything all right? Because I could always throw a few projects Rick's way. It'd allow you to give 110 percent to the Peak Performance campaign."

He stiffened. He needed those accounts, every one of them. "I'm good. I've got it all under control."

Mr. Lowe gave him a thumbs-up sign as Teresa from accounting poked her head in the door.

"Do you have a minute, Mr. Lowe?"

Trent used the opportunity to make his escape before his boss could throw any more questions his way.

"I'll see you Monday." He maneuvered past them and hurried down the hall, through the lobby, and into the elevator. He rode it to the seventh level of the parking garage.

His phone rang as he was getting into his vehicle. He checked the number. Leila, the marketing rep for Tri-City Residentials, for the third time this week. She probably wondered why she hadn't received her promo materials yet. He'd call her on Monday and tell her they were on the way. Right after he emailed the files to the printer.

Letting the call go to voice mail, he eased out of the parking garage and onto Broadway. Men and women in business attire, satchels slung over their shoulders, cell phones to their ears, thronged the sidewalks while hipsters wearing boots and backpacks wove around them. A man in a cotton candy pink suit danced his way across the street. A few pedestrians shot the man a curious look, but most of them continued, unmindful.

Thanks to a six-car pile-up on the freeway, Trent joined the bumper-to-bumper traffic, turning a 20-minute jaunt into a nerve-wracking 50-minute crawl. By the time he made it to Matthew's, the game was already underway.

"Hey, man, thought you blew us off." Arnold tossed a chip at Trent.

"Traffic." He nodded to the other guys gathered around Matthew's coffee table and settled between Nathan and Arnold. "Spot me?"

With a crooked smile, Arnold cocked an eyebrow. "What, the wifey didn't give you your allowance?"

Trent scowled. "I didn't have time to hit the bank. Give it up, already."

Arnold slapped a $20 bill on the table. "You're going down, my friend."

He glanced at a six-pack sitting at Matthew's feet. "You hoarding or what?"

Mumbling something about money-grabbing, beer-guzzling moochers, Matthew threw him a beer.

Things started slow with conservative bets and few raises, but by the second six-pack the stakes rose and Trent quickly quadrupled his initial $20. He checked the clock—8:15. He was late. Alice was waiting for him, but he was on a roll. It'd be foolish to walk away now. He'd play one more hand. That'd put him home by 8:45, maybe a little after. No big deal. He'd tell Alice he'd gotten stuck in traffic or that a meeting had run late.

The game continued for two more hours, Trent's winnings increasing with each hand, the familiar surge of adrenaline flooding his veins. Fighting a smile, he sifted his chips through his fingers. It felt good to win. Real good.

"This is lame." Matthew downed the rest of his beer. He shot Trent a sour expression and stood.

"I agree." Nathan slid his cards to the center of the table and stretched his arms in a mammoth yawn. "It's been fun, but I gotta jet."

Yawning, Arnold dropped his cards.

Trent's pulse quickened. "Come on, one more hand?"

"Sorry, man. Maybe next time."

One by one the guys said their good-byes and pushed away from the table. Matthew walked them to the door then returned. Trent hovered over his winnings like a crazed hyena.

"Listen, man"—Matthew tossed some empty beer bottles into a wastebasket—"It's been fun and all, but the party's over. Next time?"

"Yeah, whatever." Trent stood and shoved his cash into his pockets, his fingers closing around the crumpled bills. This was nothing. Next time he'd clean house.

CHAPTER 4

Alice checked her watch. Could this meeting drag on any longer? Choose a color already. "You know, I bet Saundra's Boutique will handle all our decorations for a reasonable price. Would you like me to contact the owner?"

"I don't know." Jude, a lady with short, silver hair, fiddled with a tulle centerpiece sample she'd brought. "We've always made our own decorations. It's a tradition and a great way to encourage some of our younger women to get involved. Besides, it saves money."

"Doesn't hurt to call, though." Beth jotted notes on her legal tablet. "And I'll ask Mirah if she's up for making cheesecakes. I think 30 ought to be enough. What do you think?"

Heads bobbed, and they moved to the next item on their agenda—the keynote.

Alice flipped through her three ringed binder, years' worth of notes scribbled in the margins. "You know, maybe we should change our focus this year."

Jude cocked her head. "What do you mean? You don't like the theme we agreed upon?"

"No, the theme is fine, but I've been talking about authenticity and transparency for almost a decade. As important as that is, perhaps it's time we touched on some other needs."

Beth propped her elbow on the table and rested her chin in her hand. "Hm . . . like what?"

"I don't know. There are so many things we haven't addressed like time management, healthy living. That might draw some of the younger ladies."

"Oh, like a battle of the bulge deal!" Wendy, a larger woman with a square jaw and long, thick hair nodded. "I think that's a great idea. We could change the name to 'Grabbing Hold of the New You.'"

"I say we talk about surviving the in-laws." Eileen, a petite brunette and the youngest on the team, slapped her pen onto the table. "Did I tell you about our last family reunion? Sam and I were about to go for a hike. You know how we—?"

Alice suppressed an eye roll, not in the mood for one of Eileen's elaborate stories.

Luckily Jude cut her off before her story became too dramatic. "I remember, and I've been praying for you." She gave a tight frown. "That your in-laws would see God's *love* and *grace* through every encounter."

Eileen's mouth went slack, then closed, her gaze falling to the paper in front of her.

Jude cleared her throat. "It's already mid-April, ladies. At this point, we don't have time to make any major changes. I say we stick with our agenda."

Beth nodded. "I'm not up for rewriting our outline. Besides, we're addressing a real need here. In fact, I think we should expand our focus by adding breakout sessions. Alice, want to help me write up some discussion questions?"

Not exactly, but what came out was a mumbled, "Yeah, sure."

"All right then. Let's tackle our assigned tasks, and I'll call you all in three weeks or so to set up our next meeting. Sound good?"

The ladies voiced agreement, then closed in prayer. While Jude asked God to bless their event and prepare the hearts of their audience, Alice picked at her pinky nail. Her plan to weasel out of the ladies fellowship luncheon had failed, leaving two options: slip further into her hypocrite role or find some way to radically transform her marriage.

Of course, there was a third option—switch churches, a rather tempting thought.

Alice opened the freezer and pulled out a package of steaks. She put them back. Why bother? Trent wouldn't make it home in time for dinner, and her boys preferred frozen burritos.

Part of her wanted to call Trent, tell him what a loser of a husband he was, but that'd only make things worse. There was no sense throwing a pity party, either. So he'd be late. What did she care? Besides, there were a lot of loveless marriages. Why should hers be any different? Except that she did love her husband. No matter how hard she tried not to, she loved him as much now as the day they married. But would he say the same?

The thick silence in the house pressed down on her. She grabbed her cell and clicked on the radio app. Closing her eyes, she hummed along to Lionel Richie's soothing voice until the tension seeped from her neck and shoulders.

Her phone chimed. A text from Tim flashed on the screen.

Going to Sean's to study for a biology test.

She responded: *Good for you! Be home by nine, please.*

Hopefully these recent study dates would stop Tim's downward spiral. In two semesters, he'd gone from B honor roll to barely scraping by.

She trudged back into the kitchen and sifted through the freezer. *Häagen-Dazs, where are you when I need you most?* Alice settled for a frozen Lean Cuisine from under a frostbitten bag of peas.

Now maybe she could skip BOSU class tomorrow.

Shoving the meal into the microwave, she hit what had become her most frequently used button on her most frequently used appliance—frozen dinner. She pulled it out a minute and a half later and started to pour a glass of tea when the front door creaked open. Her gaze shot to the clock on the microwave—7:30. It couldn't be Danny. He was at the Y lifting weights, and Tim wouldn't be home for another hour and a half. Her heart skipped a beat as the only other option came to mind.

Trent stood in the doorway with a bouquet of rosebuds, laughter bubbling in his throat. His back pockets bulged. A wad of cash occupied one and his wife's recently recovered jewelry the other. His paycheck, and a lofty commission from some past accounts, came just in time. A few more checks and he'd catch his breath, as long as he didn't get fired first. Everything rode on the Peak Performance Foods account. It'd make or break him—fill his bank or send him packing.

"Alice?"

She rounded the corner and looked from the roses to his face. An unreadable expression clouded her eyes. Confusion? Curiosity? It didn't matter. She was here, he was here, and based on her soft expression, their marriage wasn't over . . . yet.

Trent smiled and held out the flowers. Taking them, Alice brought them to her nose. She closed her eyes as she inhaled. When she lifted her gaze to meet his, Trent's chest warmed. Her shiny black hair accentuated her creamy complexion, a slight pink coloring her cheeks. So beautiful.

"What's the occasion?"

"Who needs an occasion when you've got such a radiant wife?" He moved closer and grazed her face with his knuckles, her skin soft against his.

She smiled, but then, in an instant, her face hardened. Trent glanced around and tried to ignore the obvious distrust in her eyes. The smell of chicken and garlic filled the room.

"You eat already?" So much for his plan to pull a Romeo.

"Huh? No . . . I . . ." She turned and headed toward the kitchen. Trent followed a few steps behind and watched her pick up a plastic tray of food. She shoved it into the fridge next to a gallon of milk, then placed the flowers in an old mason jar. A moment later, she returned to the freezer and fished through packages of frozen vegetables and slabs of meat.

Trent encircled her waist with his hands, breathing in her vanilla shampoo. "I know I've been a real bear lately, and I want to make it up to you."

She turned and stared at him.

"I've made reservations at Cutters. What do you say?" One of her favorite restaurants, it overlooked Seattle's waterfront and stood half a block short of Pike Place Market. With windows stretching the length of it, one could watch the fog roll in across Elliot Bay, seagulls circle the pier, and local runners weave through the throng of tourists. Not to mention it had the best mahi around, Alice's favorite.

Her mouth parted, then closed, her lips hovering between a smile and frown. He watched her kaleidoscope of emotions with growing frustration. He almost told her to forget it—to enjoy her nice little frozen dinner all by herself—but then her face brightened.

"That sounds wonderful. Just give me a minute to freshen up." She turned and strolled toward their bedroom.

"No." He grabbed her arm with more force than he'd intended.

She spun around, eyes wide.

Loosening his grip, he forced a smile. "You're beautiful the way you are." Slipping his arms around the small of her back, he brought her close, nibbling her ear. "You wait here. I'll get you a sweater. It's a tad chilly tonight."

She pulled away and looked up at him. "Thank you."

Trent exhaled. That had been close. He dashed to their bedroom and emptied his pocket full of Alice's jewelry back into her box. For good. He would never hock her things again. Never.

Sitting by the window, Alice watched the Ferris Wheel lights through the thick evening fog as it made it's lazy rotation, remembering a warm summer night some 20 years ago when she and Trent had waited atop. His deep-set eyes, intense beneath thick eyebrows, stole her heart. And that was when he'd proposed—with Elliot Bay below them and the Seattle skyline lighting up the horizon. Then, they'd spent the rest of the evening walking hand-in-hand along the pier, sipping lattes and talking about what the future held for them. His focused gaze and subtle charm made her feel cherished and beautiful. Like she felt now.

Trent promised to give her the world, and for a while, he had. Until alcohol sank its claws into him. Sipping her coffee, she watched her husband as he read his menu. With his square chin, thick eyebrows, and easy smile, he was just as handsome now as the day they had met. But despite the beautiful décor, her nerves refused to settle.

"This is wonderful, Trent. But . . . can we afford this?"

"You worry too much. We're fine." His gaze swept across her face and lingered on her lips. "I had almost forgotten how beautiful you are." He leaned forward.

She closed her eyes and shivered as he caressed her face, continuing to the base of her neck.

R & B music played above the steady hum of conversations. Across from them sat a table of five—an older couple and three girls who looked to be of college age. The rich smell of garlic and teriyaki filled the air.

She fiddled with her fork. "There's a couple's retreat next weekend. At the Marriot Waterfront. Want to go?"

"I have a better idea." He brought her hand to his mouth, his warm breath tickling her skin. "Why don't we go to the mountains? Just you and me?"

"That's a great idea. When?"

He pulled his phone from his shirt pocket and studied the screen. "I'll have to get back to you on that. Maybe next month. July at the latest."

Alice pushed a piece of broccoli around her plate. Next month would turn into next year, then the following, until he forgot the promise entirely.

He lifted his Scotch glass, swished it, then took a drink. "So, what'd you do today?"

She chewed a piece of steak to buy time while her emotions raged. She wanted to leave—him, this restaurant, the anger that flooded over her like a tidal wave. And she wanted to stay, to drink in his throaty compliments and allow his hungry eyes to devour her.

"I met with the women's ministry committee to plan the final details for the ladies social."

"You speaking again?"

"Unless I can find a way to get out of it."

"You'll do great. You always do."

Tracing a droplet of water on the outside of her glass with her finger, she watched an older couple sitting at an adjacent table. The man sat hunched over, focused on his plate. Frowning, the woman's gaze swept across the room. They ate in silence.

She turned back to Trent. "So, what about you? How was your day?"

"Same ol', same ol'." He gulped down the last of his Scotch, then opened his mouth wide to allow an ice cube in. It clanked against his teeth as he rolled it over his tongue. He spit it back. "Mr. Lowe asked me to take on some new clients."

He stopped the waiter as he walked by and lifted his empty Scotch glass. "Add another one, will you?"

A band of pale flesh circling Trent's ring finger caught Alice's eye. "What happened to your wedding ring?"

A man took off his ring for one reason. Her stomach soured as a mouthful of food lodged in her throat.

Trent blanched and stared at his hand. "I lost it. The guys and I hit weights over lunch, and I took it off before lifting—gym policy. You ever seen what can happen to a finger when the ring gets caught?" He grimaced. "Anyway, I could've sworn I dropped it in the outer pocket of my duffel bag, but I searched everywhere." He reached for his glass. "I left my number, in case anyone turns it in."

Why didn't she believe him? "What about our finances? Did they ever send us new cards?"

He flicked a hand. "I told you I'd take care of it and I did."

She stiffened. "I'm just trying to understand."

He leaned forward and placed his hand over hers. "As I said, you worry too much. It's almost like you don't trust me." He scanned the room, made eye contact with the waiter, and raised his glass. The kid frowned over an armload of dirty dishes and nodded. Trent turned back to Alice. "But I know you're just stressed, with women's ministry events and all."

She studied her husband. Something didn't feel right, though she wasn't sure whether her distrust was warranted or was simply the result of a dying marriage. Either way, it was past time she addressed their problems. "We need to talk."

"Again? Come on, Alice. Everything's fine."

"No, it's not. You've changed, Trent. The drinking, the staying out late. This isn't working. We need help."

He studied her for a long moment—evidence that he was actually listening for once?

"I'm sorry. Things have been crazy at work. I've been so stressed out, so focused on my accounts, and I guess I just . . ." He sighed. "I've been a real a jerk." He cupped her chin and ran his thumb across her mouth. "I love you, sweetie. More than the world. You know that, right?"

I'm not so sure anymore.

She dropped her gaze to her plate, lined the edge of her knife with the edge of her napkin.

Touching her chin again, he lifted it until her gaze met his. "I'm trying here. I really am trying. Can't we just relax and enjoy our evening?"

"We need counseling."

He tensed. "No, what we need is to reconnect. Without fighting."

This was getting her nowhere except heading toward a fight. And besides, he was right. They needed this time together, if only to remember why they fell in love in the first place.

She smoothed her napkin in her lap. "So, tell me more about this project that Mr. Lowe has you working on."

"This is the biggest account we've had in some time. And"—he rested his forearms on the table—"if all goes well, I have a feeling I'll be seeing a promotion, along with a hefty raise."

"Oh, Trent, that's great."

The rest of the meal progressed pleasantly. They talked about the boys, Trent's career aspirations, and where they were going to spend their romantic getaway.

"We could go to the San Juans, maybe do some crabbing?" Alice wrapped both hands around her coffee cup, the warmth spreading through her.

Just then, the waitress approached with their dessert—bacon bread pudding, the flavor of the day. They normally ordered the crème brûlée, but when the waitress mentioned a dessert with bacon, Trent had insisted they try it.

"Look at that." Trent laughed, grabbing his fork. "Bread, bacon, sweet. It's like having breakfast for dinner."

"Exactly." The waitress smiled, then glanced at Alice's mug. "Want more coffee?"

"That'd be nice, thanks." She watched Trent slice into the delicate mound then dipped her spoon into vanilla ice cream drizzled with caramel, resting on top of white chocolate chunks. "So, what do you think?"

"About?"

"Visiting the San Juans?" They'd been there twice, once for their first night away after baby, and the second time for their tenth anniversary. Maybe going again would stir up old memories, restoring things to the way they used to be.

"What about Lummi Island?" Trent asked. "We could rent a cottage, have dinner at The Willows."

"Oh, Trent, that would be wonderful." She wanted to ask again if they could afford it—The Willows was a world-renowned restaurant, with a price to match—but she didn't. If a luxurious weekend getaway saved their marriage, it'd be worth it.

CHAPTER 5

Trent's heart thrashed as he made his way to the bar. Men in base-ball caps gathered in front of a flat screen television whooping and hollering while ladies sat around tall, circular tables sipping martinis and daiquiris. He squeezed between a woman with bouncy curls and a man in a pinstriped suit, his gaze darting from the bartender to the metal door on the far wall.

The bartender handed a glass of wine to a slender woman with short blond hair, then turned to Trent. "Can I help you?"

He leaned forward, his voice barely above a whisper. "I'm here to see Jay."

The bartender's eyes narrowed. "He expecting you?"

He nodded. "Tell him Trent's here."

The man turned to a girl in a red tank top and frayed jean shorts. He motioned to his customers with a jerk of his head. "You got this?"

She rolled her eyes. "Yeah, whatever."

Rounding the counter, he wove through the crowd and then disappeared behind the thick metal door. Trent followed and waited, pulse racing. A few seconds later, the door opened and the bartender's emotionless face appeared. Holding the door ajar, he motioned for Trent to go in.

Smoke clouded the 10-by-15-foot room. Jay's guys huddled around the poker table drinking and smoking while Jay occupied a desk in the back. A pudgy kid in ripped jeans and a baggy T-shirt stood in front of him, his bony arms quivering at his sides. Stacks of cash lay spread across the desk next to a torn manila envelope.

Bruce, Jay's thug for hire, stood, one eye on his boss, the other on Trent. The muscles in his arms bulged as if charged for a fight.

Jay shoved a white package at the kid in front of him. "Don't make me wait so long next time."

The kid's head bobbed like an ocean buoy at high tide. He took three steps backward, spun around, then bolted out the door.

The hair on the back of Trent's neck stood on end as Jay's gaze landed on him. "You got my money?"

As if on cue, Bruce closed the distance between them. Trent swallowed, his eyes narrowing on the man's clenched fists. He stepped backward and held out his wad of cash. "It's all here."

Jay and Henry rose and walked toward Bruce until the three of them stood shoulder to shoulder. Their hard eyes darkened. If only Trent had stuck with penny poker, he wouldn't be in this mess.

Bruce grabbed the cash from Trent's trembling hand and counted the bills one by one. When finished, he handed it to his boss and stepped aside.

Jay's scowl eased into a thin-lipped smile. "I always knew you were smarter than you looked."

Trent exhaled as his tightly coiled muscles relaxed. It was over. He turned to leave, but Jay placed a heavy hand on his shoulder.

"So, what do you say? Wanna give it another whirl? I'd hate to see you walk out of here empty handed."

Trent glanced from the thick wad of cash to the tall stacks of chips on the table. He swallowed hard. Two thousand dollars was a lot of money. If he could win it back . . . Just thinking about it flooded his veins with adrenaline. Except this wasn't bingo night, and if he lost . . .

Trent shuddered. "I don't know."

Jay flipped through the wad of cash again, slower this time. Trent's eyes followed the movement of every bill. At the table, a man wearing a long-sleeved flannel shirt and thick glasses sifted poker chips through his hand. He wore his ball cap pulled low, tufts of hair curling up beneath it.

Trent swallowed again and shifted. Logic said turn around, walk away, and never come back . . . but . . . $2,000 would go a long way.

"What do you say?" Jay rubbed the back of his hand under his neck. "Feeling lucky tonight?"

He'd be a fool not to. Besides, he'd only play a couple of hands. Just enough to get a little green. "Yeah, I think I am."

He moved to the table and sat between Henry and an older man he'd never met before. The guy, who looked to be in his late sixties, shot Trent a nervous glance then stared at the table. He twitched like a jackrabbit.

Jay lowered himself into an empty seat across from Trent, grabbed a filled glass, and took a loud slurp.

Bruce handed him a deck of cards, and Jay shuffled.

Trent wiped clammy palms on his pants. What was he doing here? *Walk away, now, before you bury yourself.*

"Ante up. We're betting $500."

The kid next to Trent pushed his seat back. "This one's too rich for my blood."

Jay eyed the guys. Two stayed in the game, two bailed. Trent rubbed the back of his neck. Five hundred was a lot of cash, but $2,000 was more.

He tossed a chip on the pile. "I'm in."

Jay dealt everyone five cards, face down, then set the remainder of the deck on the table.

Trent surveyed his hand. No pair. King high and a Jack. Could be better. He studied Jay. His dark eyes, shadowed by heavy brows, were unreadable.

Jay tossed another chip on the pile. Trent licked his dry lips. Was he willing to risk a thousand on a King and Jack?

The kid to his left dropped his cards. "I'm out."

A bead of sweat snaked down Trent's temple. It was down to him, Jay, and a punk with peach fuzz on his face. Which meant he had a one in three chance of winning.

"We're growing webs, man." The kid leaned back and drummed his fingers on the table. "Pay it, or eat it."

Trent straightened and squared his shoulders in an attempt to look confident. The kid acted cocky, like he held a royal flush. Cocky usually meant loser. But then there was Jay, and Jay was a slab of ice.

He glanced at the clock. 7:15. He didn't have time to waste on a losing hand. "I fold." He'd catch 'em on the next one. And then he'd get out of here.

Unfortunately, his next set of cards weren't much better. A pair of tens and a Queen high. Not bad, but worth risking $1,000? He had to at least get his $500 back. Besides, a man could only get so many rotten eggs.

"I'll see your five and raise you ten." He tossed two chips down. The stakes had risen to $2,000.

Jay leaned forward and sifted his chips through his fingers. "I call."

Trent's hand shook as he showed his cards. The man to his right cursed and threw down a pair of deuces with an Ace high.

The corners of Jay's mouth curled into a sinister smile as he placed two pair, Jacks, and sixes on the table. Eyes on Trent, he leaned forward and scooped up the pile of chips.

Trent's throat constricted. The ticking of the clock grated against his ears. 7:40. 7:41. He had time for one more hand. Just one more.

CHAPTER 6

Alice's mind wandered as she fiddled with the lace doily under her iced tea while Amanda, the youngest member of the Bible study group, complained about how frustrating it was to have a two-year-old running around the house.

After her romantic dinner with Trent, she'd hoped things would get better. And they had, for a few days, but then his anger had returned. Almost worse than before. Any talk of a romantic getaway had been quickly forgotten. She'd tried to talk to him, once again asked to go to counseling. But he wouldn't listen, kept attributing everything to stress, saying things would get better, that he'd try harder.

It's not supposed to end up like this. Not for us.

"Alice, you're awful quiet today." Beth rested her forearms on the table. "What do you think of the passage? What do you do to build your home?"

Alice shifted. "Wow, great question, Beth. I try to stay involved in the boys' lives. Make sure they know I am always there for them."

She relaxed when Renee interjected. "I like to plan fun family stuff, like going to Seattle Center or for a bike ride. Oh, and the kids and I craft together. As for my marriage . . ." She frowned and tapped her chin. "I haven't figured that one out yet. Josh likes to watch sports, or go to sporting events. Or talk about sporting events."

Everyone laughed, then launched into a discussion on ways to make your husband and kids a priority without spending one's life in the kitchen. Or folding laundry, although, according to Beth, leaving one's house a complete mess wasn't ideal.

Alice folded her napkin into tiny squares. When had she last cooked Trent's favorite meal or baked him a pie? Or given a compliment, for that matter. So much had changed over the past 19 years. Her mushy love notes, tucked inside his home-packed lunches, had given way to hurried emails. Romantic dinners had disappeared completely. Was it too late to save their marriage? Did she even want to?

"What about you, Alice?" Once again, Beth snatched her gaze and held it. "What are some ways to juggle motherhood and marriage? How can we keep up the romance when there's always a little one underfoot?"

Alice ran the nail of her index finger along the outer edge of her napkin. How to keep the flame going? Oh, there were plenty of flames at her house, but not any they'd want to hear about. "I . . . I'm not sure if I should answer that, Beth." Speaking in a sugared tone, she tilted her head and batted her lashes.

Everyone giggled and Alice turned to Amanda in an effort to divert the attention off herself to someone more interesting, or perhaps more emotionally stable. "I would love a copy of your brownie-pie recipe. It was very good." To add credence to her statement, she sliced her fork through the nearly untouched desert on her plate and brought it to her mouth. It stuck to her tongue like a thick, gooey blob of mud.

Before long everyone—well, almost everyone—started talking about food again, followed by a discussion on the latest diet fads.

The moment the closing prayer ended, Alice jumped up, gathered her things, and dashed for the door.

Unfortunately, Beth stepped in front of her and blocked her way. "You want to help me clean up?"

Alice watched the other ladies scurry out of the room. A few of them stopped to toss their paper plates in an overflowing trash can tucked against the wall, but most of them were too engrossed in conversation to notice the mess.

"Yeah, sure." She checked her watch, not because she had to be anywhere but because she wanted Beth to think she did.

"Did you try Suzie's coffee cake? That cinnamon streusel topping was amazing."

"It was very good, and probably requires a few more hours of BOSU class." Alice picked up a wrinkled napkin.

"Hey, thanks for coming." Beth paused to say good-bye to the last of the ladies. When the door shut behind them, she cornered Alice with an I-know-something-is-up look. "You going to tell me what's going on or do I need to figure it out?"

Alice grabbed a paper plate as her mind raced for an answer. How much should she tell her? Or, better yet, how little could she get away with telling her? Knowing Beth, not much.

She forced a smile that made her cheeks ache. "Nothing. I promise. I would tell you."

"Come on, Alice. Be real with me. I know you better than that."

Before she could protest, Beth pulled a chair out from the table and guided Alice into the seat. Neither one said anything for quite some time.

"Are you and Trent having problems?"

Alice blinked, heat climbing her neck.

Beth leaned forward and covered Alice's hand with her own. "His church attendance has been . . . sporadic, and I know he's not going to the men's group anymore."

"He's been busy."

"Ed said he saw him leaving a bar on Denny Way last week."

Alice inhaled sharply, remembering the white band of flesh where

Trent's wedding ring should have been. What else had Ed seen?

"Have you thought about going to counseling?"

"We're fine."

"Alice, don't shut me out. And don't isolate yourself. Get help, before it's too late."

Trent rolled onto his side, back to the door, and pulled the pillow over his head.

"Get up." Alice shoved his shoulder. "We're going to be late."

The morning sun poured through the slits in the blinds like laser beams. He squeezed his eyes shut and rubbed them with his fists.

Alice paced the room, banging dresser drawers and rattling closet hangers. Nothing like the Alice Goddard alarm clock to jump start your day.

With a groan, Trent propped on his elbows and stared at his wife. "Ten more minutes." His head throbbed, and his mouth felt like cotton. Her high-pitched griping wasn't helping.

"Luke's getting baptized today, remember? Considering we're his godparents, we can't be late." She placed a button-down shirt and a pair of slacks on the bed.

The clock flashed 8:15, leaving plenty of time to jump in the shower, gargle a few gallons of mouthwash, and make it to the church in time for the opening song.

"Relax." He swung his feet over the side of the bed, causing his still pickled head to spin. He paused and massaged his temples.

She glared at him a moment longer then stormed out and slammed the door.

He let his head fall into his hands as reality sank in. In one night he had gone from having $2,000 in his hand to falling an additional $5,000 into debt. All because he couldn't walk away.

He lumbered into the bathroom and gripped the sink with both hands. The mirror reflected hollow, bloodshot eyes shadowed by dark circles. A two-day beard covered his chin. Body odor flooded his nostrils as he pulled his T-shirt over his head. He tossed it onto the floor then turned on the shower. Steam rose to the ceiling and crawled over the glass door.

He stepped inside and let the hot water pelt his scalp and run down his face. A razor lying next to the bar of soap caught his eye, drawing him. In one instant, with the slightest swipe, it would all be over.

Alice stood in the church entryway as men, women, and children milled into the sanctuary in their Sunday finest. The back row, her favorite hiding spot, was already filled.

She shot her boys a smile, resisting the urge to smooth down a stray lock of Danny's hair. "Want to see if you can find Luke? Let him know you're here?"

"Sure." Danny glanced at his brother who, at six foot two, looked more like his father every day.

Tim shrugged. "He's probably upstairs."

The two disappeared up a narrow stairwell that led to the balcony and baptismal. Alice turned to speak to Trent, but he was gone. She frowned, thinking about his used-car-salesman flamboyance. It wouldn't take him long to make a fool of himself. Hopefully he'd remembered to brush his teeth. Just one whiff of his nasty beer-breath would send the entire congregation into intercessory prayer.

She scanned the many smiling faces milling about. She found Trent inside the sanctuary talking to Pastor Fred. She tensed as a million questions raced through her mind. She knew Ed had seen Trent coming out of a bar. Who else had seen him? And how many people had they told? Did the pastor know? With prayer chains and community groups, it didn't take long to get the North Harmony Church rumor mill churning.

She wove her way through the crowd until she made it to Trent. Her tightly coiled nerves relaxed when the words of a familiar story reached her ears.

"So there I stood, soda dripping down the front of my shirt and all over my tan slacks, when Mr. Su-Han walks in."

Pastor Fred laughed. "You're kidding me? What'd you do?"

"Prayed for a miracle, Pastor. Prayed for a miracle." Trent shoved his hands in his pockets and rocked on his heels.

Alice stepped beside him.

"Hello, Alice." Pastor Fred extended a hand. "Good to see you this morning. How are the plans for the ladies luncheon coming along?"

"We're making progress."

The pastor nodded. "I need to connect you with one of our younger members, a newlywed. She's looking for a mentor, and I immediately thought of you."

Lovely. "Send me an email." She grabbed Trent by the arm and dug her fingers into his bicep. "We better find our seats, before they're all taken."

Pastor Fred chuckled. "Yeah, good luck with that." He lifted his gaze to survey the rapidly growing crowd. "We've got ten baptisms today. Ten. Can you believe that? God is good."

Trent patted the pastor's shoulder. "All the time."

She forced a cough—"Excuse me"—and turned to Trent, "Shall we?"

He shrugged and joined her walking down the aisle to the pew where Beth, Ed, and practically half of Alice's BOSU class crammed between two shiny wooden armrests.

Beaming, Beth sprang to her feet. "Hey there, you two. I tried to save you guys a spot."

Alice waved a hand. "It's no big deal."

Ed stood. "Good morning." Holding out a hand to Trent, his smile faltered.

Trent grinned and pumped Ed's arm. "My man. How you been?"

"I've been good. How about you? Is everything OK?" Ed studied his friend with a wrinkled brow.

Trent spread his feet shoulder width apart and folded one arm across his chest. "Couldn't be better. Couldn't be better."

Alice and Beth exchanged glances, and Beth's face softened. Alice averted her gaze.

"Looks like you guys are busting out of the seams." She surveyed the pews for a place to sit. "Trent, why don't we try to find some empty seats?"

Danny and Tim walked up as Alice and Trent headed toward the front of the sanctuary. They all settled next to a family of four. Tim immediately pulled out his phone and started texting until soft organ music filled the room, and everyone stood. Scott, the worship leader, broke out in song. Alice mouthed the words, but her thoughts turned to Trent, his drinking, and how it affected the boys. And there was nothing she could do about it, short of divorcing him, but that wasn't an option.

Trent followed the stream of people out of the sanctuary and into the lobby. He paused to shake a few hands before making his way to a far corner where Ed talked with the Sally-do-gooders.

"Thanks for coming, guys." Beth's eyes sparkled. "I know this means a lot to Luke."

"Yeah, thanks."

Trent noted the odd look on Ed's face. What was his problem? He acted like Trent had a zit in the center of his forehead. Both he and his wife were getting on Trent's last nerve, the way they kept looking at him then exchanging glances.

Then there was Alice. Every time Ed or Beth looked her way, her face flushed red, and she lowered her eyes. It was enough to set Trent on edge. And Alice wondered why he didn't want to come to church anymore. These so-called friends were anything but friendly.

He glanced at Luke who stood at least a foot taller than his father. The teen had draped a towel over his shoulder, his wet clothes exchanged for dry ones. His father elbowed him, prodding a, "Yeah, thanks for coming," out of him.

"So what do you say we do lunch?"

Trent shoved his hands into his pockets. "I don't know." His fingers closed around his empty wallet. When he glanced at Alice, her eyes narrowed.

She spoke for him. "We've got a lot going on today. Sorry."

"Another time then." Beth waved a hand. "I'm just glad you all came. Besides, I think Luke's had about all the family togetherness he can handle for a while," She said. "You're going to Misty's on Friday, right? She's having a dinner party. Should be fun."

Trent shrugged. Not his first choice for Friday night entertainment but at least it'd get him off the hook for lunch. Nothing like begging your best friend—or maybe, former best friend—to foot your bill to make you feel like a man.

Alice eyed him then shot Beth a stiff smile. "We'll be there."

Trent sighed and everyone looked at him. Alice's face tightened, the lines around her mouth deepening. He covered with a yawn. "Excuse me. Guess it's getting to be my nap time." He shot Ed a wink. "Friday sounds great." So much for his Friday night poker game, a game he really needed right about now.

CHAPTER 7

Alice wrapped her hands around her coffee mug and inhaled the rich hazelnut aroma. The warm liquid soothed the tension from her shoulders. After taking another sip, she set it down and grabbed the sign-up sheet for the ladies luncheon. Over 80 ladies had RSVP'd, but less than half had paid their deposits. That meant most of them wouldn't show.

The doorbell chimed. Standing, she inspected the tidy living room, smoothed her blouse, and strolled to the front door. Priscilla, her neighbor, stood on the stoop. A girl with long, blond hair, gray eyes, and a slight overbite stood beside her.

Alice kept her hand on the doorknob. "Good morning. Would you like . . . Can I . . . How can I help you this morning?"

"Have you met my niece, Sarah-Jane?" Priscilla wiggled her way inside, dragging the young girl behind her.

Alice followed them into the living room. "I don't believe I have."

Priscilla dropped her purse—a whale of a tote large enough to swallow the woman whole—on the coffee table and sank into the couch. Her niece sat beside her, knees pinched together, back straight.

"You still helping to organize the women's dealy-wheely?"

Alice nodded and grabbed a flyer from the shelf beneath the coffee table. "Would you like to come, Sarah-Jane?"

"Oh, she'd like to come all right." Priscilla patted the girl's leg. "She'd like to help with the premeal entertainment."

"Entertainment?"

"Mm hmm. This girl has the voice of a canary." She nudged her niece. "Let her hear you, sweetie."

Sarah-Jane studied her hands.

Her aunt nudged her again. "Come on, darling. You can't pursue your singing career hiding away in that room of yours."

Career? The girl looked all of 13.

Priscilla crossed her arms. "Now Sarah-Jane, I didn't bring you over here so Mrs. Goddard could watch you swallow your tongue. Sing already, sweetie. We don't have all day."

The teen cleared her throat and scooted to the edge of her seat. Then she sucked in air and belted out a series of notes that resembled yodeling.

I come yonder, yonder, yonder,
To follow my heart's desire
Yonder, yonder, yonder, though the trail keeps climbing higher
Though my feet stumble and my strength is wearing thin
I come yonder, yonder, yonder, for my lover's heart to win.

When she launched into the second verse, using vibrato, Alice chewed her bottom lip to keep from laughing. The girl ended with a long, high-pitched squeal, then slumped her shoulders and stared at her hands once again.

Priscilla gave her a sideways hug. "Now I know she's got some room to grow, but everyone's got to start somewhere, right? And like I told her, you want to be a singer, got to start finding opportunities to sing. Learned that in one of those mind-over-matter books my son gave me. 'Course, she'll be taking voice lessons soon. By the time of your little function, she'll be a regular pro."

Alice cleared her throat and stood. "Thank you for the . . . sample." Now what? Please leave?

"Well, you have my number." Priscilla touched Sarah-Jane's elbow, then guided her out, pausing to flutter her fingers at Alice. "Toodle-oo!"

Alice closed the door behind them, leaning against the cool wood. Laughter overtook her as she thought of Jude's expression, should she ask Sarah-Jane to sing at their event. Classic!

"Morning."

Trent glanced up as Mr. Lowe approached his desk. A toothy grin spread across his face as he waved a check in the air. Trent's eyes widened at the number printed in the box on the right. Twelve hundred and fifty dollars?

He straightened. "What's that for?"

"A well-deserved bonus. From the Medford-Howard account."

He grabbed the check and tucked it into his front pocket. "Seriously? I finished that project almost a year ago."

Mr. Lowe laughed. "Yeah, that's headquarters for you."

A smile tugged at the corners of Trent's mouth. His luck was finally starting to turn around. "Hey, I'm not complaining. Better late than never, right?"

"So true, Mr. Goddard. So true." Mr. Lowe studied a stack of papers spread across Trent's desk and frowned. "I haven't seen any updates on the Peak Performance Foods campaign. Found an angle yet?"

Trent's pulse quickened as he thought about his blank computer screen, but he quickly covered with a smile. "No problem. My gears are running overtime." He tapped his temple with his index finger.

"I imagined as much." Mr. Lowe threw him a thumbs-up sign before disappearing out the door and down the hall.

Trent leaned forward and massaged his temples. He had less than a week to create an amazing media campaign for his biggest gig to date, and as of yet, he'd come up blank.

Sports drink samples provided by Peak Performance Foods cluttered his desk. He grabbed a red bottle, took a gulp, and swirled it around in his mouth. Awaken your taste buds? No, that sounded cheesy. Burst into action? Get the flav?

Get real. They were expecting more than that. He popped a track and field video into his computer's DVD player, then leaned back to watch the runners. Next, he skimmed through two basketball clips, football footage, and extreme cage fighting, but by six o'clock he still had nothing. Nothing but tired eyes and a looming deadline.

CHAPTER 8

"You got any cash?" Alice's son Tim grabbed a pair of gym socks from the laundry basket and stuffed them into a duffel bag.

She placed a neatly folded dishtowel on the couch. "Not on me. Why? What do you need?"

"Food." He scowled. "There's nothing to eat in this place."

She set the laundry aside and walked into the kitchen. She searched the cupboards, then pulled out various food items. "There's some crackers and peanut butter in here." She opened the fridge and rummaged through the near-empty shelves. "And some cottage cheese and celery."

"I'm not in preschool, Mom."

With a sigh, she returned the items to their proper places. "Like cottage cheese would kill you? What time's your lunch period?"

Tim snorted. "I don't think so."

She peered around the corner. "What?"

"Hey everyone, Tim's mommy brought him lunch today. Isn't that adorable?"

Alice marched into the living room and jammed her hands on her hips. "OK, Mr. I'm-so-grown-up-I'd-rather-starve-than-let-anyone-know-I-have-a-mother, what would you like me to do? Leave a bag of food on the hood of your car?"

"Forget it." Tim threw his backpack over his shoulder and stormed out.

"Don't—" Alice flinched when the door slammed behind him— "slam the door."

"Gotta go." Danny set his cereal bowl down, slung his backpack over his shoulder, and stood.

"Wait." Alice faced him. "What are you doing for lunch?"

"I'm good." He grabbed his phone from the coffee table and slipped it in his back pocket.

"You can't go all day without eating. Hold on." She dashed into the kitchen for the crackers and cottage cheese, but by the time she made it to the fridge, the front door had already opened and shut. A moment later, a car engine hummed to life.

Alice exhaled and kneaded her forehead. Just another cheery day in the Goddard family. Leaving partially folded laundry on the couch, she grabbed her purse.

She crossed the room in long strides and threw open the door. Beth stood on the other side, finger poised on the doorbell.

"Good morning." She grinned, then glanced at Alice's handbag. "Did I catch you at a bad time?"

Alice offered a tight-lipped smile. "Hello, Beth. Did we have plans?"

"Huh? Oh, no. I just . . . I thought I'd stop by and see if you wanted to get coffee. My treat. Then, if we finish and find ourselves twiddling our thumbs, I thought maybe we could jot down some discussion questions." She pulled a book from her purse and Alice read the title: The *Battle for Truth and Love: Why Peace at All Costs Leads to All Out War*. "I picked this up at the library, along with *Ten Steps to Increased Intimacy*."

Alice frowned. Beth certainly was persistent. "I would but . . ." She held up her purse. "I'm heading out. I've got a lot of errands to run."

Beth's face fell. "Maybe later?"

"Yeah, sure. I'll call you." She couldn't deal with Beth this morning. Getting through the day was hard enough.

Friday afternoon, Trent leaned back in his office chair and rubbed his face. His eyes burned and his head throbbed. It had been quite a week. A good week but long. Although he still hadn't found the winning angle for Peak Performance Foods, he wrapped up a couple minor accounts Mr. Lowe tossed his way. Neither of which—one for an emerging gymnastics academy and the other for a national teen crisis center—offered big incentives, but money was money.

He glanced at the time on his computer screen. Two more long, mind-numbing hours. Time for a late afternoon pick-me-up. His gaze shot to the office door, and his ears strained for the sound of voices or approaching footsteps. Nothing.

He yanked open a desk drawer and fished around for the vodka bottle hidden in the back. The tension drained from his neck and shoulders the minute the warm liquid touched his tongue. After another nervous glance, he took a second swig.

The steady clicking of wooden soles on the linoleum signaled someone's approach. His hands went slick as he screwed the lid back on the bottle and returned it to its hiding spot. Pens rattled in a plastic desk organizer as he slammed the drawer shut. Popping a handful of mints in his mouth, he swiveled his chair, turned to his computer, and clicked on his email account.

Messages filled the screen by the time Mr. Lowe poked his head into the office. "I saw the work you did for House of Healing. I think it could be stronger with a few minor changes, but it's a good start." He crossed the room. "Did you get a chance to look at those Power Juice commercials I sent you?"

"Yeah, they were great, thanks. Gave me a lot of ideas." *Not*. There was nothing like watching what he couldn't use to shrivel his creativity.

"Glad to hear it." Mr. Lowe's eyes narrowed, and he cocked his head.

Trent held his breath, exhaling when Mr. Lowe's tight expression smoothed into a smile.

"Keep it up." And with that, he left.

Trent's shoulders went slack. Friday couldn't have come any sooner. Why waste time staring at a blank computer screen? Today was payday, and his check had already been deposited. He'd checked. With money in the bank, he could finally let off some steam. Besides, with their dinner engagement at Misty's later, he'd need a few shots just to get through the night. A couple hands of poker wouldn't hurt, either.

Guilt soured his stomach as he thought of all the times he'd left Alice hanging over the past month, but this time would be different. He would stay out of trouble and keep his eyes on the clock. Hopefully he'd win a few, but if he didn't, if he happened to lose, he'd walk away before it got bad. In fact, he'd only bring 50 bucks in with him. The rest of his cash would stay in the car. And he'd be home by 6:30 at the latest.

He scrolled through his phone and paused at Larry Bellue's name. Maybe he'd give him a call to see what kind of game he had brewing. No, that wouldn't work. Bellue and his guys didn't get going until after nine; Misty expected him and Alice by eight. Besides, the Bellue gang played penny poker, and even though Trent wasn't looking for a high-stakes game, he didn't want to sit around sucking lollipops either. Not for his one night, maybe even his last night, at the table.

After scanning through all his contacts and coming up with nothing more than a handful of unimpressive prospects, most of whom he owed money to, Trent decided to head to his favorite hole-in-the-wall pub.

The clock read four. That gave him plenty of time to get his game on, build up his wad, and head home. A quick change later and he and Alice would be off to the see the pinky-lifting cappuccino sippers, a thought as appealing as shoe shopping on Christmas Eve. At least Ed would be there, although truth be told, things had been a little strained between them lately. He didn't know why, but it was like the guy was analyzing his every move. So much for that transparency and open-arm acceptance Ed always preached. Not that Trent expected much else.

After answering one last email, he closed his laptop and slid it in its case. Grabbing his computer in one hand and his briefcase in the other, he headed into the hallway where he ran smack-dab into Mr. Lowe.

"There a problem?" Mr. Lowe eyed Trent's briefcase.

Busted.

"No, sir. Everything's great. I just . . ." Had a meeting? Needed to pick up more footage? What? "Alice called and there's . . . I've got some personal business I need to attend to."

Crossing one arm, Mr. Lowe tucked his other hand under his bicep. "How you doing with the Peak Performance Foods account? Ready to blow them out of the water? D-Day's just around the corner, you know. "

Trent's grip tightened around his computer bag. "I've got it covered."

"Let me see what you've got."

Trent swallowed. "Sure thing." Now what? Maybe he could pull up an old account, except he'd need to manipulate things, remove names, logos. "Last week you said you had some designs you wanted to show me?"

Mr. Lowe studied him. "I did? For what?"

Trent shrugged. "Something to do with their new drink labels."

Mr. Lowe frowned, staring at him for a long moment. "I said that?"

Trent nodded, working the story in his mind, searching for another stall tactic. Not that delaying would do him any good, except give him more time to sweat. Moving toward his desk, he glanced from the clock to the hallway, wondering where Theresa, Mr. Lowe's constant shadow was when he needed her.

"So, I spoke with their guys at length yesterday, to make sure I understood their angle. Their brand. You know, the tone they were going for and the feelings they wanted to invoke in their customers." He kept talking, barely pausing to take a breath. "Remember what Dave Jenkins said at the marketing seminar you sent everyone to last winter?"

Mr. Lowe shook his head and checked his watch.

"He gave a presentation on using color schemes to convey emotion. The effects are subtle but brilliant. Let me show you." He sat behind his desk and pulled open one of his drawers, rummaging through it, as if some brochure or pamphlet lay within it. "Hm . . . Where did that go?" He swiveled his chair to face the small filing cabinet to the right of his computer.

Someone rapped on his opened door. Releasing a gust of air, he glanced up, relieved to see Reba from human resources standing in the doorway. "Mr. Lowe, do you have a moment? I need to talk to you. It's important." Probably about the harassment suit the lady from accounting was filing. Perfect.

"Yes, of course." He gave Trent a brisk nod then hurried out.

Trent dashed down the hall toward the elevators. He thought about all the catching up he was going to have to do—nearly a month's worth. Nothing like a slew of deadlines to get the heart pumping. But he could put in some hours this weekend and catch up.

After a quick stop at the ATM, he headed toward his favorite bar. Fifteen minutes later he pulled into Casey's parking lot and grabbed a deck of cards from his glove box. Reaching into his back pocket, he ran his fingers over the smooth leather of his wallet.

Thinking about the $725 tucked inside, he smiled. Then hesitated. Maybe that wasn't such a good idea, walking in with that much cash. Only $50. That's all he'd spend. If he won, great. Otherwise, he'd walk away. He tucked $675 into his glove box for safekeeping; but what about drinks? That could cost him another $20. Tips could push him to $30. And leaving cash in your car, visible or not, was asking to be robbed. No, it made more sense to take it with him.

He paused to survey the parking lot with its handful of cars. Based on their rusted paint and dented fenders, it'd be slim pickings tonight. Maybe he should've hit the pool halls, although he wasn't much of a billiards man. Besides, he was here now, and the clock was ticking. He'd have to make the best of it.

A girl with shiny, black hair, dressed in a tight jean skirt and shimmering blouse crossed the lot and disappeared into the bar. He followed a few paces behind, pausing at the entrance. Tiny pricks of adrenaline shot through his veins.

Breathing deeply, he raked a shaky hand through his hair, rotating toward his car. Common sense told him to turn around, get back in his car, and head home to Alice. Cash bulged in his pocket and more waited in his bank account, maybe even enough to placate Jay and his thugs.

"You going in, or what?"

He spun around to find himself face-to-face with a heavy-set man whose crooked nose and mangled ears told of one too many bar fights.

CHAPTER 10

Alice dialed Trent's number. It went to voice mail.

"Hey, it's me. I'm checking to see what time you think you'll be home. Don't forget we're meeting Ed and Beth at Misty's this evening." Of all nights for him to pull a no-show, tonight wasn't it.

Tucking her phone in her purse, she paced. Although Trent wasn't late—yet—she wasn't holding her breath. And the fact that he refused to take her call didn't make her feel any better.

She grabbed her brush off the dresser and ran it through her already combed hair. Setting it down, she studied her reflection in the mirror. Her pale cheeks looked more washed out than usual, the dark circles beneath her lashes evidence of the many sleepless nights spent waiting for Trent to come home. Pathetic.

She rummaged through her makeup case until she found her favorite lipstick. The soft, shimmering pink thickened her lips without accentuating the tiny lines around her mouth. A few strokes of rouge to her cheeks went a long way toward brightening her face and intensified the blue in her eyes.

Finishing with some mascara to her thick lashes, she prepared for the inevitable. It could be midnight before Trent finally wandered home, slobbering drunk and smelling so foul it'd make her gag. But she couldn't go to Misty's alone, not without adding momentum to the rumor mill. Although, she might not have a choice.

She glanced in the mirror one last time and moved to her jewelry box. If she had to play the fool tonight, at least she'd look good doing it. Lifting the smooth mahogany lid, she sifted through the delicate necklaces and bracelets tucked inside. The sterling silver slide pendant Trent gave her for their fifth anniversary shimmered in the dim light. She picked it up and ran her fingers across the tiny diamonds as memories of that day resurfaced. She could still see the passion in his eyes when he had draped it across her neck.

"You know, you're just as beautiful now as the day I married you."

She closed her eyes. She could almost feel the electricity that had surged between them when he wrapped his hands around her waist and drew her closer.

"Forever and a day, right?" was her breathless response.

"Forever and a day."

His warm lips trailed across her shoulder as he hummed the tune to their favorite song. Then he'd spun her around and cupped her face in his hands, causing her spine to tingle.

Shoving the memory aside, she inhaled a breath and trudged into the living room to grab her purse. Trent wasn't coming. And now she had to figure out an excuse to feed the gossip-hungry ladies. Maybe she should call to cancel. There was always the "I don't feel well" line, but that'd only make things worse. Knowing Beth, she'd organize a chicken-soup-and-Kleenex thing. No, Alice needed to go, with or without her lying husband.

Trent looked inside the bar, then back to the man holding the door, scanning his leather vest, broad shoulders, and bulging arms in one sweep.

"You going in or what?" The man repeated, his muscular jaw tightening into a firm frown.

"Sorry." Trent looked away and dashed inside, making a mental note not to play poker with the guy no matter how desperate he became. Last thing he needed was another muscle man added to his list of pursuers.

A man with a beard that extended to midchest sat in a far corner nursing a beer. A pair of bikers with long hair and thick beards filled a small table to the right. One of them, a man with a mustache that dipped below his chin, met Trent's gaze, his expression blank.

Trent looked away and scanned the room for a friendly face. He paused to watch a lady dressed in a painted-on tank top and miniskirt flirt with a man in a suit. She looked up as Trent approached and smiled provocatively.

He paused, taking in the soft contours of her body with his eyes until his gaze met hers. In response, she lifted her chin and tilted her head, painted lips parted.

She stirred her drink. "Want a taste? I'll share."

Yeah, for a price. When a girl responded that easily, it only meant one thing. They were looking to get paid.

He shook his head and stepped back. "No, thanks." He came to let off steam, not tangle himself in a net.

Turning away, he strode to the back of the bar. If anyone came looking for a game, that's where they'd go.

He chose a table in the far corner. After ordering a gin and tonic, he pulled out his deck of cards and placed them in the center of the table. And there he sat, for 45 minutes, sipping drink after drink until he no longer noticed the smell of the moldy carpet and mildewed walls. People came and went—a couple that looked like they had just jumped off the rail; two young girls who walked in, glanced around, then ran out; a bunch of biker dudes covered in leather and chains.

Five or six cocktails later, he lost count, a group of kids meandered to the back and filled two small tables next to him. They looked fresh out of high school, barely old enough to grow peach fuzz.

A guy with spiky blond hair and a cartoon-super-hero jaw glanced at Trent's cards. "So, you a betting man?"

Trent stifled a laugh. He wasn't into cheating a bunch of kids out of their lunch money. "I've played my share."

Chuckles erupted and Blondy turned back to his friends. "What'd ya say, boys? You all up for a friendly hand of poker?"

This got everyone's attention and within seconds they pushed all three tables together and huddled around Trent's deck of cards.

He raised an eyebrow. "I don't know about this. I'd hate to take your money."

The boys laughed. "What do you mean 'take our money,' old man? We're about to clean house, ain't that right, boys?" The blond kid gave a pink-faced redhead a high five.

"You know that's right." The redhead flipped his Mariners ball cap backward and turned to Trent. "You aren't afraid to get schooled by a bunch of college kids, are you?"

Their laughter returned, hardier this time. Heat climbed Trent's neck and settled in his face. If there was one thing he couldn't stand, that was being laughed at, especially by a bunch of stupid kids.

"All right, but don't say I didn't warn you."

Alice gathered her things and headed out the front door. The sun hovered above the horizon, covering the evening sky in vibrant pinks and oranges. The tall spruce tree centered in her yard cast an elongated shadow, birds chirping from somewhere within its branches. The air was crisp and carried the scent of pine and newly bloomed lilacs.

Priscilla, her neighbor, knelt in the dirt with her torso buried in her dahlia bushes. Her silver head snapped up the minute Alice stepped onto the front steps.

"Good evening." A grin widened her cheeky face. She used the small shovel in her hand to push to her feet, her plump body rocking on swollen legs. "You talk to your committee about my niece yet?"

"I'm sorry. I haven't."

"Oh. I see. When you get a chance then. How are the boys?" Wiping her gloves on her paisley shorts and favoring her right leg, she walked toward Alice. Her eyebrows furrowed as she surveyed Alice's uncut, dandelion-infected lawn. "And Trent? I haven't seen much of him lately."

"Good. They're good, Mrs. Tanner. Thanks for asking." She motioned toward Priscilla's purple and blue blossoms. "Your flowers are looking beautiful."

"Why thank you, dear. You know, I bet I could make a bouquet for your event. Do the ladies still get together to make centerpieces?"

"As of now, that's the plan, though we haven't set a date yet. How about I call you?" With a parting nod, Alice retreated to her car and slid behind the steering wheel.

Standing on Misty's stoop 20 minutes later, she took a deep breath and smoothed the front of her dress. She rang the doorbell.

Misty greeted her with a plastic smile. Her rainbow colored taffeta sundress deepened her salon tan and made Alice's pale blue frock look like a pleated garbage sack.

"Alice, so glad you could make it." She raised purple-shadowed eyelids to stare at her empty van parked at the curb. "Where's Trent?"

"Running late." Which was true . . . sort of. She hurried by before Misty could ask any more questions. In the kitchen, everyone clustered around a bowl of chips. They glanced her way as Alice entered.

"Hey, there!" Beth waved. "And now the party begins." She smiled and wiped her hands on a napkin. The soles of her leather sandals squeaked as she strolled over to Alice, pulling her into a hug. "Where's Trent?"

Alice repeated what she had told Misty. Everyone, well, almost everyone, seemed to accept her answer. Beth and Ed, on the other hand, exchanged glances. When they turned back to Alice, the obvious compassion in their eyes made her want to bolt for her car.

Misty popped open a soda can. "That must be hard, to have your spouse gone so much of the time." She reached over, wrapped her arm around her husband's waist, and gazed into his eyes. "I don't know what I'd do if Drew worked that much. I think I'd ask him to get another job."

"And I would never let that happen, my love." He placed his free hand against the small of her back and pulled her closer.

Alice gave a mental eye roll then turned to Beth. "Where's Luke?"

"With friends. You know how teens are—avoiding adult socialization like the bubonic."

Alice nodded and nibbled on a carrot stick. Nice to know her boys weren't the only ones dodging the adults. "So, how'd he like his baptism?"

Beth smiled. "I think he felt very special to have so many people show their support. Although I know he was a little disappointed Jake didn't show up."

Luke, Tim, Danny, and Jake had grown up together, and for a while, Beth and Alice had been close to Nancy, Jake's mother. Then she went through a nasty divorce, and things got weird. Beth tried to stay in contact for a while, but after about a year of unreturned calls, finally gave up. Alice pulled away almost immediately. Nancy's failed marriage served as a constant reminder of how far her own had fallen—and where it was headed, unless things changed soon.

"Did he really expect him to, with all they've got going on?" Misty popped a cherry tomato in her mouth. "I mean really, he knows we're aware of his family problems, with the divorce and everything. It's not like we didn't see *that* coming."

"It's so sad." Some girl Alice didn't recognize shook her head. "You know, it's always the kids who suffer. Jake will be out of the house in a year. The least they could have done is wait."

"Or sought help." Beth sipped her iced tea.

Feeling exposed, Alice feigned sudden interest in scooping a precise amount of dip on her celery stick.

"Yeah, but some marriages are beyond fixing," Misty said. "I certainly don't blame Jake for not coming. Seeing Luke with both of you"—she waved her hand toward Beth and Ed—"the Cleavers of the twenty-first century. That's gotta sting."

An awkward silence followed.

"Anyway," Beth scooped some dip onto a piece of broccoli, "Luke had a special baptism and was very happy you all took the time to share such a monumental moment with him."

"Of course." Misty flicked her hand. "We wouldn't have missed it. And I'm sure you'll do the same for us, when our kids . . ."

Alice waited for the end of Misty's sentence, knowing she rarely went to church.

Misty's face tightened. "Have some sort of special event going on."

Alice made small talk for the rest of the night, but her thoughts centered on Trent and her marriage. By ten p.m., she was more than ready to head home to bed.

"I hate to be a party pooper, but I need to be getting home." She forced what she hoped to be her final smile for the night.

Everyone stood. Misty's glossed lips upturned. "Sure. I understand. I imagine you're worried about your husband."

Was that a stab?

Beth squeezed Alice's hand. "I'll call you."

She nodded, said her good-byes, and hurried out. She paused on the front porch to inhale the crisp, spring air. A light drizzle misted her face and thick storm clouds advanced across the sky, hiding most of the stars from view. A half-moon glowed behind a cluster of pine trees.

A bolt of lightning flashed, and in an instant, the clouds burst open. She raised her hand to shield herself from the rain. Icy drops flooded her face and soaked through her thin cotton dress. Slouching forward against the downpour, she ran to her van and jumped inside. Goose bumps erupted along her arms as she slammed the door behind her.

After one last glance at her "friends" through Misty's living room window, she turned on the ignition and put the car in reverse.

CHAPTER 11

Trent stared at the mound of green in the center of the table and clamped his mouth shut, fighting a smile. Three winning hands had accumulated quite a wad of cash, and he was just getting started. Boy was he glad he hadn't pulled a pansy and walked away. Nope. Coming here, playing cards, was the best decision he'd made all week. He'd turned his $725 into $1,500.

"I'll raise you two." Trent slapped two wrinkled 100-dollar bills on the table and waited for the last kid in the game to fold.

"Let's lose the training wheels." The kid dropped three crisp bills. "I'll match your two and raise you five."

Trent's eyes widened. "What, you get a hold of Daddy's money or something?" Where did these young punks get so much cash?

"Don't you worry where I got it, just be ready to pay up." He leaned on his elbows and twisted his mouth into a cocky smile.

Trent frowned. He was not about to let a couple of kids show him up. He tossed $500 in the center of the table. "I call."

His jaw tightened as a toothy grin widened the kid's face.

"Now looky here, three of a kind." A flick of the wrist revealed a pair of Aces, pairing with his Ace on the table.

"You got to be kidding me." Trent scowled and sent his cards fluttering across the table.

Laughter erupted as his opponent leaned forward and scooped up his winnings. Trent's gaze darted from face to face, infuriated by the laughing eyes that stared back at him. These kids were nothing but a bunch of hustlers. Now that he knew they had money, he'd wipe them clean.

"So you wanna play with the big boys, huh?" He tossed $500 more down.

Blondy raised his eyebrows and glanced at his friends. They pulled their chairs closer, their heads dipping in agreement. Handfuls of cash flew Blondy's way. So they decided to pool their money. Good. The more green the better.

The kid gave Trent a cocky smile. "Let's go."

Unfortunately, Trent's plans of making bank were shattered three consecutive losses later. Throwing his head back, he poured gin and tonic down his throat then yanked his sleeves up to go another round. "Deal 'em."

Blondy shook his head and stood. "Gotta bail, but thanks for the game, man."

Trent's muscles tightened. "What do you mean, 'thanks for the game'? We're just getting started."

"Sorry, man, but we got to go. Finals." The others stood and followed Blondy toward the front of the bar.

Trent sprang to his feet. "Wait. You can't leave. Just one more hand."

The blond kid turned and flashed a peace sign before disappearing into the night.

Trent slammed his fists on the table. He'd been had, by a pack of snotty-nosed kids, no less. He considered chasing them down and letting his fists do the talking, but he didn't need assault charges added to his mounting problems. Besides, there were four of them and one of him, and sitting behind a desk all day didn't exactly pump up the biceps.

He raked his fingers through his hair and weighed his options. In the span of four hours, he'd doubled the $750 he came with, and then watched it dwindle down to ten bucks. Which negated his chances of finding another game. Unless he hit the ATM. He glanced at the clock. 10:15.

Oh, man! He slapped his forehead. Alice and her socialites had been waiting for him for over two hours. She'd be furious. No, she'd be broken. Totally broken. Letting his head fall forward, he rubbed his face with his hands. *Oh, Alice.* Why did he keep doing this to her? And how long would it be before she no longer cared?

By the time Alice returned home, the heavy downpour had waned to a steady drizzle. Fighting back angry tears, she fished in her purse for her house key. Fatigue seeped into her muscles and settled into her bones, signaling the onset of depression. Key in hand, she glanced down the dimly lit street. Curtains were drawn and lights were out, minus the occasional flicker of a television set.

She turned the lock, pushed the door open, and stepped inside. Her spirits lifted when she heard the familiar rise and fall of the television. Good, Tim and Danny were home. A comedy and some popcorn with her boys was just what she needed to get out of her funk. But when she entered the living room and found half the soccer team camped out on her sofa, her heart dropped. Apparently, it was boys' night out, and Tim's scowl said moms weren't invited.

"Hello, boys." She waved to the group, then faced her oldest. "Where's Danny?"

"Mariners game."

Right. He'd asked about going last week. And Trent had said he'd pick Danny up. Her stomach tightened as she glanced at her phone screen. She released the breath she'd been holding. No texts or missed calls, which meant Trent had actually shown up. Hopefully sober. He'd never drink and drive with Danny in the car, would he?

She shot her youngest a text: *You OK?*, then turned to Tim. "I need to speak with you for moment."

He tossed a handful of popcorn in his mouth. "What?"

"Come into the kitchen, please."

He huffed and lumbered after her, then leaned against the counter with his arms crossed. "Yeah?"

"I'd appreciate it if you'd let me know when you plan to bring your friends over."

"Whatever."

"I'm serious, Tim. You need to stop with the attitude and the . . . the . . . sense of entitlement."

He stared at her for a moment, a tendon working in his jaw. Then he sighed and shrugged. "OK, so I'm sorry. What do you want me to do? Kick them out? We could be doing worse things, you know."

"Thirty minutes, then they have to go. Deal?" She liked her boys here, and she was pleased they felt comfortable inviting their friends, but she didn't have the energy to deal with the mess they always left. Nor their noisy laughter, which would inevitably keep her awake.

"Fine."

Alice's phone chimed a text, from Danny. *Game's over. Waiting for Dad. Eating duck wings at Quality Athletics.*

That restaurant was three blocks from the stadium, and though she was glad they were in a safe location, she didn't like to think of Danny walking around downtown so late. She responded: *Sit tight. I'll come get you.*

Danny: *Waitress said it was last call.*

Great. She'd need to hurry . . . but the restaurant wouldn't toss a couple teens out, would they? She hoped not. Although she was more worried about Trent showing up drunk before she could arrive.

Telling her son not to get in the car with his father felt . . . felt . . . traitorous. But what choice did she have?

She sent another text: *If Dad comes, please have him wait. Tell him I'm coming. Please wait.* She paused, then repeated: *Please, wait for me.*

Danny's response came quickly: *OK.*

Heading toward the door, Alice surveyed the mess that had become her living room. Shoes and dirty socks were scattered across the floor. Candy wrappers, chip crumbs, and crushed, overturned soda cans littered the coffee table, as usual.

Crossing her arms, she caught Timmy's eye. "Make sure to clean up after yourselves."

He grunted an acknowledgement.

A brisk wind swept over her as she stepped outside, causing goose bumps to erupt on her arms once again. What if Trent arrived before she did and acted stupid? What if he got angry? She thought about the times he'd snapped at her, of the times he'd come in staggering, acting nothing like the man she'd fallen in love with. Alcohol could do crazy things to people. Make them say and do things they'd never consider sober.

And if Trent showed up drunk, and Danny got into the car . . .

She could lose them both.

Lord Jesus, please keep Trent away.

The irony of her prayer sliced through her heart, leaving a hollow ache. Had it really come to this?

Trent stepped out of the bar into a starless night, rain pelting his face and chilling his skin. Large puddles dotted the parking lot potholes and flowed down the oil-slicked streets. Minus the occasional lowrider, the roads were empty. And quiet, the silence disrupted only by the steady squeak-scrape of the windshield wiper.

Massaging his forehead to clear his stupor, he thought about Alice waiting for him at home. Sweet, gentle, beautiful Alice. Why did he treat her like this? Again and again and again? She deserved better, much better. He longed to be the man she needed, if only he could figure out a way to climb out of the mess he made. Instead, he kept making things worse.

Easing onto the street, he leaned forward and squinted, fighting against the thick fog of intoxication. The light ahead turned red. Grip tightening on the steering wheel, he considered gunning it and sending his car flying into oncoming traffic—but there wasn't any. He slowed to a stop. Tall brick buildings with boarded windows loomed on either side of him, trash scattered near rusted doors.

The occasional streetlight cast long shadows across the broken sidewalks. An old man sat under a dark awning, his form barely visible in the pale glow radiating from the streetlights. Drinking from a bottle hidden in a brown paper bag, he rested against a bent-up shopping cart. Trent stared at him, his stomach twisting into a nauseating knot as the rain pounded against his car roof and flooded his windshield.

The light turned green.

CHAPTER 12

Alice glanced at the snoring lump beside her, covered her nose, and swallowed back a gag. The pungent smell of booze and body odor wafting from Trent overpowered her desire to stay in bed. Her nose demanded fresh air. A strong cup of coffee wouldn't hurt either. Besides, the boys' soccer game began in Puyallup at ten.

A good wife would wake Trent, remind him of the game, and tell him how important it was to the boys that he came, but at this point she really didn't care. In fact, she preferred he stayed home. That way she wouldn't have to deal with him and the feelings of bitterness he evoked. Nor the backlash he created for her boys. She had half a mind to grab Tim and Danny, her things, and split, but where would they go? Crashing at her parents was not an option.

The night before, Trent hadn't arrived until after midnight, full of excuses and apologies for leaving their son stranded downtown. No wonder the boys were beginning to hate him.

She swung her legs over the side of the bed and slipped into soft, fuzzy slippers. Following the sound of the television, she found Tim and Danny lounging on the living room couch.

"You fellas up for pancakes?"

Focused on the television screen, they answered in the affirmative.

She shuffled into the kitchen. "You two want to hitch a ride with me this morning?" She pulled eggs from the fridge, then rummaged through the cupboards for pancake mix.

"We're going with Alex," Tim answered.

Alice tossed an eggshell into the sink and poked her head around the corner. "I'm surprised you don't want to drive."

"Don't have any gas money, remember?"

She grabbed her purse off the table and fished out her last 20-dollar bill. Good thing she'd made it to the ATM early, before Trent's paycheck dwindled to nothing. He was up to something—had to be seeing someone. And she planned to figure out who.

Then what? Leave him? Confront him and beg him to leave the other woman? Or avoid him entirely until she figured out a game plan?

She returned to the living room and handed Tim the cash. He shoved it in his back pocket.

She crossed her arms. "You're welcome."

"Thanks."

"Bacon or sausage?"

"Can we have both?" Danny, her human vacuum, gave a sheepish grin.

She smiled. At least one of her boys didn't hate her. "Absolutely."

His expression sobered as he glanced toward the hall. "You gonna wake up Dad?"

Alice gazed down the hall, a lump lodging in her throat. Anger rode its tails, but she kept it hidden. "Your father's got a lot going on today—with work."

Danny's scowl deepened, and he glared at her. As if he blamed her for his father's absenteeism. Or maybe for putting up with it, making them do the same. Tim grabbed the remote and flicked the channel.

Fifteen minutes later, Alice placed a steaming plate of pancakes, a large platter of eggs, and a mound of meat in the center of the table. The boys devoured it all—every last crumb—within minutes, leaving a sink full of dishes in their wake. By the time she cleaned the kitchen, Alex had come and gone, taking her boys with him.

After tidying the living room and starting a load of laundry, she headed to her bathroom to shower.

By the time she arrived at Puyallup High, the bleachers were packed. She surveyed the stands and frowned. Apparently she'd get the bird's-eye view. At least her camera came with a telephoto lens. She started to climb the metal stairs when a familiar voice stopped her.

"Alice. Alice, over here."

She turned. Beth stood a few spaces down, waving.

Ugh. She wasn't in the mood for company. It was all she could do to keep from crying. Or screaming. Or both.

Beth had saved her a seat, right between Misty and a couple of her PTA friends.

Seeing no polite way to avoid them, Alice tucked her hair behind her ears and worked her way through a maze of legs, knees, and duffel bags.

Beth's smile widened as Alice approached. "I worried you might miss the kickoff."

She settled onto the metal bench. "Yeah, I passed by the exit and had to turn around, then got stuck in a work zone."

Misty scanned Alice's jeans and T-shirt. "Alice, good to see you." She pulled a compact from her purse and dabbed her nose.

Fans sprang to their feet in applause as the home team ran onto the field. Kirkland High followed a few moments later, eliciting a slightly fainter cheer. Alice shaded her eyes and searched the bouncing heads for Tim and Danny. It didn't take long for her to spot her oldest leading his team across the field in long, easy strides. Danny jogged four players back. His face swiveled as he searched the stands. Alice waved her arms and bounced on the balls of her feet, but he didn't see her.

Spectators sat as the players took their positions.

Beth turned to Alice. "Tim's doing a great job as captain. Luke said he really knows how to keep the guys united and motivated."

Alice nodded. "He's always enjoyed leadership positions."

"Danny's not doing too shabby, either. Especially for a sophomore. I'm glad to see Coach Davis give him so much playing time."

"And I am glad they're both on varsity. Cuts my drive time, and bleacher time, in half." She laughed.

"I think we've got a shot at state, as long as no one gets injured."

Alice leaned forward as Travis, a junior, stole the ball and kicked it to midfield, where Tim stood ready and waiting. Trapping the ball midstride, he dribbled to the right. He wove past the opposing team, setting himself up for a perfect goal shot. Alice moaned when an opponent slide tackled him.

Beth frowned. "Seems today's game might be a little closer than we'd like."

The tension in Alice's shoulders eased as they continued to make small talk. For once, Beth didn't drill her on her marriage.

Alice turned her attention back to the game. Puyallup's striker dribbled downfield. Kirkland's best midfielder ran in from the side and cross-fielded it. Micah chest-trapped it, and it dropped at his feet in perfect position.

Rhonda jumped to her feet and cupped her mouth with her hands. "Way to go, Micah!" She grinned at Alice. "Did you see that play?"

Micah passed the ball to Danny, who popped it off to Luke. The crowd erupted with a mixture of moans and hoorahs as Luke slammed it into the goal.

One of the PTA ladies turned to the group with a toothy grin. "I'm gonna get some popcorn. You guys want anything?"

"Oh, I'd love a diet soda." Alice grabbed her handbag and pulled out her wallet. She flipped it open and stared at the empty fold, her cheeks burning. She'd given Tim her last $20. Quickly returning her billfold, she tucked her purse under her knees. "On second thought, I better not. I had more than my fair share of caffeine before leaving this morning."

"I'm sure they have Sprite."

"That's OK. I really need to drink more water."

"I bet they have bottled water."

Her left eye twitched. "No, seriously. I'm fine." Her voice came out sharper than she intended so she covered with a nervous laugh.

"OK." The lady threw her hands up. "I was just offering."

Alice lightened her tone. "And I appreciate the offer, but really, I'm fine."

Misty stood and puckered her lips in a pout. "I'll come. I need to stretch my legs. My back end feels a bit sore."

As soon as they left, Beth zeroed in on Alice. "OK, so talk to me."

"About what?" Alice cupped her knees with her hands and focused on the game.

"What do you mean, 'about what?'"

She watched from the corner of her eye as Beth yanked her purse out from under her and plopped it on her lap. A moment later, she produced a tan wallet stuffed with cash. She plucked a 50-dollar bill from the fold and handed it over.

"What's this for?" Alice made no attempt to hide her frustration. For the second time this month, Beth offered to rescue her, and Alice still hadn't paid her back for lunch.

Beth's eyes softened as she rested her hand on Alice's leg. "Just take it."

"Why?"

"I know things are tough right now . . . with Trent."

"What, because of that?" She waved her hand toward Misty and her friends, who neared the concession stand. "I changed my mind, that's all. In case you forgot, I'm trying to watch my weight."

Beth frowned. Alice stared at the money, wishing for an escape route or an empty seat at the far end of the bleachers.

"You give any more thought to what we talked about the other day, about getting counseling?"

Her face heated as she glanced at the many faces surrounding her. They couldn't be having this conversation, not now. Not here. "I told you, we're fine."

"And I told you"—Beth leaned forward and spoke in a firm voice—"that I know you're not." She turned Alice's hand over and pressed the cash in her palm. "Take it."

Alice chose not to fight her for fear of making a scene.

"Why don't you call Pastor Fred?"

"Why? So he can add me to the weekly prayer list? No, thank you."

"And why not?"

Alice snorted. "What do you mean, *why not?*"

"You need prayer, don't you? Seriously, Alice, why are you running from the people who can help you the most? Why are you pushing us away? Why are you pushing God away?"

"I'm not."

"Oh, really?"

The sun was already high in the sky, slow-passing vehicles humming on the street outside by the time Trent awoke. His head throbbed and his tongue stuck to the roof of his mouth like a mound of cotton. He listened for the sound of voices. The silence assured him the house was empty. Good. That'd give him time to finish his work, once his brain fog cleared.

His stomach revolted as he rolled out of bed, evidence of one too many drinks the night before. The bright light streaming through the blinds did nothing to soothe his throbbing headache. Shuffling out of the bedroom and down the hall, he paused to survey the tidy living room. The empty chip bags and soda bottles he came home to were gone, and a neatly folded newspaper took their place.

He glanced toward Danny's room and frowned. Poor kid. He had to be pretty mad, and he had every right to be. How could Trent forget to pick up his own son?

He rubbed his face. He needed to get it together. For the boys' sake. Maybe he could take them both out for a game of pool tonight. So long as he finished the Peak Performance job.

Grabbing the newspaper, he flipped through the pages until he found the sports section and scanned a few headlines. He plodded into the kitchen. After nuking a cup of leftover coffee, he grabbed his computer and settled into the recliner. Time for a miracle—a divinely infused idea able to save his job.

Peak Performance . . . what was their driving angle? What color, image, font style most accurately represented the granola-eating, hippie-inspired food company that targeted sports-fanatic baby boomers—a group so far removed from Trent it was like campaigning for the seniors' shuffle board contest?

He set his computer aside and stood. He needed to get his blood pumping. Pacing, he wracked his brain for stored images. Nothing. He picked up a magazine and randomly flipped through the pages. "How to lose ten pounds in two weeks," spread across the top in bold letters.

Alice and her diet tips. Like she needed them.

Tossing the magazine aside, he resumed pacing.

A cold beer would get his creative juices flowing. He hastened into the kitchen, grabbed a bottle from the fridge, then returned to the couch. The can opened with a *swoosh*, the cool liquid bubbling down his throat in frothy gulps. He downed it, then set the empty can on the coffee table. Returning his attention to the computer, he clicked on the Peak Performance file.

Using the rectangle frame tool and the color swatch, he filled the screen with a deep shade of blue. He changed it to red, then green, then back to blue, finally settling on a deep navy background and locked the layer. Adding another layer and the gradient feather tool gave the screen a psychedelic feel.

Leaning back to survey his work, he envisioned the Peak Performance Foods logo across the top. Maybe if he added a big grape to the center of the screen surrounded by a group of bikers? Hikers?

Nothing fit. He deleted his work and started over, again and again—blue, green, bluish-green, Wide Latin, Impact, Rockwell Extra Bold—nada. By one o'clock his frustration level simmered near explosion.

Gravel crunched. He glanced out the window to see the mailman stuffing a thick stack of mail into his box. Great. Just what he needed—more bills. But at least he could nab them before Alice saw them.

Making a mental note to change the address on their accounts to a post office box, he waited until the mailman moved on to his neighbor before exiting the house. Priscilla knelt with her head in her flower garden, as usual. She stood when she saw Trent and hobbled over with a cheeky smile.

"Beautiful day, isn't it?" She wiped her hands on her shorts.

"Yes it is." Trent kept walking.

She followed a few steps behind, her thick clogs scraping against the walk. "I saw Alice and the boys leave this morning. They looked so handsome in their soccer uniforms."

Trent moaned inwardly. The soccer game! He checked his watch. What time did Alice say the game started? He couldn't remember. Had she even told him where they played?

Priscilla's chirrupy voice trailed on. "Such a fun age. Some people dread the teenage years, but not me. Nope. I cherished every moment watching their personalities blossom. Though they kept me busy for sure! They did track. My oldest ran the 440. Youngest preferred distance. Slower than a sea slug, but boy-oh-boy, could that kid log the miles."

Mumbling how sports increased one's self-esteem, Trent grabbed his mail and shoved it under his arm.

Priscilla's mouth quivered, poised with questions, but he didn't give her the opportunity to ask. "It was good talking to you."

He spun around and strode inside, closing the door behind him. His briefcase lay on top of an end table. He grabbed it and shoved the mail, unopened, inside then zipped it shut. On Monday, these new bills would join all the others stashed in his desk waiting for more commission checks to pour in.

Now for the soccer game. Hopefully it'd be a quickie, allowing him the rest of the day to work on this campaign. If he could even find it. Taking one last gulp of beer, he grabbed the phone and punched in Alice's cell number. Her voice mail kicked on. She probably couldn't hear the ring over the screaming fans. Next he tried Ed but hung up before the first ring.

How would he explain this one? "Uh . . . Ed, this is Trent. Alice and the boys left for their game while I slept, recovering from a hangover. Do you know where the boys are playing today? Because I don't."

That would go over real well. Besides, the game would probably be done by the time he got there anyway, which left nothing for him to do but grab another beer, sit back, and relax until creativity set in.

CHAPTER 13

Sunday morning, the steady beeping of the alarm clock sliced through Alice's dream and forced her eyes open. Sitting up, she stared at the lump lying next to her. He lay on his side with one arm stretched out, one leg bent, and the other extended to the foot of the bed. His loud snores and snorts sounded like a freight train.

They'd barely spoken three words the day before. Once again, he apologized, profusely, for messing up, not only for missing the game but for pulling a no-show on Danny the night before. This had led to a fight, during which she accused him of what she knew to be true—he was having an affair. Of course he denied it, as she'd expected.

She was done listening to his lies and stupid excuses. And she refused to let him drag her down, not today. Today was Mother's Day, and she intended to enjoy every moment of it.

She smiled, thinking of her youngest. He always had something special planned. One year he'd made her breakfast in bed. Alice spent the rest of the morning scrubbing egg off the counters, but one look at his sparkling eyes as he brought her the tray made it all worth it.

She slipped out of the room and eased the door closed behind her. Both boys' doors were closed and soft snoring drifted from Tim's room. She padded down the hall and into the kitchen. Fog blanketed her backyard and the early morning sun peaked over the horizon, chasing the crescent moon away. A raccoon leaped from a trashcan and disappeared through a hole in the fence.

She started the coffee. While it brewed she set to work straightening the kitchen. Then, she nestled into the corner of the couch, steaming mug in hand. Tucking her feet under her, she wrapped a blanket around her shoulders. A Bible sat on the end table next to a wilting plant. She picked it up and ran her hand across its smooth leather cover. The corners were frayed and many of the pages slipped from the binding. She opened it and randomly flipped through it until she landed on Psalm 46. She read the first three verses.

"God is our refuge and strength, an ever-present help in trouble. Therefore we will not fear, though the earth give way and the mountains fall into the heart of the sea, though its waters roar and foam and the mountains quake with their surging."

The Holy Spirit pricked her heart, beckoning her to kneel in prayer. She closed her eyes and pinched the bridge of her nose.

Hold it together.

She snapped the Bible shut and returned it to the end table. Grabbing her mug once again, she nestled deeper into the cushions.

"Happy Mother's Day."

The sound of Danny's voice startled her. She turned to see him holding a card and a gift bag. She recognized it as one he'd received from his birthday.

His boyish grin warmed her heart and made her smile.

"Danny, that is so sweet." She stood and enveloped him in a hug.

He stiffened beneath her embrace and she suppressed a giggle. He was at that awkward age that lingered between boyhood and manhood—the age where his voice squeaked and hugs seemed childish.

She pulled away to look him in the eye. "What do you have there?"

He shrugged. "Nothing fancy."

She removed the tissue and pulled out what appeared to be a handmade, rustic picture frame. Inside, he'd placed a photo of her and both boys together. It'd been taken two years before, when they'd taken the day to hike Deception's Pass. Tall evergreens stretched in the back, the sky a pale blue streaked with wispy clouds. Wearing cut-offs and an orange tank, and grinning like a kid at Adventureland, Danny looked so young. He'd grown at least a foot since then, and had filled out considerably.

"I love it." She gave him a sideways hug. "So, you hungry?"

Before he could respond, her phone rang. It was only 7:50. Who would call so early on a Sunday morning?

Reading the return number, she answered. "Hello, Stephanie." The church secretary.

"Good morning. Did I wake you?"

"Not at all. What can I do for you?"

"I wanted to remind you about Jaya's baby shower tomorrow. I took the liberty of buying a Little Treasures gift card. I put it on Visa. I'd like to collect everyone's contributions today."

"Yeah, sure. No problem." Minus her empty wallet, although she could always write a check. "How much do you need?"

"If everyone gives ten, we should be good."

"Sounds great, Stephanie. I'll see you at service."

Alice glanced at the clock on the DVR. Should she wait? No. Her mom was an early riser. She'd probably been up for a couple hours already.

She tapped her mom's number.

"Alice, good morning."

"Hi, Mom. Happy Mother's Day." Moving to the kitchen, she cradled the receiver between her ear and shoulder to free her hands to cook breakfast.

"Happy Mother's Day to you, too, dear. What are your plans for the day?"

"I doubt anything could top my morning." She told her mother about the picture and frame. "The wood looks repurposed, like maybe he got it from an old fence or something." She set the burners on medium and scrambled eggs with a whisk. The bacon sizzled and popped in a nearby pan.

"That sounds lovely. I can't wait to see it." Her mom paused. "You're coming for dinner tonight, right?"

Bam—the million-dollar question. "The boys and I will be there, but I'm afraid Trent's not feeling well." It wasn't technically a lie. "You know how hard Mother's Day is for him."

"He's still not talking to his dad? You know, you need to help him get over this. For your boys' sake."

Alice sighed. "I've tried, Mom. He doesn't want to hear it." Besides, her father-in-law wasn't exactly a great influence.

Trent's mother had committed suicide five years ago. Everyone said his father's alcoholism drove her to it. Since then, Trent refused to speak to the man, which wasn't altogether a bad thing, considering how tumultuous their relationship had been. Even so, the man was family, but Alice had given up trying to play peacemaker. All that ever got her was a headache and a hostile husband.

"I understand. Maybe another night."

Awkward silence followed.

"Mom?" She longed to talk to her about everything that was going on with Trent, but wasn't sure how to begin.

"Yes?"

How would her mom respond if Alice told her of her suspicions? She wasn't the most . . . understanding person. Which left Alice with absolutely nowhere to turn. An unemployed, uneducated housewife with a husband who was spending all their money on another woman.

She cleared her throat. "Never mind. I better go. Got to get ready for church."

"OK, dear. Have a good day."

Alice bid her the same and ended the call, dropping the phone on the counter.

How long could she keep playing this game?

"Breakfast is ready," she called out to her boys. "Might want to eat it before it gets cold." She checked the clock once again.

She'd give her oldest son 15 more minutes.

Fifteen turned into 20. Twenty turned into 40. When she could delay the inevitable no longer, she straightened the storage jars on the counter, folded a hand towel, and then headed for the hall. In the living room, Danny sat on the couch playing a video game. She offered him a smile before continuing toward her oldest son's bedroom.

Pausing in front of Tim's door, she inhaled and tucked her hair behind her ears. At 16, he had become just as explosive as his father. His reactions were so unpredictable they scared her. Swallowing hard against her nervous stomach, she pushed the door open and poked her head inside.

He lay with his knees tucked up and the pillow shoved under a gaping mouth. A puddle of drool seeped into the green and blue striped pillowcase.

She crossed the room and gave his shoulder a gentle shake. "Tim?" He didn't move. She raised her voice a notch. "Tim, it's time to get up."

Tim moaned and pulled the pillow over his head with two man-sized hands.

"Honey, it's getting late. We've got to get to church."

"Dad going?"

"Of course he is." Alice tossed a dirty towel into a nearby hamper.

"Still lost in the dream, huh, Mom?"

Happy Mother's Day to me. "Aren't you cheerful this morning?" She grabbed a fast-food cup off his dresser to throw it out. "There's bacon on the table. Getting cold."

Tim ignored her.

"Tim!"

"Lay off already!" Throwing the covers aside, he jolted to a sitting position. A deep scowl shadowed his face as he waved her out of the room. "I'm up. I'm up."

Alice left and closed the door behind her. What happened to that sweet little boy that used to crawl into her lap and shower her with kisses?

Shaking her head, she soft-stepped to her bedroom and paused with her hand on the knob. She eased the door open and stepped inside.

Trent lay sprawled across the bed, hair matted on one side. Even from the doorway, the thick stench of alcohol and body odor sickened her. She tiptoed to the dresser. She grabbed a pair of socks and underwear and set them on the edge of the bed before turning to the closet. A pair of jeans lay crumpled on the floor. She stared at them for a long time.

Reaching down, she searched through the pockets until she felt the smooth leather of his wallet. A small slip of paper—it looked like a beverage napkin—was tucked into the fold where a wad of cash should have been.

Her hands trembled as she smoothed it flat, blinking at the phone number written across the napkin. After copying the information into a small notepad lying on her dresser, she tucked the napkin back into his wallet and returned it to his jeans. She folded her copy then clutched it in her sweaty palm. Tears pricked her eyes as she turned her attention back to their closet.

Don't cry. Not now. Not today.

Trent stirred then pushed himself to a seated position, looking at Alice with bloodshot, red-rimmed eyes. "What time is it?"

She didn't answer right away, her hands fisted by her sides. "8:15. Where's the checkbook? I can't find it."

"What happened to all that cash I gave you?"

Alice crossed her arms. "You mean the $50 you gave me last week?"

"Yeah." He lumbered to his feet and reached for the slacks, swaying.

"It's called groceries."

"Is that all I am to you, a paycheck?"

She rolled her eyes. "Whatever."

She stormed out and slammed the door behind her. Danny stood in the hall, eyes alert and sorrowful.

Alice touched his shoulder. "You almost ready?"

He nodded, watched her a moment longer, then shuffled down the hall.

She waited until he disappeared into his room, then grabbed her cell phone and ran downstairs. Standing in the dim hallway, she paused. What if the number belonged to a woman? What then?

The television seeped through the ceiling, muffling the sound of footsteps overhead. A door creaked, and then clicked shut.

She moved into Trent's office, fell into the desk chair, and spread the number before her. Her hand felt slick around the phone. She dialed then waited.

"Hello?" A male voice, low and scratchy. "Who is this?"

"I . . . wrong number." She hit call end and dropped her phone onto the desk.

A man? That didn't make sense.

What in the world was going on?

Trent Goddard, you're driving me insane. And she was letting him. But what recourse did she have? She had nowhere else to go, no game plan, no job, and no money.

CHAPTER 14

Monday morning, Alice clutched her purse to her chest and watched an old lady with wide, pink curlers tucked under a shower cap talk to the blonde cashier. She glanced around at the men and women lined behind her. A man in a pinstripe suit caught her gaze and smiled. She looked away.

She needed cash—as much as she could get. Enough to hold her over until she got a job.

Like anyone would hire her. If only she hadn't blown off college 19 years ago. Her mom tried to warn her. Told her not to get married until after she'd finished her degree. But she'd been so googly eyed in love over the dark and dashing graphic design major, college seemed like nothing more than a distraction.

"May I help you?" A lady with a flawless milk-chocolate complexion offered Alice a bright smile.

"Yes, I'd like to make a withdrawal, please." She placed a deposit slip and her driver's license on the counter.

"For $2,000?"

"Yes, ma'am."

The teller typed on her keyboard then stopped. "It appears that your account is overdrawn."

Already?

"What do you mean overdrawn?"

"Three checks were returned for insufficient funds. Adding the overdraft and returned check fees—"

Alice blinked. "Could you just print out the statements, please?"

The girl hit a button, and a large printer behind her hummed. Watching one sheet after another spit out of the machine reminded Alice of all the companies they wrote checks to in a given month.

Which payments had bounced? To the water department? The grocery? Their tithe? How many lists held their names, printed in bright red ink, taped beside the cash register? And what about their mortgage? They could lose their house. She gripped the edge of the counter, her stomach churning.

Her thoughts turned to Danny. They'd talked the other night, at first about his classes, his friends, sports. But then Danny'd grown quiet and had looked so . . . sad. After some prodding, he'd shared his fears, and pain. Apparently, she hadn't done a very good job of hiding their financial struggles. Somehow he blamed himself for his dad's emotional withdrawal. What would her boys do if they lost their home, on top of everything else?

"Is there anything else I can do for you?" The teller's voice jolted Alice back to the present. She handed over a stack of papers. "Should I—"

"Thank you." Alice grabbed the statements, spun around, and marched out of the bank.

That evening, Trent handed Alice two $100 bills. "Here."

She studied her husband. He had aged considerably in the last five years. Thick bags sagged under his eyes and his skin held a bluish tint. A stark contrast to the clean-shaven, sharply dressed graphic designer she had married.

"Where'd you get this?" Because according to the long list of debits and overdraft fees printed on their bank statement, they were broke.

His eyes narrowed. "What do you mean where'd I get it? Where do I always get it?"

I have no idea.

She wanted to throw the cash in his face and storm off, but she needed the money. "Thank you." Shame burned her cheeks as she tucked the bills into her back pocket.

She deposited her purse on the coffee table and glanced at the clock—10:30. "Why aren't you at work?"

"Don't act so thrilled. If you must know, I'm working from home." He waved a hand toward his computer case lying on the floor next to an opened beer bottle.

"Really? And why don't I believe you?"

"Always looking for a fight."

She crossed her arms. "No, Trent. You're behavior instigates our fights."

His scowl deepened, and a dark shadow fell across his eyes. He lumbered to the recliner and fell into it. After settling his computer bag on his lap, he reached for his beer.

"It's kind of early to be drinking, isn't it?" She picked up an empty chip bag lying on the coffee table. Crumbs scattered across the smooth wood. She wiped them into the palm of her hand.

"What? You the beer police now? Can't a man kick back once in a while?"

She huffed. "You know what? It's not worth it." She started to walk away, but he grabbed her hand.

She flinched. Stiffening, she glared at him.

"Hey, come on. Let's not start our day like this. You don't want me drinking a beer this early, I'll put it aside. No big deal."

She sighed and kneaded the back of her neck. She studied her husband for a long moment. "I'm going to the store."

"Maybe when you get back we could go for a walk or something. What do you say? It's such a beautiful day, and some fresh air would do me good. Do us both good."

Silence stretched between them as her thoughts raged. Watching her, his expression softened, and for a moment, she caught a glimpse of the man she'd married. But that man had walked out on her the moment he took off his wedding ring.

She shook her head and walked out, pausing on the front porch. She wanted to walk away, for good. But she wasn't ready to take that step. Not yet.

CHAPTER 15

Trent's head throbbed. Warm blood spilled from his lip and nose and flooded his mouth. The wet pavement pressed against the side of his face like sandpaper. Pain stabbed his chest as he pushed himself onto all fours. He reached a shaking hand across his torso and ran his fingers along his ribs. His lungs and gut hurt like crazy, but his breathing, raspy as it was, told him nothing had been broken. This time.

Jay's men wouldn't be so merciful next time; not that getting his face bashed in was a walk in the park.

He staggered to his feet and shot a glance behind him. A dim stream of light flickered from a rusted lamppost and cast long shadows across the trash-littered alley. An overflowing Dumpster sat beside the crumbling brick wall next to a mound of partially broken down boxes. He looked the other direction. Rusted metal pipes and cement blocks piled beneath a boarded up window. Something metallic clanked, followed by a soft rustling. He spun around, his heart thrashing as his gaze darted from one shadow to the next.

A calico cat leapt from behind the Dumpster and ran across the alley.

He released the breath he'd been holding. They were gone. Jay and his thug-for-hire were gone. For now. But they'd be back, sooner rather than later. And Trent had learned his lesson well—partial payments were unacceptable. He didn't need a refresher course.

Alice tucked her feet beneath her and wrapped a blue blanket around her shoulders. Danny sat on her left stuffing his face with hot, buttery popcorn. Tim sat to her right, chuckling. She reached over and squeezed his shoulder. He glanced at her, and for once, laughter, not resentment, filled his eyes.

She smiled. This had been a great idea. She couldn't remember the last time they'd all watched a movie together. Well, almost all of them. She looked at the empty recliner a few feet away. If only Trent were here—the old Trent—the evening would be perfect.

"Oh! Watch this!" Danny bounced in his seat, pointing at the television screen. "Blam! Gotcha!" He let out a chesty laugh, sending popcorn flying in every direction.

"Way to make a mess there, dweeb." Tim picked up a handful of popcorn and pelted his brother with the kernels.

Danny fired back and Tim angled his head and opened his mouth. He jerked his face right and left as popcorn pelted his cheeks and bounced off his lips.

More laughter filled the living room. Alice giggled so hard she choked.

She shook her head. "You boys are crazy."

This was all the invitation they needed, and within seconds, Alice became their target. Laughing, she shielded her face with her arms and fell backward beneath an arsenal of buttery kernels. By the time they caught their breath, the bowl sat empty and white puffs decorated the carpet.

"And now, my sweet boys, you get to help your mother clean up this mess."

Tim started to rise when the front door clicked open, followed by the familiar squeak of rusted hinges. Frowning, he plopped back onto the couch and grabbed the remote. Alice began to pick popcorn off the carpet. A soft swishing sound grew fainter as footsteps made their way down the stairs and into the "cave."

Tim grumbled under his breath and turned up the volume. Alice stood, her stomach tightening. She looked at her boys, but neither returned her gaze. They acted like Trent's behavior was all her fault.

Well, she hadn't done anything wrong, and she wouldn't feel guilty for something she had no control over. If only her boys, her precious boys, would see it the same way.

"I'll be back." She patted Danny's knee. He visibly tensed, and his eyebrows pinched together.

Alice crossed the room. She paused at the top of the stairs to take in a calming breath before descending into the basement. It was dark, except for the small beam of light drifting from the entryway. At first, she could see only the outline of vague forms. Eventually, the forms took shape as her eyes adjusted to the darkness, revealing her husband hunched over in the recliner with his head in his hands.

"Trent?" She spoke softly, barely above a whisper. "What's wrong?"

He didn't respond. Didn't move. She stepped closer, her pulse quickening at the tremors that rippled through him. Rushing to his side, she knelt on the carpet and touched his shoulder. His thick hands hid his face.

"Trent?" Had he been fired? Was that why he spent so many days "working from home"? Without his next paycheck, they'd lose the house for sure.

He lifted his head, and the dim light revealed red, swollen flesh surrounding his left eye. Blood oozed from a busted lip and inflamed nose. Cupping his chin in her hands, she turned his face toward her. "What happened?"

He pulled away and shook his head.

Alice jerked back, muscles constricting as one explanation rose to the forefront of her mind. He'd been in a bar fight? Forty-six years old, and he'd been out throwing blows like a teenager.

"Forget it." Trent straightened and grabbed the remote. The television came on, and two feuding sportscasters bellowed from the screen.

Alice massaged her temples. "This is stupid." They weren't in high school anymore, and she was tired of being married to a drunk. "I'm too old for these games. Way too old." She fisted her hands on her hips. "I'm telling you right now, you need to stop this. Now."

Trent stared at her, his eyes hard. "Or what."

"Or I'm gone. And I'll take the kids with me."

"Quit with the threats already."

It was only a threat until she put feet to her words.

Leaving could cost her everything, much more than her marriage. Because everyone knew good Christian women didn't get divorced.

But maybe she was tired of playing the saint.

CHAPTER 16

Alice sat in her usual spot in the far corner of the couch with her feet tucked under her. The opened window behind her allowed a gentle breeze to tickle the ends of her hair. A steaming cup of chamomile tea sat on the end table. And next to that, a list of options, which felt few. Her biggest stumbling block? Fear. She'd never really been on her own before. Had gone straight from her parents to college to marriage. And as bad as things were between her and Trent, the uncertainty of what lay ahead, should she leave, paralyzed her. Because once she took that step, she knew there'd be no undoing it.

Stillness settled in the house, pressing in around her. Danny was at a friend's for the night and Tim went to a Mariner's game with some soccer buddies. And Trent—she had no idea where he was. Nor did she care.

Maybe if she told herself that often enough, she'd begin to believe it.

But she'd get over him, in time.

If only she knew what to do from here. She had no way to support herself. Maybe she'd get alimony, but that'd take time, right? She could tell Trent to leave, most likely initiating a scene. And what if he refused to go? What if she waited, went back to school, maybe got a job and started saving up money?

That could take months. Could she really live this way that long?

Closing her eyes, she rubbed her temples. She didn't have the energy to think about that right now. She grabbed the television remote and flipped through the channels, hoping something would capture her attention and help her forget about the drama that had become her life.

A knock sounded at the door. After a quick glance at the clock, she leaned over the back of the couch and peered through the long, rectangular window behind her. A dark car parked along the side of the road. She couldn't make out the model—not that she'd know. But it didn't look like a car Tim or Danny's friends would drive.

She pressed her palms against the windowsill and raised a notch to get a better view of the front stoop. Two men with broad shoulders and block-like chests stood on the stoop dressed in dark clothing. They had short hair, crew-cut short, and wore what appeared to be, in the dim lighting, black clothing.

It was too late for salesman.

Did those men have anything to do with the phone number written on the napkin, and the male voice it belonged to? Staring into the kitchen, she eyed her cell on the counter.

Should she open the door? They were probably at the wrong house. Maybe one of her neighbors was having a gathering or something.

Three more knocks, louder this time.

"I've got it, honey." She spoke loudly, hopefully so the guys outside would hear her and assume she was talking to a man. "Just a minute." She dashed into the kitchen and grabbed a spray can of Lysol to use as makeshift mace, if necessary. Then, finger on the ready, she opened the door partway.

"Can I help you?"

The men looked her up and down, their eyes cold.

"You Alice Goddard, Trent Goddard's wife?" asked the one on the right, a short guy with a boxy torso and pointed ears.

Swallowing, she nodded. "Can I help you?"

"Tell him his buddies stopped by. And that we're looking forward to seeing him again real soon. Real soon." He dragged the last part out, rubbing his fist with his other hand.

"Who are you?"

"Oh, he'll know." The men gave a crooked smile then left.

Alice closed the door then returned to the couch, a shiver running through her. There was something strange about those men. Something . . . unsettling.

What was Trent up to? She intended to find out, somehow. Regardless of what happened with their marriage—or more accurately, when and how soon she left him, because she *was* leaving—she needed to know. Something a woman said on an old talk show swept through Alice's mind: You need to build up your case, so you have ammunition once you go to court.

She wasn't that spiteful, but she did need to be prepared.

Another hour ticked by. She froze, holding her breath, when a vehicle eased into her drive. A door slammed and footfalls ascended the stairs. Keys clanked in the lock. Releasing a puff of air, she allowed her shoulders to slump forward. Tim was home. Or Trent. But more likely, Tim.

She wiped her hands on her thighs and crossed the living room. Turning the corner into the foyer, she froze in midstep and watched Tim stagger past her. He swayed, using his arms to steady himself. She stumbled backward.

"Have you been drinking?" Stupid question, but the one that came out.

He laughed and pushed past her, mumbling profanities.

"Don't walk away from me." She followed half a step behind, flinching when he slammed his door in her face. A second later, loud music shook the walls.

She stormed in and snapped off his radio. "Pay attention when I'm talking to you."

Tim's eyes flashed and a hard grin spread across his face. He stood, towering over her. "What're you gonna do? Turn me over your knee and spank me?"

CHAPTER 17

Trent was late to the Monday morning staff meeting. Very late. Intentionally late. His meeting with the Peak Performance guys hadn't gone well. Understatement of the year. Mr. Lowe would be breathing down his neck, expecting answers, but Trent didn't have any to give. If he had half a brain, he'd turn around, get back in his car, and head home. But he needed this job, even if Mr. Lowe reduced him to a grunt man. Which would happen in about an hour and a half, if not sooner.

The thick mahogany door leading to the conference room and the soundproof glass flanking it prevented him from hearing the conversation inside. But based on the nervously twitching faces lining the oblong table, this was far from a morning pep talk. And the tension level would soon raise a notch.

He released a burst of air through tight lips, straightened his tie, and threw open the door. Entering inside with feigned confidence, he tried to avoid making contact with all the eyes that latched onto him like a pack of wolves. Apparently, news of his campaign bombing had circulated the break room. And the cocky smirks on a few faces reminded him of his precarious position as high man on the totem pole.

He scanned the room, locating the last available chair. Unfortunately, getting to it would be anything but inconspicuous. It stood at the far end of the table between Reba and an intern.

Mr. Lowe sat three feet from the door. His eyes, narrowed beneath pinched brows, locked on Trent.

Trent offered a slight nod. Heat rose in his neck sending his sweat glands into overdrive as he made his way around the table. Sitting, he lifted his chin and flipped open his briefcase. He sifted through the stack of papers inside.

Lucky for him, Mr. Lowe hated public demonstrations and would wait until they were alone to annihilate him. That'd give Trent plenty of time to create a diversion of some kind, and perhaps even come up with a believable story to account for his tardiness. And for his major fail with the Peak Performance Foods account.

Mr. Lowe cleared his throat. Trent stared at his thick, wrinkled lips, purposefully avoiding his cold blue eyes.

"As many of you know, we have been working with Cyber Executives for ten years now, which in turn has led to an influx of business, including our most recent, lucrative account with Peak Performance Foods, among others."

Trent shifted and stared at the table.

"This morning I received a phone call from Mr. Lexington, the vice president of advertising and public relations. He informed me that he will be terminating our contract, effective immediately."

Trent's mouth went dry. He wanted to hurl. Gasps and hushed whispers surrounded him.

"I suspect they'll be taking half of our current clientele with them." Mr. Lowe's commanding voice quieted the room. "And when word gets out to the rest of our clients, which it is sure to do"—Mr. Lowe pressed his palms into the glass tabletop and leaned forward—"I am certain many more will be close behind."

More gasps, punctuated by verbal protests.

Mr. Lowe continued, but Trent stopped listening. One look at his boss's blotchy face and hot eyes said it all. He was fired.

And dead. Bruce would tear him limb from limb. Trent needed to find a way to get money. Fast.

As soon as Mr. Lowe closed the meeting, Trent grabbed his brief-case and sprang to his feet. He hoped to make a quick exit before anyone cornered him, but unfortunately, Rick jumped up and blocked his way.

"Trent, my man. Get a chance to hit a bank yet? 'Cause I told the fellas I'd get them the money you owe them."

He swallowed. He looked from one face to the next as everyone milled out of the conference room—anything to avoid Rick's gaze.

"Yeah, sure." He stepped aside and inched toward the door. Retrieving his wallet, he pretended to go through it then threw his hands in the air. "Oh, man. I totally forgot! I gave all my cash to Alice this morning."

Rick frowned.

"I'll stop by the bank tonight." Trent spoke quickly. "Tomorrow at the latest."

Rick's scowl deepened as he studied Trent. Then his face relaxed. "All right. Tomorrow then."

"Will do, my man. Will do." He gave him a hearty pat on the back and then hurried out of room, down the hall, and toward the elevator that led to the parking garage.

A woman in a coral blouse and khaki skirt sat in the reception area flipping through print work samples. Cherice, Mr. Lowe's secre-tary, spoke on the phone. She smiled as Trent approached. He nodded and dashed to the elevator.

When the metal doors closed, he fell against the back wall and brought his hands to his face. He massaged his temples fiercely as a stabbing pain shot across the back of his eyes.

The elevator doors opened to a dark parking garage smelling of exhaust fumes. His car was parked in the far right corner next to a shiny blue Lexus. A man in a blue suit carrying a brown leather brief-case got out of an SUV and gave Trent a passing nod. Dipping his head in acknowledgement, Trent continued to his car and fell inside.

The sharp pain in his skull increased as he eased his vehicle around curve after curve, following the bright red exit signs toward the busy street. Heading south, he drove aimlessly around skyscrapers and glass buildings as if in a trance.

The light turned red. He pulled to a stop and reached into his glove box. The tension in his neck and spine eased as his fingers latched onto the full bottle of Scotch hidden behind the car manual. After a quick scan for cops, he unscrewed the lid with trembling hands and brought the bottle to his mouth. He took four gulps before screwing the lid back on.

The light changed to green. He accelerated, jerking the car forward. His cell phone rang sometime between Front Street and Commercial, but the sound barely registered.

An hour—and a quarter of a bottle of Scotch later—he pulled into an empty carport and staggered up his front walk. Reaching for the door handle with key in hand, his eyes widened when it swung open. Had Alice forgotten to lock it? An image of Jay's jagged face flashed through his mind and sent bile shooting up the back of his throat, but the house was quiet. Inching his way toward the living room, he clamped his mouth shut and forced his raspy breath through his nostrils.

Adrenaline moved him to full alert as he paused at the end of the hall and strained his ears for the slightest sound of movement. Silence. Laughing at the extent of his paranoia, he threw open the hallway closet door, reached behind a navy wool jacket, and pulled out a suitcase. He brought it to the bedroom and hoisted it onto the bed.

His heart ached as he removed his shirts from the closet and stuffed them into the suitcase. Memories flashed through his mind—

of him and the boys playing catch. Of him and Alice dancing under a Hawaiian moon on their seventh anniversary. Of all of them squished in the back of the van laughing as they gorged on popcorn and watched an animated movie play across a drive-in movie screen. Shaking his head, he closed his eyes on the memories. Those days were long gone.

He had to leave. No other options made sense. It was for the best—for Alice and the boys.

In route to his sock drawer, he paused in front of the dresser to inspect a picture of Alice. It appeared to be recent. She sat, torso caved forward, on a park bench watching a young girl with auburn hair feed ducks. He picked it up and studied her lifeless expression. She looked so broken, empty.

Oh, Alice, what have I done?

He turned the picture over. His chest tightened as he stared at the message scribbled on the back: "Trent, I hope you enjoy the photo I took as much as I enjoyed taking it. You have a very lovely wife. Jay."

The image dropped from his trembling hand and fluttered to the floor. This was a warning. Jay was watching—him, his family, Alice. Most likely their house. Trent stepped backward and fell against the bed.

CHAPTER 18

Friday night, Alice watched through the window as Trent's car eased out of the driveway and down the street. When he turned the corner, she hurried into the bedroom. No more playing games. She needed to find out, once and for all, what was going on. Closing the door behind her, she paused to still a wave of nausea before beginning her search.

She started with Trent's top drawer but found nothing of value. A few toothpicks, some buttons, and a couple of receipts lay scattered beneath the mess of unmatched socks. Searching his T-shirt drawer proved futile as well. Moving on to his closet, she sifted through various shoeboxes lining the shelf.

They contained old movie stubs, a rusted railroad spike Trent found in Oklahoma while they were on a multiday biking trip, and other random items that should have softened Alice's heart but only served as painful reminders of how far they had fallen. The half empty vodka bottle tucked in the far corner didn't surprise her.

She returned the boxes and moved on to a row of pants that hung next to a bunch of ties. She went through the pockets one by one. More receipts and a wadded up tissue, but other than that, nothing. Faded blue jeans dangled from a hook in the far back corner. Trent wore them the night before—the night he came home smelling like a sour pickle—like always.

Grabbing the pants, she searched the right front pocket, finding lint. From the left pocket, she retrieved a book of matches from a place called The Spiny Cactus.

She tucked the matches in her pocket and resumed her search. When she got to the back pockets, her fingers brushed against a neatly folded piece of paper. She pulled it out and read the address written in blue ink, followed by the words: *Saturday, 9:00*. She studied the rough handwriting. The small, blockish letters looked masculine. Backing into the bed, she sat on the mattress edge, her eyes locked on the tiny slip of paper until the numbers blurred together.

I don't know what you're trying to hide, Trent Goddard, but I'm about to find out.

Standing on Ed's stoop, Trent glanced at the empty driveway and closed garage. Hopefully Beth wasn't home. That would only make things harder. As if begging your friend for money wasn't hard enough, not that Ed raked in the dough. But he certainly had more than Trent, enough to get him by until his final paycheck came in anyway.

He would have ditched, taken what little he had left and headed as far away from Jay and his thugs as possible, if it hadn't been for that photo Jay left on the dresser. This wasn't just about him anymore. Jay had made sure of that.

Lifting his chin, Trent knocked three times.

Footsteps approached, and the door swung open.

"Trent." Ed stood in the entryway with raised eyebrows. "Good to see you." He studied Trent a moment before moving aside. "Come in."

He led the way to the living room.

Trent followed a few steps behind studying various objects and knickknacks. He calculated the value of each. A blue and green glass vase stood on the mantel next to two long white candles. Probably from the local home goods store. A Wyland acrylic of a breaching whale stood on the end table next to what appeared to be a Tiffany lamp. Worth some. A set of car keys lay on the half wall separating the living room from the entryway.

Ed sat on the edge of a leather recliner and motioned for Trent to sit in the couch across from him. "You OK?"

"Yeah . . . I mean . . . no." Trent's ears burned.

"What can I do for you?"

Trent stared at the maroon carpet in front of him. "I need money." He looked up in time to see Ed's face fall.

He ran his fingers through his hair. "What's going on?"

Trent shifted. "I got myself into trouble." How much should he tell him? No matter what he said, Ed wouldn't understand.

"What kind of trouble?"

"I . . ." Trent cleared his throat. "I wish I could explain . . ."

"How much are we talking?"

"How much can you spare?" He felt like a strung-out doper begging for a hit. But it wasn't like that. He needed to do this—for Alice and the boys.

Ed stood and walked over to a small accent table tucked behind a long leather couch. He opened the top drawer and pulled out his checkbook and a pen. His hand moved fast as he filled it out. He tore it off and handed it over.

It was less than Trent had hoped for, but better than nothing. "Thanks." He looked down. "I'll pay you back."

Ed started to sit when his phone rang.

"Ed Martin."

Trent sank into the couch cushions and waited for an opportunity to politely excuse himself.

"The Newman account?" Ed's brow furrowed. "I don't have the figures on hand. Can I call you back later? I understand. OK, fine.

Give me a minute." He stood and offered Trent a tight-lipped smile. "Excuse me. Apparently my boss wants me to find four-year-old documents I probably shredded two years ago." With a sigh, Ed strolled down the hall toward his office.

Sweat beaded on Trent's forehead as he watched Ed round the corner. The moment he disappeared, Trent lunged for the accent table and opened the drawer. He grabbed Ed's checkbook, flipped to the back, and tore off a blank check. After tucking it into his back pocket along with the check Ed gave him, he sat back down. Wiping his hands on his pants legs, he concentrated on slowing his breathing.

Ed returned, occupying the recliner once again. "Sorry about that." His smile faded as he locked eyes with Trent. "How are things with you and Alice? Beth says she hasn't been at Bible study in two weeks."

Trent averted his gaze. "We're good. She's just busy. Got a lot going on with the boys and all." He looked at his watch and coughed into his fist. "I'm sorry to bust in and out like this, but I've really got to be going. Work's been a bear."

Ed frowned. After an extended silence, he stood. "I hear ya. Another time, then."

"For sure." He hurried to the door.

"How about Friday?"

He spun around. "Huh?"

"How about this Friday? You, Alice, and the boys should come by for dinner."

"Yeah, sure. I'll talk to the boss-lady and let you know."

CHAPTER 19

Saturday night, headlights flashed in Alice's rearview mirror as a lowrider advanced, loud music pulsating from it. A blur of color moved through her peripheral vision as a red two-door drifted into her lane. She swerved, nearly sideswiping a motorcyclist to her left. The man flashed his lights and laid on his horn. She jumped and gripped the steering wheel tighter. Flashes of light blurred her vision as the overhead signs reflected the glare of each passing car.

She strained to read the white lettering on the freeway signs nearly obliterated with graffiti, which grew more pronounced with each passing exit.

With a quick check in her rearview mirror, she eased off the freeway and under the overpass. A man lay huddled in the shadows surrounded by shiny black garbage bags. A few feet away, two men gathered near a burned out streetlight dressed in dark clothing with bandanas tied around their heads. They looked up when Alice passed, sending a shiver down her spine.

Death-gripping the steering wheel, she drove passed minimarts, liquor stores, and gas stations with security-encased windows and sagging roofs. The light turned red. She slowed to a stop next to a Conoco station packed with teenagers dressed in hoodies.

The light turned green and she accelerated, continuing past two-story buildings with dark windows. She rounded an empty lot and shot a nervous glance toward the brick apartment complexes on either side of her. Another right followed by a quick left led her to a series of abandoned warehouses with boarded up windows and heavy metal doors. Three of the four streetlights lining the narrow road stood unlit, making it difficult to read the rusted numbers dangling from the abandoned buildings.

She looked from her GPS to the slip of paper taken from Trent's pants. In the dark, her eyes struggled to focus. Was this it? She searched for Trent's Honda Civic among the few cars parked along the curb and hidden in the shadows. It was parked next to a pile of concrete blocks and metal pipes 200 feet down the street. He was here.

What had Trent gotten himself into? Drugs? That would explain a lot.

Cutting the lights, she turned the minivan around and parked behind a Dumpster.

An engine hummed behind her. She sank down in her seat as a man in a Jeep Cherokee approached. He parked a few feet from a flickering streetlight and got out. His head jerked from side to side as he scanned the alley. Moments later, a pit bull climbed from the back of his vehicle, a thick metal chain around his neck. They dashed across the street and stopped in front of a dented metal door. The man glanced around a second time before raising a fist. He pounded the door twice, paused, then banged again, exactly two more times.

Alice cracked her window, listening.

The door opened to reveal a heavy-set man with tree-trunk arms. Angry barks, high-pitched yelps, and human shouts filled the air. She stretched her spine to see past the men into the warehouse. The doorman moved aside to allow the guy and the dog in. The door slammed shut behind them, blocking all sound.

Alice held her breath, then lowered her window farther and strained her ears against the silence. A distant car hummed by. The angry shouts and growls were gone, replaced by ordinary city sounds, but she knew what she had heard.

Squeezing her eyes shut, she leaned back against the headrest. *Oh, Trent, what are you doing here?*

The screech-slam of a door opening then banging shut forced her eyes open. She turned to watch a wiry man with tattoos covering both arms like sleeves cross the alley, a plastic bag filled with a lump thrown over his shoulder. Alice shuddered as the streetlight illuminated his blood-splattered face. He opened his trunk, tossed the mound in, and slammed it shut. Then he left.

Dog fighting?

Nausea overwhelmed her and she opened the car door and leaned out. Taking in quick, deep breaths, she swallowed down the heave. She started the car and headed back toward the freeway on autopilot. At the first red light she came to, she reached into her purse and pulled out her cell phone.

"911. What's your emergency?"

"I want to report a dog fight."

CHAPTER 20

Y ou really lucked out on that one, my man." Dijon, a short, stocky kid with scarred knuckles and bloodstained jeans held out a wad of cash. Trent grabbed on to his winnings, but Dijon held tight.

The kid licked his bottom lip. "How about making this cash grow? 'Cause I got a feisty little two-year-old about to do major damage. Killer ain't lost a fight yet."

Trent rubbed a knuckle against his bottom lip and watched a pair of muscular dogs attached to thick chains walk past. The $500 he'd just won was great, but another $500 would be even better.

He glanced at the fighting pen at the other end of the warehouse. Men pressed against the wooden planks, punching fists into the air. Bellowing voices merged with deep-throated growls. There was a flash of fur, followed by a high-pitched yelp as Maniac, a three-year-old pit bull sank his jagged canines into his opponent's throat.

A loud crash made Trent jump. He turned to watch a mob of uniforms surge the room.

"Seattle Police Department! On the ground, now!"

People and dogs scattered in every direction. Some fell prostrate with their hands behind their heads. Others dove for boarded-up windows, fingers scraping at the rotting wood. Dijon dropped the wad of cash and bolted down a dark, narrow hallway. Trent grabbed the money and followed through the hall, up an unlit stairwell, and around the corner. The shouting behind him dimmed with each panicked step until he found himself in an empty room.

Gasping, he searched the shadows for Dijon. His gaze landed on a dark frame scurrying up a metal ladder beneath a busted window. Lengthening his stride, Trent raced toward him.

Dijon draped his arms around the final ladder rung and kicked the glass with the heel of his boot, sending the remaining window fragments flying.

Following close behind, Trent wiped his sweaty hands on his pants legs then gripped the cold metal. His heart pounded. His lungs burned. Muscles quivering, he clamored up the ladder and teetered at the top. He swung his leg over the sill. Glass shards tore through his clothes and scraped his skin. Metal clanked as he landed on the fire escape.

Twenty feet below him, Dijon hit the ground running. Trent followed, descending the fire escape as fast as his legs allowed. He leapt off the last step, landing on the cement with a jarring thud. Ignoring the sharp pain shooting through his ankle, he fell into a full-on sprint. At a backstreet, Dijon turned left. Trent raced right, heading down another alley. He dove behind a Dumpster and waited.

A police car drove by, lights dimmed. Trent held his breath. An hour turned into two. Everything went quiet. Faint light streamed from a single pole on the corner. After another 30 minutes of silence, he rose onto stiff and shaky legs, wiped the sweat from his face, and ran, dodging from one shadow to the next, toward his car.

He huddled behind another Dumpster until his breathing slowed and his racing heart dulled to a pulsating throb. Exhaling, he reached into his front pocket and closed a trembling hand around his newly multiplied wad of cash. He'd been lucky. Very lucky. A few more nights like this and he'd have Jay—and the long line of creditors lighting up his cell phone—off his back for good.

Gravel crunched on the driveway, followed by the shutting of a door. Alice hit the mute button on the television remote, stood, and held her breath. Was it the cops? Had Trent been arrested? Closing her eyes, she brought a trembling hand to her temple. She'd called the police on her own husband. But what else could she do? Besides, he'd brought this on himself. Those poor creatures, tearing each other limb from limb, to be tossed into a garbage sack once their scarred and beaten frames succumbed to death. She shuddered even now to think about it. But with Trent in prison . . .

With a deep breath, she walked to the front door. She prepared herself for the humiliation that was sure to come when the cops described her husband's horrific acts, but the familiar sound of clanking keys stopped her. Before she could process everything, she stood face to face with Trent. His hair stood in matted clumps. Tiny specks of blood clung to the bottom of his shirt. Alice swallowed down a rush of bile.

"How did you . . ." She clamped her mouth shut. If she said anything, asked anything, he would know what she had done. Balling her hands into fists, she spun around and stormed into the living room. Trent's footsteps followed.

"Sorry I'm late. I should have called."

Alice spun around. The man was totally clueless.

A hint of a smile lifted his lips. "I've got something for you." He reached into his pocket and pulled out a wad of cash. His grin widened, bunching his whiskered cheeks, as he held it out.

Alice's mouth went dry. Her mind replayed the horrid images she had seen, and a few she'd imagined in rapid, blurring succession. How many dogs had died for that money? She stepped backward and brought a fisted hand to her mouth.

His eyes darkened. "What? You're not going to take it now? After all your nagging about having no grocery money? Unbelievable." He threw the money onto the floor, jerked around, and stomped off to their bedroom.

The door slammed behind him.

Her eyes burned as she stared at the wad of cash lying on the carpet. She needed that money. Her boys needed that money. And even though everything in her revolted at the thought, she picked it up with a trembling hand. Closing her eyes, she tucked the crumpled cash into her back pocket.

CHAPTER 21

Alice spread the newspaper across the counter and searched the want ads for jobs that didn't require past experience or a formal education. If she could find one that paid more than minimum wage, even better. Although, after 19 years of "housewifery," she'd be lucky to get hired at all.

She finished circling a telemarketing position when her phone rang. She glanced at the screen. Beth. This was the third time she'd called this week. And there was no point hitting the ignore button. She'd call back again and again and again until Alice answered. Besides, annoyed or not, she felt guilty for blowing her off.

"Hello?" She lightened her tone to hide her irritation.

"Alice, how are you?"

That was a loaded question. "I'm good, thanks."

"I haven't seen you in a while and we still need to nail down those discussion questions for the ladies lunch."

She sighed. "Right. How about I send you an email later this afternoon."

A pause.

"You're not turning hermit on me, are you? We missed you at Bible study last week."

Alice continued to scan the classified ads, circling those that looked promising. "Yeah, I've been pretty busy."

More silence.

"Are you coming tomorrow? We're starting a new unit on the all-sufficiency of Christ."

She focused on an ad for a nurse's aide position. It paid well, and offered full-time hours, although it probably required special training. "I'm not sure. I'd like to . . ." *Liar, liar, pants on fire.* "I'll certainly try."

Another awkward pause.

"I . . . What are you doing this afternoon?"

Alice cleared her throat to buy herself time. "I have . . . I'm sorry, Beth, but can I call you back? I'm kind of in the middle of something right now." *Like trying to plan the rest of my life.*

"Of course."

Ending the call, Alice set the phone down and planted her elbows on the counter, dropping her head between her hands.

I need a 20-year rewind.

Trent put his car in park and fixed his gaze on the moss-covered brick wall in front of him. At 11 o'clock, only a handful of cars filled the bank lot. Maybe the lack of crowds would ease his anxiety, not that anything could make robbing your best friend easy.

Reaching into his back pocket, he pulled out the neatly folded check he'd forged so carefully a few weeks ago. Hopefully Ed hadn't noticed it was missing. The way he and Beth shared checkbooks, and her tendency to be less than conscientious with record keeping, there was a good chance he hadn't. Yet. And even if he had, he'd never suspect Trent of taking it.

Right?

That was the chance he had to take. He'd initially tucked the check into his wallet, hoping he wouldn't have to use it, that he'd hit a streak of luck. But here he was, broke again.

He set the check on the passenger seat and wiped sweaty hands on his pant legs. After another two breaths, he picked it up and stepped out. His heart hammered against his ribcage as he walked across the parking lot, his lungs tightening despite his focused, methodical breathing. What if they questioned the authenticity of the check? What if Ed found out? Trent would deny it. Besides, he'd rather deal with Ed and his seventy-times-seven forgiveness than Jay and his show-no-mercy thugs.

Countless other potential problems raced through Trent's mind, but he shoved them aside. Worry showed, and he needed to put on his poker face.

Adrenaline surged as he gripped the door handle.

"My man! Where you been?"

He froze at the familiar voice. He turned around to find Rick standing two feet behind him with his head angled and his forehead creased.

Trent thought quickly. "Been going full steam ahead, pedal to the metal, doing my thing from the home front." He flashed a grin that remained skin deep. After going over every possible scenario in his mind, he came up with an excuse that, if spun correctly, could quite possibly get him his job back. If Rick repeated it, which he would. One thing Trent learned early on, never assume bridges had burned until you saw the ashes. Even then, look for a fire extinguisher before grabbing the shovel.

"Yeah? 'Cause I heard you walked out. Up and quit on us."

"Nah." He waved his hand. "You must have heard wrong. You know how rumors fly." He looked at his watch in an effort to appear busy. The last thing he needed right now was Rick riding him over the green he owed him and his friends. Not that he could dodge that one. They were at a bank, of all places.

Rick smiled. "Yeah, you're right. Those guys can sure tell it, huh?" He looked at Trent's hand white-knuckling the shiny brass handle and motioned for him to open it. "You going in, or have they given you door duty?"

Trent squeaked out a chuckle, swinging the door wide, then stepped aside to let Rick through. He swallowed hard, scanning the nearly empty lobby. So much for his, "The bank's too busy for me right now. I'll have to come back later," excuse. He glanced at his watch one more time as his mind raced for a solution—anything to get Rick off his back.

"Glad to see you here, though." Rick pulled a pen from his front pocket and twirled it between his fingers. "Been running short on cash lately—my girl's got some big shindig coming up she needs a new dress for."

"Yeah, Alice is always finding reasons to go shopping, too."

Three young cashiers stood behind the long mahogany counter. The lady on the right had dark, silky hair tucked into a low-riding bun. Thin glasses rested on top of her tiny nose, her pink blouse crisply pressed. Likely her work was as meticulous as her appearance. He would have to avoid her.

The lady in the middle appeared more relaxed, if her soft, V-neck sweater and long, dangling earrings were any indication. But neither of them looked as laid back as the woman manning the far booth near the vault doors. Dressed in a flashy red and orange blouse with wide, swooping sleeves, the brunette's high-pitched laugh could be heard from the other end of the room. Yep. She was the one.

He stepped in her direction, but Rick grabbed his arm.

"So you think I can get that money you owe me? And for the fellas? They've been hounding me pretty hard."

His jaw tightened. He hadn't even cashed his check, and already it was as good as gone. If only he'd made it out for more, but not knowing how much money Ed had in his accounts, $500 seemed the safest way to go.

"What do I owe you all?"

"Total?" Rick scrunched his face and ran his fingers through his hair. "Well, you owe me $70, and I think Scott said you owe him $50." He paused. "Don't remember how much TJ said you owed him. How many hands did you lose?"

Trent grimaced. "I don't know." Like he really kept a running record of losses. Get real. "But I got your $70 and Scott's $50." Although $120 swallowed a hefty chunk, it still left him $375. "Then, if you could ask TJ how much I owe him"—which tripled what he owed the others combined—"I'll get that to you next week." If he saw him next week, which was unlikely. Trent would make sure of that.

Rick studied him, the creases on his forehead returning. "Yeah, all right."

Trent exhaled, his coiled muscles going slack until the teller with the immaculate hair and nails called out, "I can help the next in line."

He looked at the other tellers, all busy with customers. Maybe he could tell Rick to go first, although that would only raise suspicions. No, he lacked options, and the time for stalling had come and gone. Squaring his shoulders in an effort to exude confidence, he strode to the open cubicle. He locked eyes with the woman and slapped his wrinkled check on the counter.

"I'd like to . . ." He swallowed, glanced at the security guard who appeared to be watching him, then turned back to the teller.

Don't do this. Walk away. Just walk away.

His hand closed around the check, turning it into a tight, wrinkled wad. "I'd like to verify a deposit." If his last paycheck had been deposited . . .

The lady smiled, revealing a set of perfectly straight teeth. "May I see your ID please?"

"Yes, ma'am." He pulled out his wallet and produced his driver's license. "Can you print a list of my recent debits and credits please?"

The lady turned and began to type on a keyboard to her right. She hit a button, walked to a large wireless printer against the far wall. The teller to Trent's left motioned Rick forward. Trent breathed in, resisting the urge to drum his fingers on the counter. He needed to be done and out before Rick could hound him about the money.

Trent's teller returned with a sheet of paper and handed it over.

He focused on the numbers. More than he'd hoped, thanks in part to the addition of an old expense account check that had finally been approved. He flashed her an easy smile. "I'd like to make a withdrawal. For $1,500."

"Certainly. Mixed bills?"

He nodded. Cash in his pocket beat money in the bank any day. His blue jeans didn't charge overdraft fees, and the poker tables offered much better returns, if he played them right.

He tensed, his teeth grinding together. No. No more gambling.

Money bulging in his back pocket, he hurried for the door when Rick's deep voice stopped him. "Hey, my man! Wait up."

Trent considered bolting, but Rick was one of those hyper-fit types, so the chance of outrunning him was nil. Besides, the last thing he wanted to do was call attention to himself.

"Yeah, I gotcha." Trent turned around, pulled out his stash, and handed Rick what he owed.

There went more money, gone before he even left the bank.

CHAPTER 22

Alice followed the long, winding gravel road, past tall pine trees and through an iron gate covered with vines. A fat squirrel with bulging cheeks dashed in front of her and scurried up a nearby tree. She inhaled and regripped the steering wheel. It was just her mother, for goodness' sakes. But then again, it was her mother.

She eased into her parents' slate driveway lined with spiral bushes, marigolds, and daffodils. She parked to the left of the garage and got out. Purple asters and peach daylilies filled large ceramic vases flanking two white pillars extending from the front steps to the roof. Unlike Alice's wilting tulips, these flowers bloomed fresh and vibrant.

Her stomach flopped as she made her way up the stairs. Would her mother help her take this next step, or would she send her away with an overly cheery, "I know you can handle this, dear"?

Alice paused on the front porch to read the words etched in a garden stone to her right. "Love is like a tender flower, ever reaching for the sun." Turning back to the door, she lifted the brass knocker, clanked it, then waited. Her mother appeared wearing a floral apron and clutching a dishtowel.

"How nice to see you." She smiled and squished Alice in a hug before ushering her inside.

A candle burned on an accent table in the entryway, filling the house with the sweet scent of peach cobbler.

"To what do I owe this visit?"

Alice lowered her gaze and tucked her hair behind her ears. This wasn't something she could blurt out—especially not to her mom. "It hasn't been that long, has it?"

Her mother closed the door, then led the way to the kitchen. "Much too long, considering you live only 20 minutes away." She moved to the stove, grabbed a teakettle, and brought it to the sink. "Would you like some?"

"That would be great." Alice sat at the table and folded her hands on the bright yellow tablecloth. Freshly cut lavenders and daisies filled a pale blue vase in front of her. A few stray petals dotted the linen. She reached out and picked one up, rubbing it between her thumb and index finger.

Her mom set a plate of oatmeal raisin muffins and a saucer in front of her then returned to the stove.

She glanced over her shoulder. "So, how are the boys? How is soccer going?"

Alice made small talk, telling her mom about the boys' many events and activities, waiting for the right moment to bring up her failing marriage. How did one do that? *Hey Mom, love the flowers. Trent's an alcoholic who likes to watch dogs tear each other to shreds. I'm thinking about leaving.*

Alice grabbed a muffin and picked at a raisin. "I need to talk to you about something."

Her mother looked back at Alice, eyebrows raised. After turning the burner on high, she pulled up a chair and leaned forward. "What is it dear? Is something wrong? Are you ill?" Her eyes glimmered. "Don't tell me you're pregnant."

"I'm much too old for that, Mom."

"What is it, then? Did something happen?"

"No, well, sort of. It's . . ." She paused. "It's Trent."

"He's not sick, is he?"

"Yes, but not how you think."

Her mom's eyes widened. "What is it, dear?"

Alice fidgeted and picked at another raisin. "He's been drinking."

Her mom chuckled. "Oh, my. Is that all? I've heard what your pastor says about drinking—or alcohol of any kind—but you know, not every Christian interprets Scripture that way."

The kettle whistled as steam gushed from its spout. Her mom pushed up from the table and filled two mugs.

She handed one to Alice. "You know, dear, you should spend more time counting your blessings and less time looking for storm clouds." She took a sip of tea, peering at Alice through the steam. "Trent is a good, hardworking man." She covered Alice's hand with her own. "I imagine he's under a great deal of stress. I really think you need to give him some grace on this one."

Alice swallowed and tried again. "But it's more than that, Mom. He's . . . he's an alcoholic. He stays out all night, our checking account is a mess."

"Oh, Alice. You really need to relax. Life happens, and sometimes things get . . . challenging." She leaned forward, eyes narrowed. "Trent has shown himself to be a wonderful husband and father."

Why wouldn't her mom ever listen? "He isn't a wonderful husband. Or father. Not anymore."

"Do you remember what I told you that first year you were married, when you came running home crying with suitcases in your hands?"

"Yes. But this is different—"

Her mother held up her hand. "I doubt that. As I told you then, you can't come running home every time you have a problem. You and Trent have to work things out in your own way. Together. That's what marriage is all about."

"But Mom—"

Raising her hand again, she shook her head.

Sighing, Alice slumped in her chair. She shouldn't have come.

Her mother's face softened into a smile. "Now, tell me . . . what else are the boys up to?"

Alice blinked and shook her head. Why stay any longer? She wasn't up for storytelling. Not today. Placing both hands flat on the table, she pushed to her feet. "Thanks for the muffin, Mom, but I really need to be going."

Always good to know I can count on you in a time of crisis.

Trent sat in the Innovative Media Solutions parking garage listening to the steady hum of his car engine. He hadn't seen Mr. Lowe since the day he bailed. Could he get his job back? Or at the very least, a severance package. Maybe if he came up with a viable excuse as to why he'd ditched. Alice was sick? Yeah, right. Like that'd really send him home.

Maybe he could say Tim got in a car accident. That was a good one, if only he'd come up with it weeks ago. And he didn't call because . . . ? How about: Tim rolled his car, and they had to medevac him to the Seattle hospital. While in route to see his near-dying son, Trent dropped his phone and it landed in a mud puddle. He would've used the hospital telephone, but they wouldn't let him. And he would have called once he got home, but a drunk driver careened into their telephone poles, sending them crashing to the ground. The phone company had just recently repaired the lines.

Yep, that would work. Mr. Lowe would really buy that one, right after Trent explained how a bunch of thugs stole his computer, preventing him from presenting his amazing media campaign to Peak Performance Foods. Genius, absolutely genius.

So what would he tell him? He'd been stressed out and overwhelmed? He'd had a nervous breakdown? That had worked for Stephen, one of their new hires, but Trent was more than a new hire, and Stephen had been branded unstable ever since.

Unstable but employed.

Trent's last two mortgage checks had bounced, and even though he'd covered the charges for the first one, he remained a month behind. And then came the late fees, piling up fast. It was time to get his act together. Sure'd be nice to have that $1,500 he'd withdrawn a week ago. It'd taken less than four days to lose it. A smarter man would've learned his lesson by now.

Sitting in his car fretting wouldn't pay the bills. He needed to do some bridge checking, to see which ones were repairable and which ones had burned. Hopefully, if he spun things right, Mr. Lowe would offer him grace. As unlikely as that was.

He crossed the parking garage with long, deliberate strides before his courage faded. Inside the elevator, he worked his story in his mind, hosting a three-way conversation. His story, Mr. Lowe's response, and that nagging thing called a conscience all feuding for dominance. In the end, Trent won. Now if only he could transfer that win to real life.

Three floors later, he stepped out of the elevator and into Innovative Media Solutions's cream and black striped lobby. A new receptionist sat behind the desk. Good. That meant he'd have to deal with one less person who had heard about his colossal mess-up. It also meant that Cherice, the previous secretary, had either quit or been fired.

Maybe that could work in his favor.

"May I help you?" The woman smiled.

Trent started to ask to see Mr. Lowe when familiar voices drifted down the hall. Rick and Daniel, another graphic designer, were headed this way.

"I think I'm in the wrong office." He spun around and stepped back inside the elevator. The doors closed as Rick and Daniel turned the corner. Leaning against the cold metal wall, Trent rubbed his face. He'd come back later, maybe tomorrow. With an excuse as to why he'd bailed, hopefully one believable enough to get his job back.

CHAPTER 23

Alice perched on the edge of her seat, back straight, hands tightly folded in her lap, while Mr. Titon reviewed her application. This was her third interview this week, and based on his deep scowl, it wouldn't be her last.

She held her breath as he flipped the page over to the "skills and expertise" section on the back. As he read, his bony fingers rubbed his chin, and his lips twitched. Apparently, her "ladies tea hostess" and "luncheon coordinator" status didn't impress him.

Without much in the way of formal references, she had added a long list of volunteer positions hoping more than a decade of unpaid service would account for something. If anything, it showed she hadn't been nibbling chocolate-covered strawberries all these years. But after all the empty "We'll get back to you" responses thrown her way, she'd begun to lose hope.

Mr. Titon scanned the front and back of Alice's application a second time before setting it down. He leaned on his elbows and looked her in the eye. "Our shelving positions pay minimum wage and are only part time."

"Yes, I'm aware of that." So what if this job would barely pay enough to cover gas? She had to start somewhere—a catch-22 deal. She needed a job to get a job.

"Are you familiar with the Dewey Decimal System?"

"Yes. In fact, I often reshelve my books when I'm done. So I don't clutter up the reading area."

Mr. Titon frowned. "We prefer patrons leave the books on the tables or bring them to the check-out area so they can be filed appropriately."

"Oh. Yes, sir."

"When shelving books, what would you say is more important: accuracy or speed?"

Alice studied him. His crisp, button-down shirt with two pens tucked into the front pocket and the thin-rimmed glasses perched on the end of his nose indicated attention to detail. And yet, the frequent glances to the wall clock indicated efficiency, or perhaps, impatience. Maybe he valued both?

"I think one can be accurate and efficient simultaneously."

Mr. Titon's frown returned. *Wrong answer.* He pulled open a side drawer, pulled out a piece of paper, and gave it to Alice.

"Let me know when you are done." He stood and left the room.

She read the sheet in front of her. An alphabetizing test, much like the ones she took in sixth grade library class. The instructions: "Number these from first to last in alphabetical order as they would be shelved." A series of book titles followed. She flipped the page over and read the instructions on the back. "Put these in order as they would be shelved, from first to last." Reference numbers carried out to the fourth digit filled the remainder of the page.

She felt like she had regressed 30 years. It took less than ten minutes to finish the "test," but thinking of Mr. Titon's pressed shirt and wrinkled brow motivated her to give it a second look. After verifying her answers were correct, she emerged from the office with test in hand.

Mr. Titon stood in front of a bookshelf a few feet away, talking with a girl nearly half Alice's age. He glanced up when she approached.

She handed him the paper. He scanned it, the annoying twitch returning to his thin lips.

His face held no emotion. "I'll get back to you."

Yeah, right. I've heard that one before.

CHAPTER 24

Trent turned into the Innovative Media Solutions's parking garage for the second time this week. No more pulling a pansy. This time, he'd do whatever it took to get his job back. Hopefully, his years of faithful service, of successfully handling million dollar accounts, would carry him through on this one. If that didn't work, he'd play the victim card. Somehow.

His legs felt wooden as he made his way to the cold, metal elevator. He had rehearsed and rephrased what he would say to Mr. Lowe so many times; the words ran through his mind on autopilot. And yet, even now they sounded flat and unconvincing.

Riding to the third floor, he practiced his speech out loud, focusing on pitch and delivery. "Mr. Lowe, I know there is no excuse for my behavior. I don't know what came over me. I've been under a lot of stress lately . . ."

This ended his spiel every time. Why had he been under stress? Because he owed money to half the city, that's why. But he couldn't tell Mr. Lowe that. Scrap the whole, "honesty is the best policy" garbage. Especially in situations like this.

When the elevator doors opened, all ideas vanished. His hand hovered over the door close button. He needed to follow through with this. Focused on the thin carpet in front of him, he inhaled and took a giant step forward.

The lady sitting behind the reception desk glanced up. "Good morning. May I help you?"

He crossed the room and looked down the hall. Leaning forward, he said in a hushed tone, "I would like to speak to Mr. Lowe, please."

The woman flashed a toothy smile. "Certainly, sir. Is he expecting you?"

"Uh . . . he's . . . not exactly."

"And you are?"

"Trent Goddard."

She nodded and picked up the phone. "There's a Trent Goddard here to see you." After a slight pause, she hung up. "Three doors down and to the right."

"Thank you."

Mr. Lowe's office door stood ajar. Trent knocked then waited for his former boss, who swiveled his chair to face him.

"Come in." Frowning, he leaned back and crossed his arms.

Trent sat on the edge of his seat, hands clasped in his lap. Diving into his used-car salesman act, he inhaled and forced his shoulders slack. "Mr. Lowe, I . . ." He tossed his carefully rehearsed excuses aside as a better one emerged. Perfect. Absolutely perfect. "I stopped in to see why I haven't received any assignments from you yet. Is there a problem?"

The crevice between Mr. Lowe's eyebrows deepened. "What are you talking about?"

"Cherice told me you'd send my new assignments out some time ago, but I've checked my emails daily and haven't seen anything come in."

"I haven't sent you any files, nor do I plan to."

Trent tried to look confused. "I don't understand. Cherice said you assigned me to work with some urban development architect. A media campaign for the city beautification project, so the city council can encourage voter support." The words spilled out. "When I last spoke with her she said she would send details via email. Said I could work on it at home and," he cleared his throat, "I hate to bother you with this. I know how busy you are, which is why I waited as long as I have, but I grew nervous about a potential deadline." He shook his head. "I don't want to get Cherice in trouble, but I tried to contact her three times, and each time my email bounced back."

"Cherice?" Mr. Lowe studied him, rubbing the back of his hand under his chin. "Why haven't you returned my calls?"

"What calls?" He smacked his forehead with his palm. "Oh, my phone! I totally forgot. I had to get a new number a few weeks ago. I can't believe I forgot to tell you."

Mr. Lowe angled his head and tapped a pen on his desk.

"Are you seriously doubting me?" Trent slipped into the defensive. "After how long I've been here, all the accounts I've handled. Why would I lie about something as stupid as a phone number?"

"And a blown account."

Trent shook his head, raked his fingers through his hair. "About that. I have no idea why those execs were so upset. They didn't say a thing. Just came into the meeting, slammed my flash drive on the table, and told me I'd wasted my time."

"You saw the file, right?"

"After I sent it to Cherice, you mean?" He shook his head once again. "What was the point? I'd given those guys my best work, and they hated it. Didn't even have the courtesy to discuss it with me, tell me what they wanted me to change."

Trent held his breath, exhaling when Mr. Lowe's face relaxed. "If what you're saying is true—"

"What do you mean *if*? I've always been forthright."

"There's no beautification project."

"You mean . . . ?"

"Tell me about your files for the Peak Performance account."

"I sent the full proposal to Cherice the Friday before the meeting and asked her to email it to the company's execs. I wanted to give them time to review it before our meeting. That way they could come with questions ready. Obviously that didn't happen. Do you think Cherice sabotaged my files? I mean, I know she was pretty upset, after her friend got fired and all. I guess those two were pretty tight. And then—what happened to her, anyway?"

"She quit." Mr. Lowe's eyes narrowed, as if he were deciding whether or not to believe Trent. Hopefully his past performance, and the company's need for his skills, would win out. "I'll give you the benefit of the doubt on this one, but don't blow it."

"Of course not, sir."

Alice sat at the kitchen table going through a stack of bills. A few months ago, she wouldn't have paid any attention to them—probably wouldn't have seen them at all the way Trent kept sneaking around. Apparently, he'd rerouted their mail and changed the passwords on all their accounts, but Alice fixed all that. Although, considering all their past due accounts, she almost wished she hadn't. As the saying went, ignorance was bliss—at least temporarily. But even ignorance unraveled eventually. Like when creditors came knocking.

Thinking about all the companies they owed made her jittery; unsettled. Exposed. Worse, it felt like there was nothing she could do about it—about their finances, her marriage, the mess her life had become. Even if she found a job, which she was beginning to doubt, it'd take years to pay back all they owed. And what about money for an apartment, utilities, food, and all the other expenses involved with raising teenage boys?

Her phone rang. She set down a past due water bill and answered. "Hello?"

"Yes, hello. Is Mrs. Goddard in?"

"This is she."

"This is Mrs. Feuring from Kirkland High School."

"Good afternoon. What can I do for you?" She probably wanted help with the PTA end-of-the-year banquet.

"I'm calling about Tim."

"Is everything all right? Is he hurt?"

"No, he has not been hurt."

She released the air she'd been holding and relaxed her death grip on the receiver. "Oh, good."

"Tim is fine . . . physically. However, there have been some behavioral issues I would like to discuss with you. Is there any way you could come in this afternoon? How does one o'clock sound?"

"Yes, yes, that will be fine."

She ended the call and dropped her head in her hands. Her husband was a raging alcoholic who entertained himself by watching a bunch of dogs try to kill each other. They were so far in debt it would take a miracle to keep their house, and now Tim was falling apart. What next?

The hour hand ticked by slowly. By noon, her anxiety level grew too intense to wait a moment longer. Even if it meant sitting in her van, she grabbed her keys and marched outside. As usual, Priscilla had her head in her dahlia bushes. Alice eased the door closed and turned the key slowly, hoping to avoid the usual round of 20 questions.

Alice had barely stepped forward when Priscilla shoved to her feet and waved a chubby arm in the air. "Alice, good morning."

She nodded a quick hello and turned toward the carport. A lifted hand drifted through her peripheral vision. She turned to see a man sitting in a blue station wagon parked across the street. She paused and shaded her eyes to get a better view.

Her breath caught. It was one of the men who came to her door that night she'd been home alone.

Her chest squeezed and she brought her hand to her neck. The man responded with a crooked smile, and a chill ran up her spine. Taking a step backward, her vision narrowed on his hardened face. Was he watching their house? An image of Trent sitting in the basement with blood spilling from his lip resurfaced.

After a moment of frozen fear, adrenaline propelled her toward her van. Her hand trembled as she turned the key in the ignition. The van started with a jolt, and she peeled out of the driveway.

The 15-minute drive to Kirkland High only provided time to fuel her ceaseless what-if scenarios. When she pulled into the parking lot, her breath was raspy and her hands were clammy.

Jumping out of the van, she dashed around parked vehicles. A couple of students stopped, holding fast food bags, to watch her. Alice slowed to a half run and offered a tentative smile.

Once inside, she paused to catch her breath. Students bumped into her as she made her way through the crowded hall toward the principal's office.

The secretary, Ms. Wiles, smiled when Alice walked in. "Good afternoon, Mrs. Goddard. How may I help you?"

"Hello. I'm here to see Mrs. Feuring. We have a one o'clock appointment, but I wondered if perhaps we could meet a little earlier."

Ms. Wiles nodded and picked up the phone. "Mrs. Goddard is here."

A boy with curly, brown hair sat in a chair to Alice's right. He wore an orange T-shirt and Bermuda shorts and was chewing on his pinky nail.

"Mrs. Feuring is ready to see you." The secretary smiled and resumed her duties.

Alice nodded and walked the receptionist's counter, down a narrow corridor lined with plaques and an occasional abstract painting, and into the principal's office. Void of windows, the boxlike room had a stale green tint. Three long fluorescent bulbs flickered on the ceiling.

Mrs. Feuring stood to meet her in a crisp, tan dress suit. Her thick, black hair was piled on top of her head, save a few loose ringlets. To the right, Tim hunched in a leather chair, scowling, eyes locked on the beige carpet. Blood trickled from a cut on his left eyebrow, and his right cheek looked red and swollen. He glanced up, stabbed Alice with a hateful glare, then looked at the floor again.

"Mrs. Goddard. So glad you could make it." Mrs. Feuring gave her a firm handshake. "Please, sit." She motioned to a chair next to Tim.

Alice perched on the edge of the seat, looking between Mrs. Feuring and her son. "What's going on, Tim?"

He rolled his eyes.

"Tim was in a fist fight." Mrs. Feuring returned to her seat positioned behind an immaculate desk void of family portraits or endearing figurines of any sort. Only the bare necessities: a computer, phone, nameplate with gold lettering, and a few other office items.

Mrs. Feuring cleared her throat. "Which by itself is disconcerting enough. We certainly do not condone fighting." She leaned forward and placed folded hands on top of her desk. "But I believe this is an indication of a larger problem."

Alice swallowed.

Mrs. Feuring grabbed a manila folder sitting on her desk and flipped it open. "Tim's grades have gone from As and Bs to Cs and Ds, and teachers have complained about his reactive attitude."

A swirl of images flooded Alice's mind—Tim's angry eyes and clenched jaw, Trent staggering in the house, dead dogs shoved inside plastic garbage bags, the man parked across the street. They all blurred together in one dizzying mass.

Mrs. Feuring's lips pressed together, forming tiny lines around the edge of her mouth.

Alice closed her eyes and pinched the bridge of her nose. This couldn't be happening. Not with Timmy. And yet, she knew it was true. She had witnessed it herself—the hateful, rude comments, the disregard for authority, the sudden lack of interest in school.

"Is he expelled?"

Mrs. Feuring looked at her for a long time, glanced at Tim then back to Alice. "Is there something going on that we should know about?"

"I . . ." She shifted. "Things have been . . . tense . . . but we are working on it."

"Expulsion is always the last option." Mrs. Feuring closed the manila file. "I hope now that you are aware of the problem . . . I'm certain you and your husband will discuss this and deal with it appropriately."

"Yes, of course." Alice spoke quickly.

Mrs. Feuring turned to Tim. "And you, young man, are much too smart to throw your life away. You are at a fork in the road here, and the direction you take is ultimately up to you. You can turn things around and set yourself up for success, or you can continue down the path you're on and end up flunking out to work minimum wage jobs for the rest of your life. Not to mention, you could lose your athletics eligibility, and I know how important sports are to you."

Tim didn't respond. Didn't show any reaction whatsoever. But he had to feel some sense of apprehension. The kid lived and breathed soccer. Then again, according to the eligibility packet Alice had signed at the beginning of the year, all he had to do was pass four classes each semester, and Ds were technically passing grades.

Mrs. Feuring stood and rounded her desk. "Thank you for meeting with me, Mrs. Goddard."

Alice wiped the sweat off her palm before shaking Mrs. Feuring's extended hand. "No, thank you. I appreciate your concern."

"Hopefully next time we will meet under more . . . pleasant . . . circumstances."

Alice followed her son out of the office and into the hall. She grabbed his arm. "Tim, we need to—"

Jerking free, he whirled around, glaring.

"What's going on with you?"

He snorted. "Why? Am I embarrassing you? Ruining your Sunday School image?"

"Don't be ridiculous. I'm worried about you—about your future. Unless you start acting more responsible—"

"What? You'll ground me? Take away my spending money?"

"Watch your tone, young man. I know things have been—"

"Lay off already."

She reached for him again. "Tim, stop. Listen to me," she yelled over the noise of hurrying students. Apparently too loud, because teens stopped, turned.

Tim looked around, his face coloring. "What? What do you want from me?"

Tears stung her eyes. "I want the anger to stop. That's what I want. I want my sweet boy back."

And with that, she knew exactly what she needed to do. It was time. She needed to act, before she lost both of her sons.

CHAPTER 25

Alice's heart raced as she crammed her belongings into the suitcase. A plastic bag filled with dirty clothes lay at her feet. She didn't have time to do laundry. She wanted to be gone, with the boys, before Trent got home. Whenever that would be. If she had any decency at all, she would confront him, tell him what she knew, why she was leaving, and what he needed to do to get her back.

Running away was easier. Besides, she couldn't leave any doors open. If he conceded to her demands, if by some miracle he promised to change, she'd have no choice but to stay. And that wasn't a chance she was willing to take. It was too late for that.

Do you trust Me? Will you turn to Me? The words swept through her mind, stilling her thoughts.

And where were You when my marriage collapsed?

She didn't listen for God's response. Steeling her heart, she resumed packing. She grabbed a pair of sandals along with her red pumps, and shoved them into the outer pocket of the suitcase.

Fighting nausea, she surveyed the room. What should she take? It'd be easier to pack if she knew her destination. Now that her parents' place was out of the question, she needed an alternate plan. Beth was her next option, and Alice was fairly confident that she would take her. Although the thought of asking made her stomach clench. *"Hi, Beth. How are you? Mind if the boys and I crash on your couch . . . indefinitely?"*

After adding a few more necessary items, Alice zipped the suitcase shut and lugged it into the living room. She scanned the area again, found nothing of importance, and continued to the kitchen. Should she take the dishes and silverware? This question evoked a thousand more—was this it? Was she leaving Trent for good? Would they get a . . . she couldn't even say the word.

Unwilling to deal with the implications of her actions, she decided it was better to pack as many items as she could jam into the van. If she'd been thinking clearly, or had planned ahead in the slightest, she would have rented a storage locker, not that she had the money. Nor would for quite some time. Her next step? Save for an apartment.

She looked at the clock. School had just let out. The boys were probably on their way to soccer practice. What would they say to all this? Maybe she should have talked to them first, but she was afraid Trent might come home early. She didn't want a scene. More than that, she feared if she waited, even a few hours, she'd lose her courage. No, she'd waited long enough.

Grabbing two backpacks from the coat closet, she packed overnights for the boys. They could return for the rest later. Then, she loaded everything into her van and hurried to the high school.

Kids dotted the soccer field. The track team made their warm-up laps while the soccer players raced back and forth across AstroTurf. Coach Davis and his assistant, Mr. Puzo, stood on the sidelines talking between themselves. They looked up when Alice approached.

"Mrs. Goddard. Good to see you." Coach Davis rocked back on the balls of his feet. "How can we help you?"

"I need to speak with the boys." She shaded her eyes against the bright afternoon sun and searched the field for Danny and Tim.

Coach Davis frowned. "May I give them a message?"

"I'm sorry to interrupt practice, but it's important that I speak with them."

The coach sighed and blew his whistle. The athletes stopped, looked. Cupping his mouth with his hands, he bellowed, "Goddard boys, over here."

Danny and Tim exchanged glances, and then Tim jogged across the field. Danny trailed him with shoulders hunched, head down. A moment later, they stood in front of Alice, looking from her to their coaches.

"What?" Tim's tone was icy.

Danny stood beside him.

"I need to talk to you both. In private."

Tim rolled his eyes. "Whatever."

"Watch how you speak to your mama, boy." Coach Davis scowled at him.

With a huff, Timmy stomped toward the far bleachers, leaving Danny and Alice to follow.

Tim stood with his back to his teammates. "What do you want?"

Alice flinched at his biting tone. "It's . . . I . . ." There wasn't an easy way to say it. "I'm leaving your father. We're leaving."

Both boys' eyes widened. "What?"

"We're leaving. Tonight."

"Why?" Danny asked.

"Get real." Tim laughed, as if daring Alice to challenge him.

She faced Danny. "What do you mean, *why*? Your father—" she clamped her mouth shut. *Gambles on dog fights.* "It's better this way."

"Better for who?" Tim crossed his arms.

Danny's forehead creased, and he suddenly looked five years younger. "Where will we go?"

Her hands quivered at her sides as she fought the urge to wrap him in her arms and pull him close. "I know this is hard, but it is for the best, for all of us. We'll stay at Beth's." Hopefully. "Until I save enough to get our own place."

"Where, on their living room floor?" Tim scoffed. "You've got to be kidding me. You do what you want, but I'm not going." He flicked Danny's shoulder with the back of his hand. "Come on."

"Tim, wait!" Alice reached out for him, grasping at air. She turned back to Danny, who watched his brother retreat with sad eyes. "Honey."

When she touched his arm, he recoiled as if burned. "Leave us alone. Can't you do that?"

Before she could say more, he spun around and jogged back to the soccer field.

Chest heaving, she headed toward the parking lot on wooden legs.

Now what? Oh, Lord, now what? Her legs went numb beneath her, threatening to buckle. She wanted to shake her fists at the sky, cry out to God in the middle of the high school parking lot, beg Him for mercy—anything. But it was too late for prayers. If God cared, He would have helped her long ago.

Twenty minutes later, she stood on Beth's doorstep with a suitcase in her hand, sore and swollen eyes, and a sinking feeling in her gut.

Beth opened the door and glanced at the Alice's luggage. "Is everything all right?"

Alice blinked.

"Come in. Come in." She grabbed Alice's suitcase and led the way to the living room.

Alice followed in a daze. Was she making a mistake? Was it too late to turn back? No, she couldn't. She wouldn't. But what about the boys? Would they come after practice?

Did they hate her?

Beth set the suitcase against the wall and guided Alice to the couch where Ed sat watching the baseball game. A bag of potato chips lay in his lap.

Sliding his feet off the coffee table, he looked at Alice. "Is everything all right?"

Hugging her middle, she hunched forward.

"Everything's fine." Beth wrapped one arm around Alice's shoulder and motioned with the other for him to leave.

His gaze fell to the suitcase before returning to Beth. Her features tightened, the creases in her forehead deepening, as she shooed him away again.

Alice studied the carpet, wishing she could crawl beneath it. She sat next to Beth, silence stretching between them as Ed sauntered across the living room and disappeared into the kitchen.

"What happened?" Beth asked.

What could she say? Worse, what would Beth say? "Remember your vows." "Divorce is a sin." "Marriage isn't about your happiness. It's about your holiness."

So she'd lose the Christian-of-the-year award.

"Where are the boys?"

A dull ache lodged in Alice's throat.

Beth wrapped her arm around Alice's shoulders and pulled her closer. Silent tears shivered through her and streamed down her face.

Beth rubbed her back. "It's going to be OK. Everything's going to be OK." She bowed her head. "Holy, ever-compassionate Father, hold Alice close to Your heart. Heal her wounds and help her to hear Your voice. Watch over Trent. Do whatever is necessary to break his addiction and bring him to You in full surrender. Restore this marriage by Your power and grace."

Trembling beneath her friend's embrace, she bit back an angry retort. She didn't want a resurrected marriage. She wanted out.

"Did you talk to him?"

Alice shook her head. "I'm done talking, Beth. I'm done fighting, done listening to his lies and excuses."

Beth just looked at her with a sad expression.

An awkward silence followed.

Ed reappeared. "I'll be in the garage. If you need me."

Alice wiped her face and straightened. She glanced at the clock on the DVR. The boys should be done with practice by now. "I need to make a phone call."

"Sure. No problem." Beth stood. "I'll give you some privacy."

When she left, Alice tried Tim's cell. She got his voice mail. "Call me. Please. We need to talk about this."

She tried Danny next. Again, no answer. After repeating the same message, she dropped her phone and fell back against the couch, face in her hands.

The soft swish of footsteps on the carpet signaled Beth's return. "You get everything taken care of?"

"I'll try again later." She stood. "I'm really tired."

"Oh, of course. Let's get you settled."

Beth grabbed Alice's suitcase, led her up the stairs, and rounded the corner to a small guest room with floral wallpaper and pale pink curtains. She set Alice's belongings beside a small white dresser.

Beth gave her a sideways hug. "Everything's going to work out. You'll see."

Then she left, closing the door behind her.

A lifetime of insecurities surged to the surface as Alice sat on the edge of the bed. A grown woman with two teenage boys crashing at her friend's like a stupid college kid. Pulling a pillow to her chest, she rolled into a fetal position and stared at the wall.

Trent climbed into his car, fell against the backseat, and released a long, slow sigh. He'd been lucky. Very lucky. And thanks to Mr. Lowe's "we're all a team here" speech, the rumors and whispers at Innovative Media Solutions had stopped. In fact, the ready smiles and firm handshakes everyone sent his way indicated they bought every word of his story. Of course, it helped that Cherice had only been there a year and kept to herself most of the time.

Now that he had his job back, he could start digging himself out of the hole he'd created. A little repair work on the home front wouldn't hurt, either. He'd start on that tonight. Some wining and dining at El Bistro would melt Alice's icy heart in a flash. And this time he'd be more consistent about it, consistent enough to rekindle the flame.

Driving home employed and with a plan, he felt like a new man. His gambling days were over. No more drinking, either, except maybe an occasional beer or two on the weekends. Not that it'd be easy. His debt ran so deep—to Jay, the credit companies, their mortgage lender, pick a name—just thinking about it set his mouth watering for the juice.

But he could do it. Had to. One bill at a time. So long as he had Alice and the boys, he'd make it. Having come so close to losing it all, he never wanted to fall that far again. Mr. Lowe wouldn't be so forgiving next time.

When he got home, emptiness swallowed the house and uneasiness settled in his gut. He glanced at the clock. Almost seven. Maybe the boys and Alice were at a soccer game. A game he should have known about. But this would be the last one he'd miss.

He tossed his keys onto the coffee table and strode into the kitchen. Out of habit, he opened the fridge and pulled out a beer. Almost immediately, he put it back and slammed the door. The tendons in his neck tightened as he fought against the familiar urge, his saliva glands activated. No. He ground his molars together. No more booze.

Needing a diversion, he returned to the living room to catch up on the baseball scores. The peace and quiet felt good. No nagging, no loud music blaring from behind closed doors.

But when 10:30 rolled around and no one showed, he began to worry. It wasn't like Alice to stay out so late without calling. He stood, crossed the living room, and glanced at the calendar tacked to the fridge. There weren't any games, no meetings—nothing to account for her absence.

He picked up the phone and dialed her cell. Her voice mail picked up. Pressing call end, he stood in the center of the kitchen, countless thoughts churning through his mind. The look of hatred searing her eyes the last time they talked pressed to the forefront.

She probably went out with the girls to throw herself a pity party. He'd hear all about it come morning.

He couldn't win with her. Why try? He stomped back to the kitchen and grabbed a beer. Who was he trying to stay sober for, anyway?

Alice pulled off the side of the road and cut her lights. She scanned the street. Tim's car wasn't there, and his bedroom remained dark. Multicolored light from the television set flickered from the living room. Where had her boys gone? What if her actions drove Tim further away? She phoned him again. Voice mail. She tried Danny.

"Hello?" He sounded tired.

"Honey, where are you?"

"A friend's."

"Listen, we need to talk."

She could hear Tim in the background.

"I gotta go," Danny said.

"Wait. When will you be . . . home?"

"I don't know."

"Let's meet for a soda and fries. Red Robin tomorrow?"

"I've got to go." The line went dead.

Alice called back. No answer.

I can't lose my boys. She dropped her face in her hands and cried.

Trent woke to an infomercial and a stiff neck. Turning off the television, he stood and made a visual sweep of the room illuminated by the faint glow of the streetlights. He listened for the slightest sound, but the house remained silent. Totally silent. The queasiness he drank away earlier sank into his gut like a heavy slab of concrete as he made his way down the hall. The door to his bedroom squeaked open. He turned on the light. The bed was made, unslept in. The closet doors stood open, revealing a row of empty hangers.

He froze, unable to process the image. The conversation he'd had with Alice on the night Jay's thugs had beaten him up resurfaced:

"I'm telling you right now, you need to stop this. Now."

Trent stared at her, his eyes hard. "Or what?"

"Or I'm gone. And I'll take the kids with me."

He ran out of the room and across the hall. He threw open Tim's door and exhaled, his slackened body nearly crumpling against the doorframe. Clothes lay in mounds on the floor, crammed in the closet, and strewn across the bed. A few items, like Tim's iPod and cell phone, were gone, but other than that, his room looked like it always did—a mess.

What about Danny? Alice would never leave without their youngest. Stepping back into the hall, he closed the door behind him and moved to his other son's room. Holding his breath, he opened the door and searched the area for any sign of change. As in Tim's room, a few things appeared to be gone, but nothing major. Not that Trent could tell. Danny's "treasure chest," a shoebox full of old baseball game stubs and other things he had saved since he was a kid sat in its usual spot on the dresser. A few folded dollar bills and a pile of change lay beside it.

Wherever Alice had gone, the boys hadn't gone with her, which meant that she'd be back. Wouldn't she?

CHAPTER 26

Alice parked beside a rusted bus and crossed the parking lot.

Coach Davis met her at the edge of the field. "Mrs. Goddard, can I help you with something?"

"I need to talk to Tim and Danny."

"They're in the middle of a scrimmage. Can this wait?"

"I'm afraid not."

He sighed and trudged off toward the field, blowing his whistle. The players looked his way. "Goddard boys, your mom's here."

Laugher erupted and someone made a "your momma" joke, slamming other players with high-fives. Tim and Danny met their coach on the sidelines, talking with quick hand gestures. The coach shrugged and jerked his head toward Alice. The boys trudged toward her, frowning.

Maybe she shouldn't have come, should've waited.

Upon reaching her, Tim crossed his arms, scowling. Danny slouched beside him.

She spoke slowly. "Why won't you answer your phone?"

Tim spit on the ground then swiped his mouth. "What's there to talk about? You left and we found a new place to hang. It's all good."

"It's not good. You need to come with me."

"Yeah, why's that?"

"Because I'm your mother."

Tim laughed. "Good one." He flicked Danny's arm. "Come on."

Danny looked from Alice to his brother.

She touched his elbow. "Danny, please, we need to talk about this."

He backed away, shaking his head. "This is messed up. Leave us alone. Can't you do that?" He turned around and jogged back to the field.

Alice returned to Beth's after her failed attempt to talk to Tim and Danny at their early morning practice and stared out the window from Beth's kitchen table. Two chubby-cheeked toddlers raced Big Wheels down the adjacent sidewalk as their mother ran behind them.

Beth entered and sat across from her. "Ed said you went out last night."

Alice traced her finger along a crack in the table.

"Did you get any sleep?"

"Your guest room was very comfortable, thank you. And thank you for letting me stay over."

Ed had already left for work. Hopefully, Beth had errands to run today. Alice needed a few minutes to herself, to process everything and come up with a plan. One she should have formulated before packing her suitcase.

She wrapped her hands around her coffee cup and watched the cream disappear into a sea of brown. How long would Beth and Ed let her stay? How long did she want to? As if she had a choice. Until she found a job, her options were few. And what about the boys? They couldn't stay here in Beth's one guest room. Although at this point, her hopes of them joining her had nearly evaporated.

Obviously, they were avoiding her. She had called their cell phones more times than she could count and left messages each time. Not one returned call. Nothing. Not that she blamed them, really. Their world had been turned upside down.

What kind of mother was she, walking out on them like that? Except she hadn't walked out on them. She left Trent, and it was for their own good.

Right?

Beth moved to the fridge and pulled out an orange juice container. "You talk to the boys yet?" She poured herself a glass.

"I tried. They won't listen."

"Do you think they're at the house?"

"Danny said they're at a friend's, but I don't know for how long."

"If you need someone to talk to . . ." She placed her hand on Alice's shoulder.

Beth migrated to the living room, set her glass on the end table, and curled into the corner of the couch. She grabbed a notebook and her Bible, chewing on the end of a pen as her eyes scanned the opened page.

Alice hadn't even thought to bring her Bible with her. But that was only because she'd left in a hurry. Not that she'd been reading it much lately.

Her heart sank as she relived the afternoon she'd left. The hatred in her son's eyes . . . *Oh, sweet Timmy*. She never meant to hurt him. Either of them.

Maybe if she'd waited one more day, the boys would have come with her. They didn't understand. If only she could talk to them.

She rose and lumbered toward the guest room. Closing the door behind her, she grabbed her phone and sifted through her contacts. She needed to find out where Tim and Danny were. Though she wasn't thrilled about sharing her drama with the entire PTA, she didn't have much of a choice. Highlighting the first name on the list, she pressed call.

Rhonda answered. "Alice, good morning. What can I do for you?"

She swallowed. "I . . ." This was even harder than she had imagined. "Is Tim or Danny staying with you?"

"Uh . . . no. Were they supposed to be?"

"No, I just . . ." *Have no idea where they're at, being the wonderful mother that I am.*

"Is everything all right?"

"Yes, everything's fine." She fiddled with the handle of the dresser. "They forgot to call, that's all."

"Don't you hate that? Max did that to me once, just once, mind you. Thought his father was going to have a conniption." She laughed. "He'd been studying at a friend's, or so he said, and lost track of time. 'Course he never stayed out all night, but that's why you have to come down hard the first time. Otherwise they keep on sliding. *Woosh*, like a slippery old banana down the garbage shoot."

Alice shifted. She didn't have time for this.

"That's how we handled it, and let me tell you, that solved that problem right away. A week of hard labor and no cell phone woke Max up real quick."

"Thanks. I'll remember that." She tried to cut the conversation short, but Rhonda continued.

"Not that we haven't had other issues. Boy, have we had issues, part of raising teens, I'm sure. But poor Max, you can't blame him really. He gets so caught up in the moment, just like his father. I think it's his creative side showing . . ."

Alice stifled a sigh as Rhonda went on, tracing back at least five years. After another ten minutes of listening to her share every last detail of her life—from how Max threw his dirty socks on the floor to how Stephanie liked to keep her room tidy—Alice finally interjected. "I hate to cut you off, but I really need to get a hold of them."

"Oh, right. Sorry. Hey, did you try their cells?"

"I think they forgot to charge them."

"Oh, I hate that!" Rhonda launched into another five-minute dissertation on how Max always left his phone buried in his sports bag beneath a bunch of dirty socks at the bottom of his locker or on his bedroom dresser.

By the time Alice hung up, she'd developed quite the tension headache. Massaging her neck, she went through the rest of her contacts one by one until she got to Lisa Luttrell.

"Good morning, Mrs. Luttrell, this is Tim and Danny's mom."

A lengthy pause.

"Alice. I'm glad you called." The woman spoke through her nose.

"Have you seen Tim or Danny?"

"Yes, they're here, and we've told them they are welcome whenever they need . . . space. I planned to contact you later today."

Alice closed her eyes and pinched the bridge of her nose. Of all the families Tim and Danny could have crashed with, they had to pick the Luttrells?

"Can you come over this evening to talk about this? Patrick will be home at six."

Great, an intervention. Just what she needed.

"Actually, I . . ."

Going would be stepping into an ambush. As a licensed psychologist, Lisa loved diving into other people's heads. Her husband, a psych professor at the University of Washington, wasn't any better.

Alice opted for avoidance. And now that she knew where her boys were, even if she didn't like it, she could quit worrying and move on to fixing. Somehow. Without Lisa's help. "Can I call you back?"

"These sorts of things must be dealt with immediately. Before they become insurmountable. How does 6:30 sound? You remember how to get here, right?"

Alice sighed. The last thing she wanted was to be psychoanalyzed, but right now, that was the only way to get to her boys. "Fine. 6:30 is fine."

Ending the call, she wondered what "sorts of things" Lisa referred to. She had no way of knowing what rumors had been spread or how many people had seen Trent staggering out of a bar or at a dog fight or God only knew where else. But that wasn't her problem. Not anymore. Right now she had one concern—getting her boys back.

She turned to the oval mirror hanging above the dresser, applied tinted gloss to her lips and a few strokes of blush to her cheeks, then exited the room. In the living room, Beth still sat on the couch reading her Bible when Alice walked by.

She glanced up. "Are you heading out?"

Alice nodded, grateful Beth didn't push for more information and yet desperate for advice just the same.

"I'm going to be in and out today, but I'll leave a key for you under the front mat."

"Thanks."

She didn't have anywhere to go, but she couldn't hang out at Beth's all day.

CHAPTER 27

Alice parked outside the Luttrells' four-car garage and tried Tim's number once more. When it went to voice mail, she tried Danny. No luck.

Taking in a long, slow breath, she smoothed her hair behind her ears and stepped out onto the slated driveway. Stone pillars stood on either side of a circular walk, leading to a two-story brick house with high, arching windows.

She continued up the front steps and rang the doorbell. The lock clicked and the door swung open.

Dressed in a teal cardigan and white slacks, Mrs. Luttrell offered a stiff smile. "Alice, so glad you could make it." She stepped aside. "Please, come in."

She closed the door behind Alice then led her down the hall and into a formal sitting area. A porcelain tea set, a *Psychology Today* magazine, and a book called *Reaching Troubled Teens* sat on the glass coffee table.

"Mrs. Goddard, hello." Mr. Luttrell rounded the corner carrying a legal tablet. He was a wisp of a bald-headed man with tufts of hair protruding around his ears. Three pens were tucked in his shirt pocket. After shaking Alice's hand, he and his wife sat on a cream-colored leather couch.

Alice perched on the edge of a matching love seat.

"Tea?" Mrs. Luttrell poured a cup and handed it to Alice.

"Thank you." She set the mug down. "And thank you for letting Tim and Danny stay here."

Mrs. Luttrell nodded. "Of course. I know how trying the teen years can be. Which is why we'd like to help. We've worked with troubled families for years and have seen parents make great strides when issues are handled appropriately."

"Things have been . . . difficult for the boys, but we'll work through this." Alice glanced through the arched doorway and down the marble-floored hall. "If you don't mind, I'd like to speak with them alone."

The couple exchanged glances.

Mr. Luttrell cleared his throat. "Actually, they aren't here." He spoke slowly, much like a politician. "We sent them with our son to see a movie. So we could discuss the situation in private."

Alice blinked and folded her hands in her lap. She looked Mr. Luttrell in the eye. "I appreciate your concern, but the boys and I need to talk. And although I am thankful you allowed them to stay, they really need to come home now."

Mrs. Luttrell raised an eyebrow. "And just where would that be? Because our son tells us that you are no longer living at home. That in fact, you are living on someone's couch."

Alice's hands clasped tighter. "Not that it's your business, but I'm staying with friends. In their guest room."

"Yes, well, we do not believe the boys are . . . ready to talk with you. In situations like this, a cooling off period is best for all involved."

"A cooling off period? And just how long do you envision this period to last?"

Mrs. Luttrell shrugged. "As long as they need. We told them they are always welcome and our door is always open." She added sugar to her tea and stirred. After taking a rather long sip, she set her drink down and cupped her hands around one knee. "During that time, we can work with you on appropriate communication methods and proper behavior modification procedures. In fact"—she grabbed her purse off the ground beside her and pulled out a pocket planner—"why don't we start next Friday? Free of charge, of course."

"I'm not interested in a therapy session." So, not only were they hindering her communication with her sons, now they wanted to psychoanalyze her? "Are you saying you will not *allow* me to see Tim and Danny? As if you had the right. These are my boys and I decide what's best for them."

"Really?" Mrs. Luttrell raised an eyebrow. "Because it appears to us as if you are not *addressing* the matter at all. Rather, you are attempting to manage the symptoms without taking the time to determine their cause. Effective parenting—"

Alice held up her hand. "This conversation is pointless." She pulled a slip of paper and pen from her purse and wrote out Beth's address on it. "Here." She slapped the paper on the table. "This is where I'm staying. Tell the boys they are to come home—to our new home—tonight."

Mrs. Luttrell frowned. "This is exactly the type of behavior that leads to these sorts of difficulties in the first place. We can't make the boys do anything. And you know as well as I, if we force them to go to this place"—her gaze flicked to the address—"in their current emotional state, they'll only run away again. You must deal with the issues underlying their behavior—and yours, I might add—before things escalate."

Alice stood, using every ounce of strength she possessed to maintain self-control. "Once again, thank you for the tea and your concern. Please." She stressed the word, holding Mrs. Luttrell's gaze. "Please tell them I stopped by. And have them call me."

The couple rose, and Mrs. Luttrell smoothed her blouse. "Certainly. But remember, pushing too hard too fast will only push them further away."

CHAPTER 28

Trent shoved a gallon of sour milk aside to make room for a 12-pack of beer. He pulled out a bottle and put the rest on the top shelf. So much for kicking the booze. But with Alice gone, he didn't see the point. In anything.

Dirty dishes filled the sink, and breadcrumbs scattered across the counter—a painful reminder of her absence. He'd called her twice—once to locate her and to find out what it would take to get her home, then to invite her to a nice, candlelit dinner. No answer either time, which wasn't like her. It wasn't like her at all. If not for the empty closet and missing suitcases, Trent would have thought something tragic had happened.

He lumbered into the living room, fell into the recliner, and leaned back until the footrest popped up. Grabbing the remote, he began his nightly routine of flipping through mindless commercials. He guzzled one beer after another until the familiar fog of intoxication took over.

At 7:30, Danny arrived covered in sweat and with a gym bag tossed over his shoulder.

Trent jolted upright, snapping the footrest beneath him. "Hey. Where you been?"

"A friend's."

"Did you clear that with your mom first?" Alice probably told the boys to stay away—one of her manipulation tactics, no doubt.

"Where is she, anyway?" He spoke slowly to hide the slur of his words.

Danny shrugged.

"Call me next time, OK? You seen your brother lately?"

A tendon in Danny's jaw twitched. He dropped his gym bag and turned toward the kitchen. Cupboard doors started banging shut. The fridge opened and closed.

Trent made a mental note to hit the grocery store the next day on his way home from work. Downing the rest of his beer, he walked into the kitchen to find Danny head first in the refrigerator.

"You in the mood for pizza?" He reached around his son to grab a block of cheese covered in green mold. Tasty. Wrinkling his nose at the stench of soured dairy, he tossed it in the sink.

Danny turned around and shoved his hands in his pocket. "Yeah, sure."

"Good deal." He plucked a pizza coupon off the fridge and called the company advertised. "Think Tim will want some?"

"Maybe. If he comes home."

Trent ordered two large supremes, just in case, then returned to watching television. Danny sat on the couch, rigid, and focused on the television. Neither of them spoke, minus the occasional three-word sentence.

Tim stumbled in shortly after ten smelling like booze with a curvy blonde on his arm. She appeared to be equally drunk. Trent set his beer down—his ninth—and struggled to his feet. Danny glanced up, shook his head, then slumped down the hall. The door slammed and pictures rattled on the wall, followed by the steady pounding of drums and the squeal of an electric guitar.

Trent mumbled a few swear words and faced his oldest son. "Just what do you think you're doing?" Tim's girlfriend was dressed provocatively in a short skirt and a crop top that swooped over her shoulders.

A crooked grin spread across Tim's face. He wrapped his arm around the girl's neck and squeezed. "Brandi, meet my pops. Pops, say hi to Brandi." He lifted his elbow under her chin, causing her face to tilt toward his, and planted a long kiss on her lips.

Trent's neck heated. "Nice to meet you, Brandi." He enunciated each syllable, trying to maintain self-control and keep from jumbling the words—nothing like a drunk father telling his drunk son that he couldn't bring a girl home. "But I'm afraid you're going to have to leave now."

Brandi turned to go, but Tim held fast.

"Brandi's not going anywhere." His eyes flashed.

Trent stepped closer. The veins pulsed in his forehead, hot blood saturating his intoxicated brain. "Good-bye, Brandi."

The girl squirmed under Tim's headlock, her gaze darting between Trent and Tim. She pushed her hands against Tim's chest. In his drunken state, Tim lost his balance and fell against the wall, allowing Brandi to break free. She backed up, stumbling over the mat.

"Call me." She spun around and threw open the door.

Tim lunged toward her, but the door slammed in his face. He rotated, a dark shadow falling over his eyes as his gaze narrowed on Trent.

Trent stared at Tim's balled fists then at his bulging arm muscles quivering beneath broad shoulders, and took another step backward. Tim stood nearly five inches taller with at least 50 more pounds of muscle. The rage in his eyes told Trent he was itching for a reason to pound him.

Trent turned and shuffled back into the living room, grabbed his beer, and brought it to his mouth. Footsteps swished behind him.

Standing in front of the coffee table, he watched his son closely. After a very intense standoff, Tim let out a string of expletives, turned, and marched to his room.

"Yo, Danny," Tim called out. "Pack your things. We're outa here."

Trent sighed and plopped back into his recliner. He turned his attention back to the television. A moment later, doors creaked open and Tim and Danny emerged, scowling and lugging duffel bags.

"Don't wait up, Pops." Tim laughed and flicked his brother's arm. "Let's go."

Picture frames rattled on the wall when the front door slammed behind them. An engine revved and then tires squealed.

CHAPTER 29

"When can you start?"

Alice raised her eyebrows. "You mean . . . ?"

Mr. Wilson smiled and nodded. "You've got the job, if you want it."

Alice almost giggled. Bussing tables wasn't exactly a step up, but after 20 applications and ten fruitless interviews, she was grateful to have a job.

"And as I mentioned earlier, we prefer to promote from within."

Nice thought, except eventually she'd need to land a career.

Mr. Wilson walked over to a stack of boxes. "What size do you wear?" He pulled out a pale blue polyester dress with wide collars and puffy sleeves. It looked like something Dorothy wore in the 1939 version of *The Wizard of Oz*. Dark brown stains under the arms indicated it was far from new.

He handed her the dress. She held it against her chest. The bottom hem hit an inch below her knee. "This will be fine."

"Great." He showed her to the door. "Can you be here tomorrow morning, eight o'clock?"

"Absolutely." She tucked the garment under her arm and left.

Back at the car, she didn't know whether to laugh or cry. Visions of pimple-faced teens, arms loaded with plates of fried food, flashed through her mind, taking her back three decades—to her high school days. The pay would be low and the work tiring. But she had to start somewhere.

When she returned to Beth's, she found her sitting at the kitchen table with her nose stuck in her Bible—again. A bag of river rocks lay at her feet. Sharpies of every color littered the table.

Alice lingered near the arched entryway separating the kitchen from the living room. "Hey, listen, I don't think I'll be able to help with the ladies luncheon this year."

"I kind of figured that." Beth smiled. "Don't worry about it. We've got it covered."

"Great." She huffed. "So I'm the talk of the church, then?"

"No, nothing like that. I handled it quietly." Beth grabbed a pen and scrolled something on a 3-by-5 card.

Alice eyed the clutter spread across the table. "What's all this?"

Beth grinned. "We're going to lay our burdens down tomorrow. Leave 'em at the foot of the cross." She closed the Bible and folded her hands in her lap. "You coming?"

Alice sank into the seat across from her. "I wish I could but . . ." She raised the polyester dress.

Beth covered her mouth and stifled a laugh. "Oh, Alice!"

"I'll be fighting them off in this beauty." She lowered her eyes and pushed her lips out in a half-smooch, half-pout.

"Oh!" Beth jumped to her feet. "Ooh, I know what would be perfect with that outfit!" She ran into her bedroom and returned with a pair of chocolate-colored brown clogs. "If you wear these, you certainly will."

Alice erupted in laughter. "Where on earth did you get those? And more importantly, why do you still have them?"

Beth slipped her feet into the shoes and pranced around the kitchen with her hand under her chin. "What do you mean, why do I still have them?" She kicked them off and returned to the table. "They were a gift from my mother-in-law. To go with a lovely olive-green jacket."

"You think that's bad. A few years ago, Amanda bought me a pair of Christmas light earrings and a matching necklace. You know, the ones that flash."

"Oh, I remember that." Beth giggled. "That was for our secret sister party, wasn't it? She was trying to be funny."

"Oh no she wasn't. I saw her at a restaurant a week later, and she asked me why I wasn't wearing them. Her matching set assured me she was serious."

They spent the remainder of the afternoon one-upping each other until giggles filled the small kitchen. Alice laughed so hard her eyes watered.

Ed walked in an hour later. "Did you forget to write a check in the checkbook?"

Beth's brow pinched. "Hmm. I don't think so, but I guess I could've. Why?"

"Just trying to balance the checkbook."

"Don't envy you there." She laughed.

Shaking his head, he disappeared into the living room. Or maybe his office. Beth followed shortly after with a glass of tea, leaving Alice alone in kitchen.

The rest of the evening dragged by while they waited for Luke to get home from soccer practice. When Beth served dinner, things got awkward. Alice felt like a third wheel with a squeaky bearing. More like a fourth wheel, counting Luke.

"So," Ed popped a forkful of corn into his mouth, "you talk to Trent lately?"

She pushed a piece of chicken across her plate. "No." She could feel everyone's eyes on her.

"Have you tried?"

"No."

She glanced up to catch Beth jabbing Ed in the gut with her elbow.

He ignored her. "Maybe you should give him a call."

Beth elbowed him again, harder. "Ed!"

Corn fragments showered the table as he choked on his food. He covered his mouth with his fist. "What? I'm just saying."

Alice swallowed and stared at her plate. Had she worn out her welcome?

Luke cleared his throat. "May I be excused? Homework."

Ed shooed him off with a wave.

Beth changed the subject. "So, remember when I told you about that river rock idea I had? About having all the ladies write their problems on a stone so they could lay them at the foot of the cross?"

"Uh-huh." Ed took a gulp of tea.

"That's tomorrow." She turned to Alice and squeezed her hand. "Sure wish you could come."

"Maybe next time."

Long moments of silence and strained conversation dominated the rest of the meal. Despite Alice's missing appetite, she forced down a few more bites. To be polite more than anything. Beth made small talk about clothes, gardening, anything but Trent and the boys while Alice humored her with polite nods and smiles.

"Great dinner." Ed pushed himself up from the table.

Beth stood and reached for his plate.

Alice stopped her. "No, you go. I'll get the dishes." She welcomed the distraction.

"You sure?"

"It'll give me something to do. You go enjoy your husband. Put action to all those romance tips you give us in Bible study."

Beth laughed and gave Alice a sideways hug. "Thanks." She disappeared into the living room.

Alice cleaned the kitchen then went to her room. She sat on the bed and scooted back until her spine pressed against the headboard. Hugging her knees to her chest, she tried to ignore Beth and Ed's laughter seeping through the wall. Which only made her feel more alone than ever. If only Trent hadn't started drinking. If only he'd agreed to counseling. Maybe their marriage wouldn't have failed.

No matter how hard she tried to hate Trent, or to pretend she didn't care, she ached for the love they once shared. Even after all the lonely nights, she longed for his strong embrace.

But those days were gone. It was time to move on.

Trent flicked on the light. Walking into the kitchen, he stepped over a mound of soccer shoes, shin guards, and schoolbooks. His empty stomach cramped, arguing with his empty wallet. *No more pizzas or burgers*. He opened the fridge and gagged. Time to find whatever was fermenting inside.

Red juice dripped from a decomposing tomato, pooling in partially dried globs on the bottom shelf. This was surrounded by plastic containers filled with food in various stages of decomposition. Removing the moldy containers one by one, he tossed them into the trash. Looked like he'd have to settle for a bottle of beer and a handful of stale crackers.

His phone rang. He glanced at the screen and held his breath. Great. His bank. Letting his voice mail answer, he waited for the message alert to pop up then hit play.

"Good afternoon, Mr. Goddard. This is Leah Northrup from First American Savings. I'm contacting you to discuss your current home loan. Please return my call as soon as possible." She left a phone number and extension.

Mrs. Northrup could wait until tomorrow. Right now, he needed to scrounge up some spare change. He was almost out of beer.

Rummaging through a kitchen drawer crammed with appliance warranties and recipe cards, he uncovered a faded picture. It was of him and Alice at a Valentine's dinner ten years ago. She wore her hair long back then, and it draped across her delicate shoulders in loosely curled ringlets. Her eyes sparkled with life, the laughter they had shared evident in the flush of her cheeks.

It had been a church function. Dinner, dancing, and a fun, little not-so-newlywed game. Whoever nominated him and Alice had gotten their vote's worth, for sure. Trent chuckled at the memory.

"So, Trent" Pastor Fred gave a mischievous grin. "Tell me, which animal did Alice say you most resemble, a mole, peacock, or a chicken?"

Laughter filled the sanctuary.

Trent played into the audience. "It would be easier to answer if I knew their driving personality traits."

Ed stood, stuck his fingers in his armpits, and waved his elbows. "Baaak, baaak, baa-aak."

Trent lurched to his feet and held his arms out in a "You-want-a-piece-of-this?" gesture.

More laughter. He glanced at Alice. She brought her hand to her mouth and giggled, her blue eyes sparkling.

Pastor Fred hummed the tune to Jeopardy! and motioned for everyone to settle down.

Trent cleared his throat and returned to his seat. "All right, if it were me, I'd say I resemble a bright, socially adept, creative mole."

"Leave it to you to turn a rodent into a CEO!" Someone from the back of the room hollered. It sounded like Theo.

Trent leaned back and draped his leg over his knee. "But Alice would probably say I remind her of a peacock."

Boos, heckles, and a few "amen to that's" shot out.

"And the answer is . . ." Pastor Fred turned his attention to Alice.

She giggled again and flipped her piece of cardboard around to reveal her answer.

Trent grinned and punched the air. "What'd I tell you? I know my girl." He leaned over and planted a passionate kiss on her lips.

When he pulled away, he saw she was blushing, making her look all the more beautiful.

The shrill ring of the phone brought Trent back to the present. He returned the photo to the drawer and glanced at the number displayed on the caller ID screen. Another creditor. He hit ignore.

Sitting at Beth's kitchen table, Alice wrapped both hands around her coffee mug and watched the steam rise. "I don't know what to do." She looked at Beth, who sat across from her.

"You said Danny asked you to leave them alone?"

She nodded.

"And they're staying at the Luttrells'?"

"I assume they still are."

"Then they're safe. You called the school, right?"

She nodded again. "At least they're still taking classes. For now. But what if they get into trouble? They won't take my calls. Maybe I should go to the school. Talk to the principal . . . or the police?"

"I don't know." Beth stirred her coffee. "I'm not sure what the police would do, except maybe force the boys to go back home."

Alice shook her head. "I don't want them around Trent." Having the kids watch their father throw his life away certainly won't help them get a grip on theirs.

"If you push them, they'll probably just leave again, and who knows where they'd end up. You said Tim's pretty reactive."

"But not Danny. At least, not until now. He's been mad at me before, turned silent, but he's never shut me out like this."

"I don't know. I wish I did." She placed her hand on Alice's arm. "Honestly, right now I think the best thing you can do is pray and keep reaching out. Send cards, leave phone messages. Let them know you love them, no matter what. That you're here for them. Maybe once they calm down and the storm settles, they'll be more apt to listen."

Alice slumped her shoulders. "Maybe."

Trent closed his office door, settled behind his desk and pulled out his phone. He called the bank.

"First American Savings. This is Saundra. How may I help you?"

"Yes, this is Trent Goddard. I received a message yesterday from a Leah Northrup."

"Will you hold, please?"

Elevator music played across the line. It stopped abruptly when a woman's voice came on.

"Hello, Mr. Goddard?"

"Yes?" His stomach churned as he waited for the inevitable.

"This is Mrs. Northrup. I'm calling to discuss your delinquent mortgage."

He massaged his forehead. "I know I'm behind."

"I'm trying to work with you here, but as I told you during our last conversation, property values have dropped and as this is a refinance, you now owe more than your house is worth."

"I plan to mail a check later this month, as soon as I get paid. If I could just . . ." He squeezed his eyes shut and calculated all his potential commissions. They were thin. Real thin. But if he could get a few more accounts turned in before the next pay period . . .

Mr. Lowe entered his office, and Trent nodded a greeting. Mrs. Northrup continued but Trent no longer listened. He focused on his boss who now stood in front of the desk. A deep scowl clouded his face, and a thick stack of brochures crumpled in his hand.

Trent ended his call and swallowed past a dry mouth. "Good morning, sir. I was going to call you today to go over my ideas for the Hendell account."

"What is this?" Mr. Lowe dropped brochures Trent had recently completed on the desk.

"Is there a problem? Because if you'd like me to—"

"Seamless commutations? Commutations?"

Trent stared at the bright white lettering beneath the Astra-Owens logo. There went 30,000 copies, along with four banners and three 7-by-5-foot signs, down the drain.

"Seriously, Trent. Didn't you use spell check?"

"I . . . I . . ."

Mr. Lowe leaned forward and pressed his palms into the desk. "What is with you?"

"I'm sorry, Mr. Lowe. That was unacceptable. I will—"

"What? You'll call Astra-Owens and explain why we don't have their marketing materials ready for their grand opening? You'll cover the loss, not just on wasted print and supply fees, but on all the business this will cost Innovative Media Solutions? Not to mention all the bad publicity this will generate."

What could he say? "I'm really sorry. I don't know what happened. This isn't like me, sir. You know that."

"You mean it *wasn't* like you. You're off your game, Trent. Have been for a while now. You need to take some time off—get yourself together."

This was crazy. He couldn't be laid off now. "But sir—"

"Either you take time to get your head straight, or you find another job."

Bile flooded the back of his throat. He swallowed it down and looked at a stack of open contracts to his right, then back at Mr. Lowe.

"Yes, sir."

His mind raced as he watched his boss leave. He struggled to breathe against constricting lungs and thought, for the third time that week, how easy it would be to end it all—to slip into the dark abyss of nothingness—no more pain, no more bills, no more muscle-men breathing down his back . . .

But then there'd also be no more Alice. Beautiful Alice.

CHAPTER 31

Alice paused with her hand on the diner door and watched women in polyester scurry from table to table, steaming pots in their hands. Men in ball caps and faded T-shirts filled nearly every booth.

Inhaling, she opened the door and stepped inside.

A tall, trim girl half Alice's age took orders from a group of men. Alice's cheeks heated as she watched a broad-shouldered man ogle the girl, his mouth curling into a hungry smile. She tugged on her waistband, suddenly feeling exposed.

"Hey there, darlin'."

Alice turned to see a bleached blonde with gray roots bounding toward her. Thick folds of flesh strained against the seams of her uniform. "So you're the new busser, huh?" The woman smiled and turned to a man standing behind a long metal counter. She handed him a slip of paper. "Two up. Not too runny."

Her lips twitched as she turned back to Alice, her narrowed eyes sweeping over her like a calculating drill sergeant. "I'm Melba. Been waiting tables here for 20 years, ain't that right, Frank?"

The cook flashed a toothless grin, save a few gold-capped incisors, and grabbed the order. He stuck it to a clip dangling in front of him. "You know that's right. Old Melba been here 'bout long as me."

The woman planted her hands on her hips. "Two things you gotta remember. Keep the tables clean and the coffee mugs filled. And your rear end far from Mr. Leupold's grabbing paws." She shook her head. "Ain't no tip worth putting up with that man, I tell you." She motioned toward an old man sitting at the bar in red suspenders and a sweat-stained hat. He threw Alice a wink.

"You do that," Melba tucked her order pad in her belt, "and I'll give you 10 percent of my tips."

Yahoo, a whole ten cents on the dollar. "Yes, ma'am."

"Hey, Melba." A man at the end of the counter clanked his coffee cup against the Formica. "I'm going dry over here." He raised his mug.

She jerked her head his way. "Better get going, darling. Old Carl's like a sieve, always flowing from both ends." She shoved a pot of coffee at Alice who hurried to Carl's table, filling raised cups as she passed.

Melba lumbered by carrying a tray full of food. She pointed her elbow toward an empty table on the left. "Grab those dishes on your way back, will you, Sugar?"

By 10:30, Alice was covered in thick syrup and egg yolk, and her feet burned. She leaned against the dish station and watched as Melba and Miss Flirt made their way through the few remaining tables.

Around 11:00 things slowed. Melba handed her last customer his check, set her order pad on the counter, and walked back to Alice. "Thing's will pick up soon." She reached behind the breakfast bar and pulled out a blue-and-green-checkered tote bag. "If you wanna smoke, now's the time. Before lunch rush hits." She rummaged through her purse until she found a pack of cigarettes. "But we gotta go out by the Dumpsters, so's the customers don't see us."

Melba headed to the back. Alice stepped out front where she could soak up a few rays of sunshine before returning to the dungeon. Perched on the edge of the curb, she hugged her knees. It was almost noon. Only four more hours to go. She grabbed her cell phone and called her boys, leaving a message for each of them. "It's your mom. I love you. Call me, please."

"Excuse me, miss?"

She looked up into clear blue eyes set beneath thick, blond eyebrows. "Yes?"

"You wouldn't happen to know how to get to I-5 from here, would you?" The man ran his fingers through curly blond hair and stared at a map in his hand.

She stood. "I-5 is on the other side of Lake Washington."

"And that is?"

"West. You're going to want to head north on 202 until you get to 522." She leaned forward and traced the highway with her finger, her nose filling with the woodsy scent of his aftershave.

"I knew I missed my turn." He folded the map and tucked it into his back pocket. "After two months, you'd think I'd be a better navigator." He gave her a boyish grin and glanced at the diner. "You work here?"

Alice blushed and glanced at her food-splattered uniform. She nodded. "First day."

The man watched her for a moment, his eyes softening as if he instantly knew her life story. "Yeah? So how's it going? The food any good?"

She shrugged. "If you like stale coffee and slimy pancakes."

"They're the best." His smile quickened her pulse.

"I got to get going."

The man glanced at his watch, the heart-stopping smile lingering on his lips. "Yeah, me too." He paused. "You work tomorrow?"

She fingered her wedding ring. Was he flirting with her?

"Uh . . . I think so."

Trent shut the door behind him, threw his keys onto the coffee table, and fell into the couch. Grabbing his phone, he scrolled through his contacts until he found Mrs. Northrup's number. Slumping forward, he dropped his phone and rubbed his face. There was no point calling. With unpaid leave, credit card interest rates ballooning, and enough debt to land him in the senate, he was out of options.

What had happened? When had everything gotten so out of control? And where was Alice?

Picking up his phone once again, he tried her cell. Her voice mail came on. He sat with the phone pressed to his ear until a shrill beep ended the call.

He laid his phone on the table.

The sound of the front door crashing into the wall jolted him to his feet. Tim stomped to his room, slamming the door behind him. Loud banging echoed down the hall then stopped. Tim emerged a moment later with a large duffel bag slung over each shoulder.

Trent stared at him. "Where are you going?"

"Alex's."

"When will you be back?"

"Don't know."

"Wait. I need to talk to you."

Tim stopped in midstep, turned, and glared. "What?"

Trent rubbed the back of his neck. How does a father tell his son he is about to lose their house and has absolutely nowhere else to go?

"Never mind. We'll talk later."

Danny never made it home that night, which probably meant he'd joined Tim at Alex's. Which was good. At least Alex's parents had food in the fridge.

CHAPTER 32

After four days of bussing tables, Alice was starting to get the hang of things. She even learned how to deal with nasty old Carl. Setting her purse behind the counter, she tucked her hair behind her ears, and mentally prepared herself for yet another busy day. At eight o'clock, the morning rush was already well under way. Customers filled nearly every table and, according to Mr. Wilson, they were short handed.

"Grab an apron from the back room. You've just been promoted."

She stared at him with wide eyes.

"Come with me, sweetie pie." Melba grabbed her by the elbow and dragged her to a janitor's closet near a large metal door. White aprons dangled from a hook. Stacks of order pads and pens piled on a shelf above them.

Melba grabbed one of each and handed them over. "Hurry up. I'll be on the floor."

Alice tied the apron around her waist and tucked the order pad inside the wide pockets. Nothing like crash course in waitressing to get her blood pumping.

She emerged to find Melba loaded down with plates and a long list of drink orders waiting to be filled.

"Grab the coffee pot and hit the floor running, sugar drop. And see about getting Carl his two-egg special."

Alice complied immediately. Three tables later, Carl grabbed her arm. Glancing at the other waiting customers, she sighed, then set the coffee pot down. She pulled out her order pad and a pen.

Old man Carl's face puckered as he watched Melba rush from one table to the next. "Send Melba my way, will ya, cutie? She seems to be dodging me this morning."

"I'll be more than happy to take your order. What can I get you, sir?"

He leaned back and crossed his arms. "I thought you was the bus girl."

"I was, but they're shorthanded today."

He raised an eyebrow and studied her. But then his features relaxed. "I want that two-egg special. Not the one with bacon, but this one here." He traced the menu with a dirty finger. "Eggs over easy, but not too runny. Extra butter, two scoops."

Alice wrote down his request word for word. Carl leaned over to look at her pad.

"And make sure my bacon's crisp. Not that soggy garbage Frank tries to give me. Not too greasy, either." He shoved his mug to the edge of the table.

Alice filled it then hurried back to the kitchen, leaving half the restaurant with empty mugs.

She tore off the order and handed it to Frank.

His face twisted into a grin. "You writin' a book, pretty lady?"

Melba arrived and grabbed the order. Throwing her head back, she laughed. "Whoo-wee, girl! Never waited tables before, have ya?"

Alice shook her head.

Melba looked back at the floor and gave a shrug before returning her attention to Alice. "Let 'em wait. If I don't school you now, you'll be holding us up all morning." She grabbed a menu, set it on the counter, and placed her order pad beside it.

"Never use whole words. See here, '2 OE sp w/bc' means a two-egg special, over easy with bacon. And," she scribbled some more, "'msh/saus/sp + 2 T' means a mushroom sausage and spinach omelet with two slices of toast on the side."

"Hey Melba! Where's that decaf I ordered?" A man in a plaid shirt raised his mug.

"Comin', Abel." She turned back to Alice. "Don't sweat it, darlin'. Just scribble it down without the vowels. Frank here'll figure it out, won't ya handsome?"

Frank grinned and pushed a plate of scrambled eggs across the counter with a wink. "Don't you know it?"

Melba picked up the plate and dropped a bottle of ketchup into her apron pocket. "You take the right, I'll go left. Might wanna get those fellas that just came in some water."

Alice nodded. She grabbed two glasses, filled them, then dashed back to the floor. She was almost finished with her second table when a familiar face flashed through her peripheral vision. When she turned to make eye contact, her heart gave an odd jump. It was the guy with the map, the one she'd met her first day. And based on his amused smile, he had been watching her.

Alice looked away as heat flushed her cheeks. What was it about him that got her so flustered? Besides his icy blue eyes and rock star smile, that is.

She ran her thumb over her wedding band and turned back to her customer. "Is there anything else?" She felt the stranger's eyes on her, sending a flutter through her stomach.

Her flutter turned into a full-blown knot when she reached his table less than five minutes later. His eyes locked on hers, accelerating her pulse. Swallowing, she brushed aside a stray lock of hair tickling her forehead. "Hello. What can I get you?"

The man smiled. "Thought I'd order me some of those slimy pancakes you told me about." His sun-kissed skin glowed beneath a crisp gray and tan button-down shirt.

She fumbled for her order pad. "Pancakes it is. Anything else?"

The man studied her for a moment, his head cocked, eyelids lowered slightly.

She held her breath. Was he about to ask her out?

"How about a cup of coffee?"

Her hand trembled as she wrote his order down. "Were you able to find the freeway yesterday?"

"Eventually." He laughed. "You'd think I'd be able to find my way to the freeway by now."

"Where'd you move from?" Why was she still talking to him? Not that there was any way to avoid him. Besides, she was only being friendly. That's what waitresses were supposed to do, right?

"Emporia, Kansas."

"Where's that?"

Again, the man laughed, a throaty, alluring chuckle that quickened Alice's heart. "I get that a lot. Between Kansas City and . . ." He scratched his head. "And a wheat field."

"Ah. So what brought you here?"

Melba whizzed by, bogged down with dirty dishes, scowling when she and Alice made eye contact.

"I better go." She motioned toward her other customers.

"Yeah, OK. What time's your break?"

Her stomach flipped and she lowered her eyes. "I . . . uh . . ."

He leaned forward, and his gaze intensified, holding hers. She shifted and fiddled with the hem of her apron.

"Hey, waitress." A low voice to her right called her attention to a man three tables down. "Gotta go down to Columbia to get the coffee or what?"

"I'm coming, sir." She turned to go.

The stranger grabbed her arm. "You never told me your name."

She hesitated. "Alice."

"Good to meet you, Alice. I'm Austin."

She nodded and hurried to the man with the empty mug. She sensed Austin's eyes following her. A sideways glance confirmed her suspicions. Cheeks burning, she turned back around.

By nine o'clock Austin had left. Alice—busser and waitress rolled into one—strolled over to the empty table and began to clear away the dishes. Tucked beneath the plate she found a 20-dollar bill and a folded napkin. Printed in smooth, careful writing were the words, "Call me," followed by a phone number. She picked it up, ran her finger across the edge of the napkin, then set it down.

She smiled. After all these years, it felt good to know someone found her attractive.

CHAPTER 33

The house was quiet. Depressingly quiet. Empty vodka and beer bottles littered the coffee table and dirty dishes filled the sink. Days worth of mail lay unopened on the kitchen table.

Trent grabbed the remote and turned on the television. His phone rang, and he studied the caller ID. After a long, internal debate, he answered.

"Hello, Mr. Goddard? This is Mrs. Northrup from First American Savings Bank."

"Yeah, I meant to call you back."

"We are trying to work with you here, Mr. Goddard. No one wants to see your property go into foreclosure."

He watched a lady with raven-black hair play the harmonica on the television screen. He flicked the channel.

"As I mentioned previously, you are behind on your mortgage payments. Adding the contractually agreed upon 5 percent late fee puts you at . . ."

Trent flicked the channel again as Mrs. Northrup droned on about all the money he owed. Wasn't much he could do about it now.

"So what are my options?" He cut her off in midlecture.

"As I said, we're willing to work with you on this. Are there extenuating circumstances we should be aware of?"

Did losing his family count? How about getting laid off while the debt multiplied? Having thugs hunting after you?

"Listen, I've got to go—"

"I suggest you deal with this, Mr. Goddard. Before we deal with it for you. I'm trying to help you out here."

Closing his eyes as if doing so would make it all go away, he raked his fingers through his hair and exhaled. "All right. You tell me. What do you want to do here?"

"Perhaps it's time we talk about a short sale."

"Do what you gotta do."

"I'll need you to fill out some forms in order to prove financial hardship."

He sighed. "You can fax them to my work." He gave the number then hung up. Short sale, foreclosure. What'd he care? Either way he lost the house. The bank would probably ask for Alice's signature but considering she still avoided his calls . . . So he'd forge her name.

He grabbed his beer and brought it to his mouth.

A single drop fell on his tongue. Time for another.

He walked into the kitchen and opened the fridge. An empty cardboard box sat on the top shelf. Empty bottles littered the counter and spilled from a nearby trashcan. He needed to scrounge up a few bucks.

Moving to the living room, he searched the seat cushions for change. He found two quarters, a dime, and three pennies in the couch. Searching the recliner proved pointless. Maybe the boys had left a few coins lying around. He walked into Danny's bedroom, opened his dresser drawers, and rummaged through T-shirts and mismatched socks. Nothing.

A pile of dirty clothes lay on the floor. He grabbed a pair of jeans and checked the pockets. Empty. Two shoeboxes lined the closet shelf. He pulled them down and dumped their contents on the carpet. Old movie stubs, school photos, and soccer game brochures spilled out.

A note from Alice was tucked inside a blue-and-tan birth-day card. Trent's eyes burned as he picked up the smooth paper.

He slipped it back into the card, sifted through the rest of Danny's keepsakes, then closed the lid. Back to the closet. As he ran his hand along the dusty shelf, his fingers brushed against something cold and smooth. He moved a pile of sweaters out of the way and found a pale blue piggy bank. The day Danny had decided to save his very first dollar played through his mind like an old movie clip.

"For me, Daddy?" The boy's eyes widened when Trent handed him the crisp bill.

He ruffled his hair. "Don't go spending it all in one place."

Danny responded with a cheek-bunching grin. "I won't! I'll put it in my paddy bank right now!"

Breathing deep, he forced the memory aside. He pulled the porcelain bank down and ran his fingers over its smooth surface. It was heavier than he'd expected.

Unscrewing the bottom plug, he turned it over and shook until everything spilled out. Crumpled wads of cash and numerous coins spilled across the tan carpet. He counted through the bills. Adding it all together, it totaled $29.63. Enough to buy a large bottle of vodka, maybe two. Swallowing down a wave of guilt, he shoved it all in his pocket and left.

The streets were quiet as he made his way through the neighborhood. A woman pushing a stroller glanced up as he drove by. She flashed him a smile. Trent looked away and continued down the street.

Rain started to fall, light at first, growing heavier until large drops flooded his windshield, making it hard for him to see. He kept driving, past single story homes with white picket fences, a strip mall, a row of restaurants and trendy storefronts, and onto the freeway.

Two exits down, he turned onto a side road and into the parking lot of his favorite liquor store. The rain pounded against his roof and splattered onto the asphalt. A flash of lightning lit the sky. His hands went slick on the steering wheel.

What was he doing, robbing his own son?

He squeezed his eyes shut as his nerves cried out for alcohol.

"For me, Daddy?"

"No one wants to see your property go into foreclosure."

"You're off your game, Trent. You're off your game, Trent. You're off your game . . ."

A knock sounded on his window. He looked up to find a man with bushy eyebrows and a tangled beard staring down on him.

The man cupped grimy hands around his face and leaned into the glass. "Hey, buddy. Spare some change?"

Trent cranked the key in the ignition and threw the car in reverse.

Alice sat on the edge of the bed and counted her money. Fifty bucks in tips, largely due to Austin's generosity. Not bad for eight hours of waiting tables. It was more than she'd made in a week of bussing. If things continued, she'd have an apartment in no time. Though she needed to pay her phone bill, and in a few months her car insurance would come due. Tim's as well.

Would she need a three-bedroom rental? Hopefully. The boys still weren't taking her calls.

They just needed time. Right?

A knock rattled the door.

"It's open."

Beth poked her head in. "You up for an awesome jam fest?"

Alice set her money down.

Beth rested a shoulder against the doorframe. "Should be interesting. Sanctified and Lampstand are playing at Gas Works Park." She broke out in song, snapping her fingers and shaking her hips. "When my love, my love, my love gets hold of yo-o-ou."

Alice giggled at the exaggerated way Beth shoved her rear out when she danced. "What time does it start?"

"Eight."

She loved Gas Works. Stretching just over 19 acres, it was once Seattle's Gas and Light Company's gasification plant, and it had retained a good deal of the factory's equipment, some in original form, some refurbished.

She and her boys used to spend hours there, back when they were young. She'd read a book or snap a zillion pictures as they climbed the plant's old exhauster compressor in the "play barn." Then, they'd hike the 15-meter high hill to fly kites, pausing on numerous occasions to check the time using their shadows and the massive sundial on the ground. Sometimes, Beth and Luke would join them, and they'd have a picnic on the waterfront with geese to their back and private planes circling overhead. Often, they'd end the evening munching on potato chips and watching the sun set over Lake Union.

"Come on, Alice." Cutting through her thoughts, Beth stepped further into the room. "It'll be fun. Just like old times, well, minus toting diaper bags and sweaty boys around."

"I'm kind of tired."

"Nah. You just need a little fire under those dancing feet of yours." The corners of Beth's eyes crinkled as she gave her hips another shake. "Ed's at a men's retreat and Luke's at a youth group lock-in." She walked over and stood in front of Alice, pushing her lips into a pout. "You're not going to make me go all by myself, are you?"

Alice threw her hands up. "All right. I'll go."

"Yay!" Beth clapped and hopped up and down like an excited middle schooler, turning Alice's chuckles into rolling laughter. "It'll be fun. You'll see."

They arrived to the park early and parked across from Fisheries Supply, finding the lot nearly full.

Beth cut her engine and glanced about. "This seems like a lot of people for an unknown, independent band."

"Maybe they're here for a protest or something."

Beth made a face. "I sure hope not."

Despite it's relatively isolated location, four miles from downtown and on the south side of the middle-to-upper class Wallingford neighborhood, the park's history boasted numerous political rallies, including a seven-month vigil in the 1990s in opposition to the Gulf War.

The two made their way down a gravel road and past a row of cement support columns that resembled upside-down horseshoes, continuing toward the waterfront.

Blankets covered the landscape in a kaleidoscope of color. A handful of giggling girls chased after a group of geese, ribbons and braids bouncing off their tiny backs.

Beth stopped a few hundred feet from a rusted, 30-foot tall structure—part of the old gasification plant. "This look good?"

A gentle breeze stirred Alice's hair, a few strands tickling her cheek. With the sun warming her back, she inhaled slowly and let the fresh air pull her mouth into a relaxed smile. "Perfect."

Beth spread a blanket on the ground and sat, legs folded beneath her. Alice sat beside her and hugged her knees. She gazed above the crowd at the gold and pink reflecting off wisps of clouds on the other side of Lake Union.

When Sanctified stepped onto the concrete stage, people cheered, a few jumping to their feet. Quiet came just as quickly when Filip, the lead singer, moved to the mic and, without introduction, started to sing. Each word vibrated in his throat before pouring out in a low, husky chord.

When you close your eyes, what do you see?
When you cry on your pillow, will you come to Me?
When your world is crashing, will you reach out your hand?
In Me alone will you stand. In Me alone will you stand.

Oh my beloved, push past the pain.
My dear sweet beloved, just call My name
Lift your eyes until you see My face,
Child, surrender to My embrace.

Alice rested her chin on her knees and closed her eyes as the lyrics flowed through her, settling deep within her heart.

It'd been too long. Much too long.

Beth wrapped her arm around Alice's shoulder. "Want to pray?"

She opened her eyes. Inhaling, she straightened. "I'm fine."

"Why do you keep shutting me out?"

"I'm not." She stood and brushed grass from the back of her pants. "I need a minute. I'm going to go for a walk." She needed to think, to process. To figure out how she wanted the rest of her life to play out.

CHAPTER 34

Trent slowed the car as he approached his house. Thick shadows shrouded his front door and walk. Minus a few porch lights, the neighbors' homes were dark.

He pulled into the carport and cut the engine. The hair on the back of his neck stood on end. Was someone watching him? He jerked his head to the right. A tall alder stood between him and the nearest streetlight, breaking the beams into fragments reflected on the oil-slicked street. He looked to the left. Nothing but empty cars, and yet, the fear in his gut increased. Someone hid in the shadows, watching him.

Watching the street again, more carefully this time, he noticed a black sedan with tinted windows. Amidst the darkness, the silhouette of a man emerged. In an instant, recognition surfaced.

Perspiration beaded on Trent's forehead and upper lip. He threw the car in reverse and squealed out of the drive. With a constant eye on the rearview mirror, he punched the gas, blowing through three red lights. An approaching driver laid on his horn. The high-pitched blare electrified Trent's nerves. He checked the rearview mirror again. A car followed close behind. Holding his breath, he accelerated. Blinkers flashed. The car disappeared down a side street.

He exhaled and scanned the road behind him. Another vehicle lagged 20 feet back. Was it the sedan? Trent accelerated and took a quick right. Then a left. He slowed, eyeing the single story houses on either side of him like a trapped doe seeking shelter. Ten minutes and three turns later, he parked between a six-foot fence and a metal shed. He killed his lights and wiped sweaty hands on his pants.

His thoughts immediately turned to his boys. What if they came home? Would Jay have Bruce unload on them? Trent's hand shook as he reached for his cell phone and called Tim. It rang once. He hung up. It was after midnight. Both boys would be asleep, wherever they were. Besides, what would he tell them? "Hey, Tim. It's your dad. Don't come home anymore."

He needed to call Alice.

Alice pulled the blanket to her chin and nestled into her pillow. It had been a wonderful night. The music, Beth, watching children dance under gently swaying tree branches—all of it. Things were starting to turn around. She could feel it. Pleasant weariness seeped into her muscles. Sleep would come quickly.

She closed her eyes and let her mind drift into restful oblivion. Visions of giggling toddlers holding ice cream cones, chocolate dripping down dimpled chins emerged as sleep took hold.

The evening concert replayed, mingling with her subconscious. Tim and Danny nestled in their father's arms. Alice sat on the edge of a pink blanket sifting through a basket of food. Soft notes drifted from a faraway piano. She rose on her knees and looked toward the sound. Her children's voices grew dim as the melody enveloped her.

Across the meadow, a stone passage wound its way between clusters of daffodils and bluebells. Their delicate petals danced in the breeze. Alice stood and walked toward the path, her vision narrowing until everything else blurred and then darkened. A strand of hair tickled her cheek. She brushed it away, laughing as a hummingbird flitted between the branches of a blossoming cherry tree.

Pausing to lower her face to a hyacinth, she inhaled its soft fragrance. A flash of color to her right caught her attention. Turning, her gaze locked on two dark eyes peering through yellow-green fronds. Pointed ears protruded from the top of the foliage and a bushy tail flicked from side to side.

Alice straightened as goose bumps erupted on her arms. She stepped backward, her eyes held by the tiny slits of coal in front of her. Spinning around, she ran back in the direction of Trent and the boys as dark clouds blew in, swallowing the sun.

Trent stood, his expression flashing from smiles to hatred as if stuck on instant replay. He held his arms out to her. The boys caved by his side, their faces pale, eyes wide.

"Momma!" They clung to their father's leg, reaching for Alice with their free hands, their tiny fingers grasping at the air.

"Danny! Timmy!" She ran toward them. The wind grew fierce, ripping through the trees like an angry force. The clouds exploded with rain, pelting her face with icy droplets.

"Momma! Help us!" The boys drifted into the distance, their hands still grasping.

She shivered as an intense cold ran through her. A clap of thunder rumbled, followed by a flash of lightning.

She fell to her knees. "Danny! Timmy, come back!"

A sharp ring sliced through her dream, jolting her awake.

Alice sprung to a sitting position, damp with sweat. It took a moment to free her mind from the images of her nightmare.

Her phone rang again. She grabbed it. "Hello? Timmy? Danny?"

Silence. A shiver ran through her.

"Hello?" Her voice squeaked.

"Alice, it's Trent."

She exhaled and rolled her eyes. Shoving her hands through her tangled hair, she looked at the clock. "Do you know what time it is?"

"I'm sorry to call so late." His voice trembled. "It's . . . I . . ." He paused. "I need you to call the boys. I need you to tell them not to come home."

"What is it? Are you OK? Is everything all right? Where are you?" The words tumbled out.

"I'm in trouble."

CHAPTER 35

Trent studied the brick house in front of him. The faint glow of a porch light dangling from a wrought-iron hook elongated the shadows encasing the windows.

Behind him, a long row of fences formed a barricade between the narrow alley and the single story cottages lining the street. A Neighborhood Watch sign hung on a wooden post. He couldn't stay here. Not unless he wanted the police on his back. But he couldn't go home, either.

He thought briefly about calling his father—the drunk would be awake—then tossed the idea aside. Trent hadn't spoken to him in years, ever since his mother had slit her wrists, driven to it by his father's alcoholism.

Like father like son.

He pulled out of the driveway, down the alley, and onto a quiet road lined with streetlamps. A handful of vacant cars dotted the curb. His pulse quickened as an image of Jay and Bruce resurfaced. Gripping the steering wheel, vision dulled from lack of sleep, he saw them in every shadow and darkened window. Where could he go where they wouldn't find him? And what about the boys and Alice? Were they safe? How far would those thugs go to get their money?

It was a good thing Alice and the boys had left, so they didn't have to get all wrapped up in this mess. As if they weren't already.

Trent rounded the corner and followed the curve of the road. He searched the tree-lined street in search of shelter. An abandoned house he could hide away in, a Dumpster he could park behind, another alley—anything.

Others slept on the ground or park benches. But there was nothing but manicured lawns surrounded by garden lights and white picket fences. He was about to give up and head to the city—not that he wanted to fight off a bunch of gang bangers—when he caught sight of a neighborhood playground.

Making a quick U-turn, he pulled into the parking lot, drove to a dark corner, and cut the engine. Reclining his seat as far back as it would go, he grabbed a sweatshirt lying on the floor and shoved it under his head.

Sleep came slowly and was disrupted by unsettling images. The kind that made him sweat, causing his shirt to cling to his clammy flesh like a second skin.

A distinct tapping startled him awake.

He lurched to an upright position. Air caught in his chest as his eyes fought to focus.

A man stood over him and aimed a flashlight through the driver's side window.

Trent scanned the interior of his car. His keys, where were his keys?

He groped the seat beside him. His sweaty hand closed around the smooth plastic of his key chain.

Three more taps, louder this time.

Trent's mouth went dry. He jabbed the keys in the ignition, his shoulder muscle twitching.

"Hey, buddy. You can't stay here."

Trent dropped his hand and stared at the man standing beside him. A gold badge attached to a dark blue uniform glimmered in the dim light. Trent's muscles slackened, and he sighed. Great. He rolled down the window.

"You can't stay here." The policeman touched the handle of his gun.

"Sorry, officer. I'll leave now." To do what? Roam the streets of Seattle until he ran out of gas?

Seated at the kitchen table, Alice nursed a cup of coffee, not that she needed it. Her nerves were so fired up, caffeine would only send them in overdrive. The smell of eggs and bacon wafting from the stove where Beth cooked churned her stomach even more.

She couldn't get Trent's words from the night before out of her mind.

"I'm in trouble."

He'd gone on to tell her just how deep. Gambling, losing his job. About how a couple of loan sharks were watching their house. Because Trent owed them money he had zero ability to pay.

And now she needed to call the boys and tell them it wasn't safe for them to come home. As if they hadn't already been through enough.

"Morning, ladies." Ed crossed the kitchen and wrapped his arms around Beth's midsection.

She giggled as his lips grazed her skin. "You hungry?" She grabbed two slices of bread and popped them in the toaster.

"Always. And a few gallons of coffee won't hurt, either." He plucked a mug from the cupboard and filled it.

Beth turned to Alice. "What about you? Want a piece?"

"I'm not hungry. Thanks."

Alice watched the clock. 7:15. Was it too early to call the boys? She had wanted to phone them last night. Had spent 30 minutes fretting over it as images of muscle men scoping out their house flashed through her mind. In the end, she'd decided it'd be best to wait till morning.

"Get 'em while they're hot." Beth flashed a smile and handed a plate of eggs and toast to Ed.

"Thanks, babe. I gotta go." Taking the food, he planted a kiss on Beth's cheek.

"So much for that." Beth laughed and wiped her hands on a kitchen towel before facing Alice. "I guess I better get myself ready. Are you going to the ladies tea this morning?"

Alice shook her head. She looked at the clock again and pressed her palms together, back straight.

"If you change your mind . . ."

She offered a polite smile. The minute Beth disappeared around the corner, she called Tim. As usual, his voice mail picked up.

She sighed and rubbed the back of her neck. This wasn't something she could leave on voice mail. *Good morning, Tim. Your father called and asked that you not come home.* Or even better, *"A bunch of thugs are camped outside the house, so stay away."*

She tried Danny. Again, voice mail.

"You know what to do. Beep!"

"Hey, sweetie. Call me. Please. It's important."

He wasn't going to call. Neither of them would. Fine. If they wouldn't come to her, she'd go to them. She tucked her phone in her purse, slung it over her shoulder, and hurried out the door.

Ten minutes later, she stood face-to-face with Mrs. Luttrell.

"Alice. I'm surprised to see you this morning." The woman's face tightened as she smoothed the front of her navy pantsuit. Crossing her arms, she angled her face like a teacher addressing a wayward child.

"I need to talk to the boys."

"Have you thought more about what we discussed? Because the best way to help your boys is to help yourself first."

"I know it's early, and I'm sure you're in a rush—"

"Have you seen—?" Mr. Luttrell came to the door holding a leather briefcase. "Oh. Hello."

Alice forced a smile. "Good morning."

The Luttrells exchanged glances, and Mr. Luttrell looked like he planned to leave, but then his wife raised her eyebrows and moved aside.

Mr. Luttrell's face fell. He sighed, slouched his shoulders, and set his briefcase on the floor. He glanced at his watch. "I have a meeting at 8:30, but I suppose I can spare a few minutes."

Heat flooded Alice's cheeks. Reluctantly, she stepped inside and scanned the meticulous entryway. "May I please speak with Danny and Tim?"

Mrs. Luttrell led the way to a formal living room with burgundy curtains. A long, gold mirror stood above the mantel behind three perfectly aligned picture frames.

"Have a seat." She motioned to the couch.

Not again. Alice chose an armchair instead. She focused on the spiral stairs to her right where she heard laughter and energetic voices.

"Hey Mom, have you seen my MP3 charger?" Alex's voice traveled down the stairs. He emerged holding a blue backpack. Danny and Tim followed.

The three of them halted in midstep, eyes wide, smiles gone.

Alice stood. "Danny, Tim, good morning." Her heart ached to pull them close. "I need to talk to you. It's important."

Danny frowned and chewed on his thumbnail. Tim scowled and rolled his eyes.

"Please." She turned to Mr. and Mrs. Luttrell, who now stood at the base of the stairs. "Would you mind?"

A spasm flitted across Mrs. Luttrell's left cheek. With a sigh, she threw her hands in the air. "All right. But please make it quick. They have to get to school."

Her two-inch heels clicked across the wooden floor, her arms swaying staunchly at her sides. Her husband followed, and Alex bolted back up the stairs.

Breathing deep, Alice turned to her boys. "I've missed you." She reached up and touched her youngest's cheek.

"What do you want?" Tim asked.

"Your father called—"

Tim snorted. "And?"

"He's in trouble. And . . ." Alice tucked her hair behind her ears and swallowed. "It's best if you don't go home for awhile."

CHAPTER 36

Trent woke with a stiff neck and the impression of a door handle pressed into the side of his face. After hours of bouncing from one neighborhood to the next, he finally settled on a diner parking lot. Next to a very busy, 24-hour gas station. Needless to say, it hadn't been a restful night. Between the headlights of approaching cars and the occasional ear-splitting stereo system—a pack of kids decided to use the lot as their hangout sometime around two a.m.—he'd gotten less than three hours of sleep.

The glare of the sun burned his eyes and made them water. The tremors of withdrawal were setting in. Lifting a shaky hand to block the rays, he surveyed the parking lot. A woman in a pale blue polyester dress with black, chin-length hair made her way across the asphalt.

He sat up straighter and rubbed his eyes. Was that . . . ? No, it couldn't be.

The woman paused at the restaurant door and tucked her hair behind her ears before disappearing inside. Trent rubbed his face again. It had to be.

He jumped out, slammed the door and half ran, half walked across the lot. Pausing midway to catch his breath, he studied his reflection in a nearby car window. What a mess. Stubble covered his sweat-drenched face and his hair was matted to the side. He spat on his fingers and ran them over wayward clumps. Cupping a hand in front of his mouth, he exhaled, wrinkling his nose. His breath stank. Bad. With trembling hands, he dug in his pockets for a mint. Nothing.

A man dressed in a plaid shirt and torn jeans approached and touched the brim of his hat. Trent nodded and resumed his stride. Standing in front of a long, dusty window a moment later, he cupped his hands around his eyes and pressed his nose to the glass.

Alice stood in front of a small, round table holding a pen and tablet. A man with blond, curly hair and a square chin sat in front of her, visually devouring Trent's wife.

The man said something, the corners of his eye crinkling, and Alice glanced down once again, tucking her hair behind her ears—a nervous habit. She glanced at the man through lowered lashes and cocked her head, a slight laugh rippling through her soft body.

Trent jerked back, his hands clenching into fists. He lunged for the door and started to burst inside, give this yahoo a what-for, when the image of his reflection in the glass stopped him.

Dropping his head, he slumped, turned, and walked away.

Sunday morning, Alice closed her eyes and let the warmth of the sun caress her skin. The crisp air, filled with the soft scent of lilacs, soothed her. A lady in a cloche hat adorned with a bright blue ribbon smiled at her and held the church door open.

"It's a beautiful morning, isn't it?" She handed Alice a bulletin.

"Delightful."

It felt good to be new. Unknown. Alice nodded hello to two men dressed in heavy work boots and coveralls sitting on a bench along the far wall. Beside them, brochures, flyers, and pocket devotionals topped a long, rectangular table, above which hung a corkboard with what appeared to be missions and ministry pictures.

Alice proceeded into the tiny sanctuary. She chose a seat in the far back corner—in case she cried through the entire service. Not that she planned to. But her emotions rarely operated according to plan.

The pews filling the small sanctuary looked like they had seen their fair share of parishioners, but the dull wood and faded carpet only added to its warmth. A rainbow of color streamed through the stained-glass windows set high on the wall.

She slid her purse under her seat, leaned back, and closed her eyes, her body relaxing into the wood.

"Hello. Is this seat taken?" A stocky woman with short, gray hair held her hand out. "I'm Betty. Betty Frye."

Alice tried not to look annoyed as the lady pumped her arm up and down with enough gusto to tear her shoulder out of socket.

"This your first time?"

She nodded. "My home church is in Kirkland, but I'm thinking of changing." She needed a fresh start—someplace where she could reinvent herself without memories of Trent and their old life weighing her down.

"So you're 'church shopping' as they say? Me, I've been here 35 years, ever since I gave my life to Christ. Don't understand kids these days, the way they hop from one church to the next like they're out shopping for a new car. The body of Christ isn't supposed to work that way. Know what I mean?"

Alice shifted, feeling slightly exposed. "I guess." She watched a woman in a floral dress sit behind the organ, hoping this inquisition would soon end. Any hopes of an immediate reprieve were shattered when a man in a suit and tie, presumably the pastor, engaged the organist in conversation.

"I don't know what I would have done without my church family. When Daddy died," Betty held her hand to her chest, "and Momma got sick, I wanted to crawl in bed, pull the covers up over my head.

Up over my head!" She jabbed Alice in the ribs. "But thanks be to God, my brothers and sisters in Christ carried my burdens. Carried my burdens, child, just as if they were their own."

The man with the tie walked to the center of the stage and grabbed the mic. "Hymn number 487." His deep voice contrasted with his wiry frame.

Alice pulled a thick green book from the shelf in front of her and flipped to the assigned page while her newfound "friend" belted out a high-pitched vibrato. Three songs later, the pastor grabbed the microphone again.

"No better place to be on such a sunshiny morning, isn't that right?"

"Amen!"

"I've been coming to church ever since I can remember. Came from a long line of religious folks, and I could talk it up with the best of them." He paced as he talked. "Said my 'amens' and 'hallelujahs' like a good Christian boy. Even threw a few verses in the mix when I wanted to sound extra spiritual. I was like all those respectable Pharisees walking around in their long flowing robes. But inside, I was terrified. Terrified that someday someone would see through all my religious acts to my dark heart underneath."

Alice straightened and stared at the wooden pew in front of her.

"Then one day, I'd had enough." He walked to the end of the podium and paused. "I was done playing the religious game. I wanted more. I wanted to experience reality. I wanted to experience God."

He continued for another 20 minutes, but Alice barely heard him. Her mind remained stuck on what he said about wanting to experience God. How long had it been since she'd drawn near to Christ, craved His presence? And yet, she had lived the lie for so long, she didn't know how to be real anymore. Didn't even know what real was. But it wasn't this—her life as it was now—that much she knew.

When the service ended, Betty turned to her and grinned. "It was a pleasure to meet you. I'd love to stay and get to know you better, tell you about some of our programs—our women's tea is coming up next month. Might want to think about coming. It'd be a great way to get to know people."

Alice glanced at white and gray heads all around her, then turned back to Betty. She held her bulletin in the air. "I'll have to check that out. Thanks."

Bold typed words in the center of the page grabbed Alice's attention.

> **FOR RENT:** Mother-in-law apartment. Great loca-
> tion. Full kitchen. Prefer single mom or college
> student. Call Betty Frye for more information.

A phone number followed.

Alice lowered the bulletin and looked Betty in the eye. "Is this you?" She pointed at the bulletin. "Do you have an apartment for rent?"

Betty squinted, read the bulletin, and smiled. "Yeah, that's me all right. Why? You know someone who's needing to rent?" She frowned. "Not one of those bachelor types that like to throw parties all the time and have people coming in and out all hours of the night. Momma couldn't handle that, poor thing. Ever since Daddy died . . ."

Blinking rapidly as tears pooled in her eyes, she pressed one hand to her chest and fanned her face with the other. "Need to find some-one that won't go tearing down the place. Been trying to rent it out for a long time. Not for the money, mind you. Daddy made sure Momma never wanted for nothing. Great plug for our friends in the insurance agency, wouldn't you say?"

Alice offered an awkward laugh and glanced around. Most everyone had already left, and she was beginning to feel out of place.

"Once Daddy died, Momma got forgetful. Distracted and real lonely. Tried to get her to go to one of those 'retirement' places. Found a real nice one, too. With Friday socials, craft days, you name it. But she wouldn't hear of it. Said she'd birthed four kids and buried one husband in that home and wasn't about to walk away now."

The woman pulled open her purse, grabbed a stick of gum, and popped it in her mouth. "And I would have moved in with her if it wasn't for my husband." A sour expression spread across her face. "Charles don't come to church no more. Not since he lost his leg. An old farming accident that left him tied to his wheelchair. Always thinks people are looking at him—pitying him."

Betty rolled her eyes. "I told him to get over himself. Like anyone's got the time of day to get all caught up in his life. But he's stubborn that way. He likes watching those 'how things are made' programs. You know, the ones that show you how they put computer chips inside calculators or something crazy like that. Like it'd kill him to miss one once in awhile."

"The apartment? Can you tell me more about it?"

"Oh, I'm sorry. My husband always says I'm like a bag of popcorn kernels let loose on a hot-iron stove—popping in so many directions it makes you dizzy just trying to keep up with me."

Alice smiled.

Betty sat and set her purse beside her. "It's got three bedrooms, nothing fancy. Two of the rooms are pretty small, but they're big enough to get a full and a dresser in 'em. Other one's almost master size. Only one bathroom. Comfortable living area, and it's got its own kitchen."

It sounded perfect, but it probably cost a fortune. Certainly more than Alice made waiting tables.

Betty's eyes narrowed. "Why? Who you thinking of?"

Alice swallowed and sat up straighter. "Me. Me and my two boys."

Betty's face erupted in a fleshy grin, until her gaze landed on Alice's wedding ring. Then her expression hardened. "You on the run? 'Cause Momma sure don't need any crazy wife-beaters pounding down her door in the middle of the night."

"Oh, no! We're . . . I . . . It's complicated."

Betty leaned back and crossed her arms.

Alice held her breath. Was she about to lose an apartment because of a wedding ring? Really?

After a few moments, Betty relaxed, her smile returning. "I'm heading that way now, if you'd like to see it. Wanna check on Momma anyway. Make sure she took her meds." She grabbed her purse and pushed herself to her feet. She grimaced when her knees popped. She pressed her hand against her spine. "All these visits are wearing me thin. It sure would be great to have someone right there, to check on her." She paused. "Would you be willing to do that? Check on Momma every now and again? Make sure she's doing the things she's s'posed to?"

"Certainly."

"Then come on."

Alice grabbed her things and followed Betty to the parking lot.

Maybe God was watching out for her after all.

CHAPTER 37

Trent spent most of the night driving through the streets of Seattle only to begin again as soon as the sun peaked over the horizon. His muscles ached from exhaustion, yet sleep refused to come.

He needed to return to his house to get his things before the bank threw everything to the curb, but just thinking about it sent his heart racing. Not that Jay's boys would still be there. Surely they'd given up by now. Unless Jay intended to make an example out of him. Trent shuddered.

He checked his gas gauge. With just over a quarter tank and not a dime to his name, he'd be running on fumes soon. He needed to find a place to park. He snorted. Why? So he could go for an afternoon stroll? Greasy hair and all? That would go over real well. Unless he headed south to Pioneer Square, formally known as Skid Row. He'd fit right in there. Emptiness wrapped around him as he glanced around at the tree-lined streets and steeply sloping yards on either side of him.

Used to fit in here, too.

Living in the has-beens wouldn't do him any good. He turned the corner, passed a playground, and followed the curve of the road through another residential area. On his left stood a white, one-room church with a cross shooting up from its roof. Slowing, he pulled alongside the curb. Men and women dressed in their Sunday finest filed out of the double doors, smiling, rosy-cheeked children tagging along behind.

A man with short dark hair and broad shoulders carried a giggling toddler. A little girl with blue and white polka-dot ribbons scampered along beside him. Her plump little legs took three steps for every one of his. Following close behind, a woman with dark curly hair framing her heart-shaped face lugged a Bible in one hand and an overstuffed diaper bag in the other. A sweet, happy family, like Trent once had. His eyes stung, pain stabbing at the back of his throat as he watched the four of them cross the street and pile into a silver minivan.

He grabbed his phone lying on the passenger seat. A black screen stared back at him. The batteries were shot and his charger was at the house. Now he had to return home, unless he wanted to lose all connection with the outside world. Not that anyone would call him, except creditors. And he had their numbers memorized, all five of them. Hit ignore after the first ring. Mrs. Northrup had begun to call almost daily, probably with details on proceeding with the short sale. Although based on her last message, she'd finally made the decision for him.

Meaning, most likely, he was now officially homeless, with a lifetime of belongings sold on auction or tossed into a Dumpster.

The one call he'd been waiting for hadn't come. His heart cramped, the pain constricting his lungs, as he thought about the possibility of losing Alice forever. An image of the curly-haired man at the diner—his hungry gaze locked on her as she giggled and blushed—flashed through his mind.

She wouldn't call. She'd moved on.

Trent opened his wallet and pulled out an old family photo. The color had faded, and a tear spread through the right corner. He traced his finger across Alice's face and studied her laughing eyes. It had been a long time since he had seen her laugh, since they had laughed together. His chest ached as he thought about the day of the photo and the flustered look on the photographer's face. Young Timmy had blinked every time the camera flashed. And whenever Danny smiled, his face scrunched up until his eyes nearly disappeared amidst a mound of pudgy cheeks.

Trent glanced back at the church. The crowd had started to thin. Then a man in a suit and tie slipped out and locked the door behind him. Trent waited to step out of his car until the man climbed inside a station wagon and pulled away. Slowly, he made his way across the street and up the concrete stairs to the tiny steeple.

The peeling paint on the window trim and doorframe revealed dry rotted wood and moss grew in the corners of the windows. He touched the door with a shaking hand. Running his fingers along the rough wood, he squeezed his eyes shut. It wasn't supposed to be this way. When had everything gone so wrong? His dear, sweet Alice. What had he done?

He fell to his knees and pressed his forehead against the door and sobbed. Lifting his face toward the sky, he cried out, "Help me, God! Please, help me! I can't do this anymore."

He cried until his throat ached and his eyes burned. Spent, he pushed to his feet and turned to go. A pale yellow slip of paper laying on the top step caught his attention. He picked it up. A bulletin: "Church of the Open Door: Transforming Lives with the Love of Christ."

Yeah, well, some lives were too far gone for transformation. He started to toss it aside when a blurb asking for help at a local food bank caught his attention. His stomach gurgled, reminding him how long it had been since his last meal. An address was provided. Second Street, less than a quarter tank of gas away.

Alice followed Betty east on 105th Street to Aurora, then turned left. They continued south at a snail's pace to North Green Lake Drive where diners and concrete parking lots gave way to lush floral gardens. Quaint cottages set behind limestone retainer walls nestled between Cape Cods and late 1800 Tudors with their heavy chimneys and steep roofs.

She allowed a smile as the road curved around Green Lake Park dotted with massive elms and alders. Much better than the dilapidated houses she had envisioned.

Betty stopped in front of a pale green cottage with white trim and a tangerine door. Odd-shaped stones lined the moss-covered walk leading to a covered porch. A stone chimney centered between two block windows gave the property an enchanted feel.

Alice parked behind Betty and stepped out.

"It needs some work." Betty shaded her eyes from the sun. "But it's stable. And quiet." She tucked her purse under her arm and walked up the front steps made from railroad ties. "Mind if I pop in to check on Momma before I show you the apartment?"

"By all means."

Not wanting to intrude, Alice walked over to the porch bench to wait, but Betty beckoned her with a jerk of her head. "Might as well meet her now." She paused, hand on the doorknob. "Don't say nothing about checking up on her or nothing. She'd throw a fit if she thought you were here to keep an eye on her. She's stubborn that way."

Alice nodded and tucked her hair behind her ears. The idea that this lady might be counting on her to watch out for her mother unsettled her. It was a commitment she wasn't ready to take on. She had enough to worry about getting her own two feet on the ground. But Betty and her mom had made it just fine without her for quite some time, and should Alice move, for whatever reason, they'd do it again. Besides, how hard could it be to pop in every once in awhile?

"Momma, it's me!" Betty cupped her hands around her mouth and yelled so loud Alice thought the doors would rattle. "Momma?"

A few moments later, a woman dressed in a housecoat with a shawl draped around bony shoulders shuffled into the kitchen. Her wrinkled face erupted into a toothless smile.

"Oh! You didn't tell me you were bringing company. I'll make some coffee. Decaf OK?" She reached for a small pot on the counter but Betty grabbed her arm.

"No, Momma. We don't have time for that. Alice here is thinking about renting out the granny suite."

"Oh, I see." The woman's face fell. She turned back around, swayed slightly, then grabbed Betty's hand for support.

"Alice, this is my momma, Gertrude. Momma, this is Alice . . . ?"

"Goddard. Alice Goddard."

"Good to meet you, dear." Gertrude squeezed her hand and held it. "I'm so glad you came. It's always nice to have company, whatever the reason." She turned to her daughter. "Surely you can spare a few minutes. I have cake. Cindy brought it by. I asked her to stay and have a piece, but she had to study or some such thing as that. You know how busy she is."

Betty shot Alice an apologetic glance.

Alice covered a giggle with her hand and shrugged.

"I really do hate to eat alone." Gertrude pulled a cake from the fridge and set it on the table. She placed three small saucers and a silver knife next to it. "I do hope you like the apartment. Although it isn't as clean as I would like. If I'd known you were coming, I would have spruced it up a bit." She sliced the cake into three thin slivers. "'Course, I could always tidy it up while you eat. At least clear out a few of those nasty cobwebs."

Betty raised her hand. "No worries. Alice is capable. I'm sure she won't mind."

"Not at all." A little Alice could handle, but if they were looking for a handyman, they needed to keep searching.

"Such a dear you are." Gertrude's face brightened. "I'd forgotten all about Betty's rental conditions. Do you like to garden?"

"I—"

"Did you show her the garden in the back, Betty? I can hardly stand to look at it myself. It's gotten so overgrown. Used to be the talk of the neighborhood. Back in the day, everyone wanted to spend time in my little patch of heaven, isn't that right, dear?"

"Yes, Momma." Betty shoved a forkful of cake into her mouth.

Gertrude set her fork down. "It'll be so nice to have someone to enjoy it with. Are you a bird watcher, Alice? I love to sit out there and watch the hummingbirds fly between the flowers. My favorites are the roses. Though I don't like pruning them much, not with all those thorns. Maybe you could help me with that. Always thought an extra set of hands would do that garden good." She spoke herself breathless.

Alice smiled. The woman was absolutely adorable.

After they finished their cake, Betty stood and rubbed her stomach. "That hit the spot, Momma." She turned to Alice. "Ready?"

"Hate to see you eat and run." Gertrude spoke fast. "Why don't we go into the living room where it's more comfortable?"

Betty shook her head, eyes firm. "No, Momma. I need to show Alice the apartment."

"Yes, you're right." She squeezed Alice's hand. "So nice to meet you, dear. I do hope you like it. It will be so nice to have someone to talk to once in awhile."

"All right then, if you don't need anything." Betty glanced about, as if taking a mental inventory.

Gertrude shooed them away with both hands. "Go on. Don't let me keep you."

Betty kissed her mom's cheek then led Alice out the door and along a stone walkway. The sound of trickling water alerted her to a pond on her right surrounded by rhododendrons and a few low-lying ferns. Wicker furniture decorated a paved patio a few feet away.

They rounded the corner and stopped at a door that could use a fresh coat of paint. Betty opened it to reveal a tiny living room filled with mismatched furniture.

"Don't let the dust and cobwebs fool you. The rental really is quite nice. Cozy."

It had a peaceful, homey feel. Its quaint little kitchen, tiny living area, and full bath were perfect. As long as the price was right. But considering the location, Alice wasn't holding her breath, even with the "momma-watching" discount.

CHAPTER 38

Trent followed a series of small cardboard signs to the back of a large industrial building. Men, women, and children formed a line from the warehouse doors to the end of the parking lot. Sweaty-faced toddlers clung to their mother's legs, and slouching men stared at the cracked concrete. Trent fought off a wave of shame as he filed behind a woman in a yellow top and calf-length skirt.

She smiled at him. "Think we'll get peanut butter this time?"

He didn't answer.

"I like the crunchy stuff, but you never know what you'll get." She craned her neck to see around the long line of people. "Clifford said he got oranges." She licked her lips. "Can't remember the last time I had a good orange!"

Trent focused on the ground and inched forward. The sun climbed higher in the sky, biting at his back, neck, and shoulders. Two girls played a patty-cake type game in a stretch of grass near the edge of the lot. A group of children, they looked to be siblings, lined the curb, hopeful eyes glued on a man standing behind a long table. Dressed in jeans and a navy T-shirt, he handed out food. Iced water bottles filled a bucket to his right.

Trent shifted and tapped his left toe on the pavement. Sticky sweat accumulated between his shoulder blades, trickling down his back. A man in a black jumpsuit looked at his watch, then at the mass of people in front of him. He spat a slew of curse words and left. The line moved another two steps. Trent wiped the sweat off his forehead. He contemplated leaving, but his hunger prevented him. Besides, he didn't have anywhere else to go. And he really needed to conserve every drop of gas he had.

He looked around. A few cars parked along the street, and a rusted pickup sat beside two large Dumpsters. Maybe he could stay here, at least for the day. It'd give him easy access to water, anyway.

The line moved another step forward. And then another, until Trent reached the front.

The man in the T-shirt flashed him a coffee-stained smile, his chestnut eyes bright. "You must be new."

Trent nodded, eyeing the man. His long, brown hair, tied in a low ponytail, gave him the appearance of an '80s wannabe rock star. Pockmarks dotted his sallow cheeks. Minus the clean clothes and hair, he looked like all the other yahoos crowding the parking lot.

The guy studied Trent for a moment, his gaze sweeping across Trent's striped polo shirt before lingering on the country club emblem. The man raised his eyebrows.

He handed Trent a clipboard and a pen. "Gotta fill this out to get the grub."

Trent read the long list of questions printed on the front page. Name. Address. Employed: Y/N. Number of dependents currently under your care.

He glanced at the line behind him, now extending past the end of the parking lot.

The man laughed. "Don't worry, I won't make you get back in line." He tossed Trent a water bottle. "Give me a holler when you're done, and I'll get you hooked up."

Trent moved to a curb a few feet away and sat. He downed his water in deep gulps before focusing on the questionnaire.

Address? My car.

He jotted down his street, even though his home was heading toward a short sale, if it hadn't been auctioned off all ready. Like these folks did credit checks.

Employed? He wasn't technically unemployed. Just suspended. Without pay.

Who was he kidding? This was about as rock bottom as it got.

It took him all of five minutes to finish and return the form. The man looked it over then traded it for a bag stuffed with bread, powdered milk, and various other nonperishables topped with two plump oranges.

"You get one bag a week. There's a day and evening shelter on South Main. And the folks from Holy Trinity should be around Friday handing out backpacks filled with water bottles, deodorant, stuff like that. If you see 'em, don't be afraid to grab a pack. You need shelter?"

Averting the man's gaze, Trent mumbled that he didn't and turned to go.

The man grabbed him by the arm. "Wait." He pulled a pen from his back pocket and wrote a number on a slip of paper. He handed the paper and a glossy brochure to Trent. "Call me anytime." His expression sobered. "Anytime."

Trent stared at the number scrawled beneath the guy's name and tucked it into his pocket. "Thanks, Ethan." He waited until he reached the curb to read the brochure.

Grace-filled recovery: breaking the bondage of addiction one life at a time.

Beth rested her shoulder on the doorframe and shot Alice a grin. "Wow, that apartment sounds perfect. And the price—I can't believe you found a rental in Green Lake for that."

"No kidding. But I think it's more about Gertrude. I could tell Betty worries about her."

The two of them walked into the living room where Luke stood stuffing a wad of dirty gym cloths into his duffel bag.

Beth scrunched her face and pointed to the laundry room. "Toss 'em, buddy."

"But I've only worn them once."

She pinched her nose and pointed again. "Grab a T-shirt and pair of shorts from the laundry basket."

Luke obeyed.

Beth turned back to Alice. "So, you going to get the rest of your stuff from the house now?"

Her stomach dropped. She had to . . . eventually. But the thought of seeing Trent unsettled her.

Beth walked over and squeezed her shoulder. "Let me know if you need someone to go with you." She glanced at her watch. "Wow, I better get going. The ladies will pound down the church doors if I don't get there soon." Laughing, she grabbed a spiral notebook and her Bible off the coffee table. "You sure you don't want to come?"

"I would but . . ." Alice swept her hands over her uniform.

"Right. Observant, aren't I?"

"I understand. Blue polyester has a way of growing on you." She paused for effect. "Like cancer."

"Guess I better schedule a fashion biopsy soon then, huh?"

And then she left. Luke followed a few minutes later, leaving Alice alone in the house.

Was she really taking this step, getting her own place? And what did that mean? Was her marriage over? Really over? After 19 years, two boys . . . But what else could she do?

She grabbed her phone and checked for missed alerts. Nothing. The boys hadn't called. She'd leave another message this afternoon with her new address. Maybe now that she had her own place, things would be different.

She straightened a quilt draped over the couch, her fingers running along the soft fabric, then slung her purse over her shoulder and left.

Standing on the front step, she breathed in and exhaled slowly. The sun peeked over the roofs of nearby houses, casting a warm glow over the neighborhood. Dew glistened on the grass like tiny diamonds. She plucked a seeded dandelion and brought it to her mouth. Its delicate tufts tickled her lips. Closing her eyes, she blew, like she used to as a little girl. She watched the seedlings float on the air.

Everything was going to be OK. She and the boys would get through this one step at a time.

Sitting in the diner parking lot 20 minutes later, she checked her reflection in the rearview mirror. A steady dose of sleep had restored the color to her cheeks and diminished the bags and circles under her eyes. In fact, she felt almost pretty. Her thoughts turned to Austin, and her heart skipped a beat. Would he stop by today? Did she want him to? She huffed. She was acting like a giddy schoolgirl chasing after the high school quarterback. Yet, it was nice to be noticed. Although she wasn't going to do anything foolish.

She grabbed her purse, hopped out, and crossed the lot in long, quick strides. Melba met her at the door with a pot of coffee and a sour expression.

"They're chomping at the bit today." She wiped the sweat from her brow with the back of her arm. "Might as well get a funnel going, the way they're slurping it down."

Alice tucked her purse behind the breakfast bar. "I'll fill them up." She grabbed the pot and began making her rounds—pour coffee, pick up dirty dishes, take orders, fill more mugs, pick up more dishes.

She wiped down a food-splattered table, straightened the salt and peppershakers then darted toward a newly occupied table to her left.

"Fine, be that way."

The familiar, deep voice sent a flutter through her stomach and stopped her in midstride.

She turned to see Austin smiling at her. "I'm sorry. I didn't see you come in. Have you been here long?"

"Long enough to watch you scurry around like a busy little rabbit."

His tone sent a rush of blood to her cheeks. "I'll be right back to take your order."

"I'll be here."

She made her way to the kitchen, stopping at the dishwasher to catch her breath. What was she doing? Was she flirting with this guy? Was he flirting with her? She was married for goodness' sakes. OK, so maybe on paper only, but still, adultery was adultery.

"You all right?" Frank studied her with a wrinkled brow.

Alice squared her shoulders and smoothed a lock of hair behind her ear. "I'm fine. Just taking a breather."

"I know that's right." He flashed a grin. "Never made so many cakes in one morning in my life! And that's the truth."

"Yeah, well here's two more orders to add to that list." Melba approached and handed Frank two slips of paper then turned to Alice. "I think your Romeo's getting antsy for you."

Alice's gaze fell to her wedding ring as a war of thoughts raged through her mind. So much was happening so fast. Was she really about to throw 19 years of marriage away?

She smoothed the front of her dress. She couldn't think about that now. She had more important things to worry about, like making as much money as possible and moving her junk out of the house.

Lifting her chin, she grabbed a plate of bacon and eggs then headed back to the dining room. Three table-stops later, she stood in front of Austin again, the familiar flutter returning. Her stomach bottomed out completely when he leaned forward, eyes intensifying as his gaze dropped to her lips.

She cleared her throat and shifted. "The usual?"

"Surprise me."

She stepped back. "Burnt toast special it is."

His deep-throated chuckle sent an electrifying jolt through her.

Spinning around, she passed old man Carl and his waving coffee cup and headed into the kitchen.

Things were getting too intense. She could see it in Austin's eyes, the way they fell to her mouth when she spoke, his head cocked to the right like a mischievous child about to talk her out of a bag of candy. Well, it took two to tango. All she had to do was stay out of the dance.

She returned to his table a few minutes later with a spinach omelet.

"How did you know?" He leaned forward, inhaled, and settled back against the seat. He glanced around the restaurant. "Pretty busy today, huh?"

"Yeah, Fridays always are."

"Guess everyone's getting a jump start on their weekend?" He opened his napkin and placed it on his lap. "So, what about you? What do you have cooked up for this weekend? It's supposed to be beautiful." His eyes swept over her, lingered on her wedding ring for a moment before returning to her face.

So he knew she was married? She almost laughed out loud. Obviously she'd misread him. So desperate for attention that she interpreted a simple question as a pick-up line. What a relief. No more what-iffing, dancing on the edge of sin. He was simply a nice guy.

"Yeah, well, I doubt I'll get much of a chance to enjoy the sunshine." This time her smile came easily. "I'm going to be moving."

His face fell. "Seriously? Where to?"

"Really far away." She laughed. "Green Lake."

His smile returned. "Had me scared there for a minute. You need a hand?"

She nibbled her bottom lip. So he knew where Green Lake was? Odd, considering when they first met, he didn't know where the freeway was. Apparently he'd done some navigating.

"You're not going to turn down free help, are you?" He cut his omelet into squares and brought one to his mouth. "Besides, I don't have anything better to do, being the resident newbie and all. And there's nothing more depressing than spending a Friday night alone."

"Oh, all right. I get off at four."

CHAPTER 39

By the time Trent forced his eyes open, it was near midday. His head felt like it'd been leveled by a Mack truck. The air, heated to near boiling by the rays penetrating his windshield, weighed heavy in his lungs. His sweat-drenched shirt smelled like decomp. Which was why he needed to get to a gas station. A splash of water to the face and some soap-laden paper towels to the pits and he'd be good to go. Might even be able to get a few drops of gas.

He grabbed a can of chili out of the paper bag and popped it open. After sifting through the other food items, he gave up on finding a spoon. Oh, well. As the saying went, beggars can't be choosers. He threw his head back and poured the cold contents down his parched throat. With a few gulps, he emptied his last bottle of water. He snorted. An entire bag of food and only four water bottles. But then again, most of the other moochers probably weren't living in their cars.

Last night he got the first restful sleep since he started bumming it three weeks ago. Maybe cockroach havens were good for something after all. Their parking lots made perfect crash pads. No security guards or policeman banging on your window. Although the lowriders and punks with spray cans were almost as bad, but even they knocked off by two a.m. They'd caused the hairs on the back of his neck to stand on end a couple times, when their beady eyes gave his shiny four-door a once over, but in the end, they'd left him alone. Pathetic really. He was so down-and-out even the local punks wouldn't give him the time of day.

He turned his key in the ignition and headed south. He pulled in to the first gas station he saw. A woman stood at the pump. Two toddlers were strapped in car seats in the back of her car. She glanced up as Trent drove by. He looked away, cheeks hot.

Eying an attendant smoking a cigarette just outside the store's entrance, he drove around back in the hopes of finding an unlocked bathroom. He lucked out. The door was ajar, propped open by a crushed beer can. He got out of the car and slipped inside. Swallowing back a gag as the stench of urine and feces wafted from the yellow floor, he flicked a switch, turning on a single bulb dangling overhead.

Gripping the sink with both hands, he let his head sag between his shoulders. Nearly two decades of graphic design work and hundreds of campaigns under his belt, and he was reduced to dodging in and out of gas station bathrooms?

He turned on the faucet and splashed cold water on his face. His rough whiskers scratched his palm. Body odor wafted up when he peeled off his sweat-drenched shirt. Grabbing a wad of paper towels, he soaked them with sudsy water. His skin tingled as he scraped the rough paper against his armpits, chest, neck, and stomach. Next, he thrust his entire head in the sink, closing his eyes as cold water poured over his scalp and down his face. Lathering a handful of soap into his hair, he scrubbed until his skin burned.

A knock rattled the door.

He startled, smacking his head on the faucet.

"Just a minute." He grabbed his T-shirt and shoved it under the water, working the fabric with his fingers.

Three more knocks, louder this time.

"Hold on!" He twisted his shirt into a tight cord, large drops of water spilling over the sink and onto the floor. Grabbing more paper towels, he made quick work of the mess. He tossed the towels in the trash and pulled his damp shirt over his head. Casting a quick glance in the mirror, he smoothed his hair and opened the door.

A short, boxy man stood on the curb with raised eyebrows. Trent ignored him and rushed to his car, slamming the door behind him.

Any chance old Ethan had dropped some deodorant in the bag? Not likely, but the thought warranted a quick search. Dumping the contents onto the passenger's seat, Trent rummaged through the cans and miniature bags of chips and crackers. A bright red gas card captured his eye. Gas-Mart and Go was printed across the top in white lettering. With a chuckle, he lifted his gaze to read the sign at the edge of the parking lot. Gas-Mart and Go. *Merry Christmas to me.*

What a loser, excited over a $20 gas card. That and an unlocked bathroom.

The brochure Ethan gave him lay on the passenger seat underneath a tub of peanut butter. An address was printed on the back. Should he go? It beat hanging out in his car all day. Besides, maybe they'd have coffee and donuts.

After adding a few gallons of gas to his tank, he pulled onto East Madison and headed to Union. Turning left, he continued south until he reached the location noted on the brochure. It looked to be an abandoned warehouse. Cars and trucks lined the curb—some shiny as if straight off the lot, and others rusted and dented with duct-taped windows. He parked between a brown station wagon and a silver SUV.

Two heavy metal doors with unlocked chains dangling from the handles stood in the center of the building. It looked to be the only way in. A quick glance in the mirror did nothing to settle his nerves, although if Ethan handed brochures to all the beggars he met, Trent's hairy face would fit right in.

He crossed the street and paused at the curb to look around one more time. After finger-combing his hair and straightening his shirt—

as if anything could make him presentable—he heaved the door open.
A group of people—some in business suits, others looking like they'd
slept in a Dumpster—sat with their backs to him. A man with a long
gray beard and thick, bushy eyebrows hovered over a metal podium
blubbering like an idiot. Trent stepped inside and stood with his back
against the wall, listening as the man spilled his entire life's story.

"One night I passed out, face down, in my own vomit. Woke up
to find my six-year-old kid kneeling over me with a bowl of water and
a washcloth. Wasn't the first time, either." He closed his eyes for a
moment. "One day my oldest had enough. He grabbed his things and
his siblings and headed to my sister's. Couldn't go to their mother's.
She was just as bad as me. Left them a long time back—once the juice
got hold of her."

"You coming in?"

Trent turned to find Ethan standing by his side, grinning.

"Yeah, I guess." At least the place had air-conditioning.

Ethan led the way to a pair of chairs halfway down and to the
right. He paused to say hello and shake hands with people on the
way. They threw smiles and knowing nods Trent's way. He bristled at
their assumptions—that he was just like the company he kept, that he
belonged here—and the fact that they were right.

"Guess we got the last seats in the house, huh?" Ethan sat and
motioned for Trent to join him.

Trent clamped his mouth shut. *Yeah, a real happening place.*

Claps followed the speaker's closing. A thin woman with long,
blond hair took his place. She scanned the crowd and her cheeks colored. Girl looked like she belonged in the church choir. Not here.

Her hand shook as she lifted the microphone off the stand. "Hello.
I'm Lindsay. I'm an alcoholic saved by grace." Her voice trembled.

"Hello, Lindsay." Everyone spoke in unison.

"I've been drinking for as long as I can remember." She cleared her throat and tugged at the hem of her blouse. "In many ways, my story's a lot like Chip's. Only difference is, when I hit rock bottom, I didn't care. The idea of dying didn't scare me. As long as it didn't hurt. Drinking seemed a painless way to go. Drinking and pills, but pills were hard to get ahold of, so most times I turned to the bottle."

Her voice grew stronger as she talked. Eventually, she lifted her gaze off the podium and made eye contact with the crowd. "I heard that you could die from alcohol poisoning. So I tried it." She gave a harsh laugh. "Failed that one, just like everything else in my life. Every day was the same for me. Tore my parents up. Mom about had a nervous breakdown, but I didn't care. Didn't feel anything, really. Only thing I cared about was the booze and not feeling."

She went on to talk about a slew of counseling appointments, interventions, and rehabs. "It got to be a game, really. I'd go, to get the folks off my back. Sometimes I even stayed sober for a week or two. Longest I quit was three months." She made a part giggle, part snort sound. "Would have thought that'd be enough to get me on the straight and narrow, huh?" Her voice tightened. "But there's no reason to stay on the wagon if you don't want to live."

Silence hung in the air, disrupted by an occasional nervous cough or shifting seat.

"A friend"—she laughed—"as if I had friends back then. People were nothing more than a means to an end. If they had booze, we were cool. If they'd drink with me, even better. If they started talking smack about how I should clean myself up"—she waved a hand—"I was through. But for some reason, this girl was different. There was something about her . . . an inner joy and peace . . . and a love for me."

She pressed her hand to her chest and closed her eyes. "This woman didn't even know me, and she loved me. Not with the selfish manipulative love I got from my mother or the explosive love of my father. Only now I know it wasn't her that loved on me. It was Jesus Christ, pouring out His love through her." Gripping the podium with both hands, her gaze intensified. "That gave me a reason to live."

Lindsay returned to her seat. Claps followed along with a few "amens."

Ethan walked to the front and set a leather Bible on the podium. His gaze swept across the sea of faces, maybe two dozen in all, before landing on Trent's, making him squirm. "We've all been where Lindsay was, haven't we?"

More "amens" filled the room.

"If we're honest with ourselves. Whether consciously or not, everyone who feeds the dragon dances with death. And at times, welcomes it. Oh, we may act like we have it all together. I know some of you play the part really well. Fancy cars, nice homes, beautiful wives, or Bruce Lee husbands. But our hearts don't lie, do they? And when we close our eyes at night, we know. We're living a lie. Reaching, grabbing, crying out for life, settling for bondage.

"But then there are those who have found the ladder. Our ladder is Jesus Christ and only He can yank us out of the pit." He flipped his Bible open. "In the New Living Translation of John 10:9–10, Jesus said, 'Yes, I am the gate. Those who come in through me will be saved. They will come and go freely and will find good pastures. The thief's purpose is to steal and kill and destroy.'" Ethan looked up. "Your family, your job, your very soul." He turned back to the passage. "But Jesus said, 'My purpose is to give them a rich and satisfying life.'"

He closed the Bible. "So which is it going to be? Will you let the devil steal your life from you, or will you give it God?" He held the Bible in the air. "Ask yourself this question: Have you found your lifeline? Are you climbing to higher ground or are you clinging to the mud?"

CHAPTER 40

Austin was waiting in a green pickup when Alice got off work. He leaned out the window with a boyish smile, making her feel like a teen on her first date. What was it about this man that sent her heart racing? And was the attraction and excitement she felt a sin? Or had Trent's alcohol and gambling released her from her vows? Were his addictions adultery—if it stole his heart and shattered any hope of reconciliation? At what point could she walk away . . . for good?

Or had she already?

"Hop in." Austin slapped the outside of his door with a strong hand.

She picked at a cuticle. "Maybe it'd be better if you followed me."

"Nah. It'll be easier this way. Save gas."

Old news broadcasts about the Green River killer came to mind. She tossed them aside as evidence of her paranoia. Austin was nothing more than a businessman from the Midwest offering to help. She'd be crazy to turn him down. Besides, he'd been coming in the diner long enough. She knew him. His easy smile and laughing eyes. The man didn't have a mean bone in his body.

At one time, she'd said the same thing and more about Trent.

The man was offering a ride, for goodness' sakes, not a marriage proposal.

Alice climbed in and Austin waited for her to buckle her seatbelt before turning on the engine. "Where to?"

"Kirkland. Not far from Crestwood Park. Head to 85th and I'll show you the rest of the way."

He put the truck in drive and draped his hand over the steering wheel. Hands folded tightly in her lap, Alice glanced back at her van parked in a far corner of the lot. How well did she know this man? She thought of Trent and the way he had swept her off her feet, promising to give her the world wrapped in ribbons and bows—bows that eventually unraveled into a tangled heap.

"You going through a divorce?"

She stared at him, mouth slack.

"I noticed how you always tug on that ring. Like it's eating away at your flesh."

Her cheeks heated. She shrugged. "Haven't thought that far yet."

"Marriage can be a funny thing. Kind of like a shiny, red apple. Never know what you're getting until you take a bite."

"What about you? Ever been married?"

He gave her a sideways glance, his eyes filled with an expression she didn't understand.

"Once. She went missing a year and a half ago. The authorities found her car in the woods. Never did find her body."

She brought her hand to her mouth. "I'm so sorry." At the upcoming intersection, she pointed. "Turn right."

Austin followed her directions onto 88th. "It's all right. I don't mind talking about it. The cops think something happened to her, say she'd never leave her car in the middle of nowhere like that, but they didn't know her. I say she up and left. She was wild that way." He looked at her with cold, lifeless eyes, all traces of laughter gone. She shivered. And then, just as quickly, his shoulders relaxed and an easy grin returned.

He settled back against the seat, continuing through neighborhoods until Alice's house came into view.

"It's the gray one on the right."

He pulled along the curb, and Alice scrambled out. As usual, Priscilla knelt in her yard with her head stuck in her flowerbed.

Priscilla shoved to her feet and waved. "Alice, how have you been? I haven't seen you in awhile."

"Fine, Mrs. Tanner. I've been fine." She crossed the yard in long strides and bounded up the front steps. A for sale by auction notice was attached to her door.

No. Not their home. Trent, what have you done?

Her eyes burned as she fumbled in her purse for her keys.

Austin came to her side. "Something wrong?" He pulled down the notice and studied it. The wind whipped between them. "Oh. I'm sorry."

She stumbled inside, moving to the couch in a daze. "What can I do?"

Austin sat beside her. "I don't know. Maybe you can call the mortgage company, see if they can't work something out?"

She rubbed her temples and stared at the carpet in front of her.

They sat in silence for a while, cars humming by on the street outside, the clock ticking.

Pull it together, girl. You knew this was coming. "No sense moping." She stood and straightened her blouse. "I'm done with this house anyway." She trudged down the hall, countless memories swimming through her mind, and entered Tim's room. Everything looked much like it had the day she'd left. Dirty clothes scattered the floor, the unmade bed, an empty soda can lay between sports trophies on the dresser.

She picked up a foam football sitting on the bookshelf, turning it over in her hand. "Do you have enough room for all this?"

Austin nodded and rubbed her back. "I've got all the room you need. We can always take two trips."

Three hours later, clothes and boxes filled the truck and they headed to Alice's apartment in Green Lake. The loss that consumed her only hours before lessened into a dull ache. There'd be time for tears later. Right now she needed to focus on rebuilding her life.

Gertrude met them on the porch with a wide-eyed expression and a pitcher of lemonade. She looked Austin up and down, the corners of her mouth twitching between a smile and a frown. "Don't believe I've had the pleasure." She set the lemonade on a small, round table and shuffled forward. "Is this your husband?"

Alice's cheeks burned. "No, ma'am. He's a friend. Came to help me move my things."

Gertrude's face gradually smoothed into a smile as Alice made introductions.

"Pleasure to meet you, son." She grabbed a glass off the table and filled it an inch from the rim. She patted Alice's arm. "Glad you had someone to help you, dear." After handing the glass to Austin, she filled another one. "I worried how you'd go about moving all your belongings by yourself. Not that you needed much, with the apartment being furnished and all. But I know how you kids are, always wanting your own things. You ask me, I say it gives you more junk to take care of." She handed Alice a glass, then lowered into a white rocker. "My husband was like that. Always grabbing on to some gadget or other, trying to tuck it away somewhere."

Alice glanced apologetically at Austin, surprised to find him watching her. The intensity in his eyes drew her in and knotted her stomach at the same time.

"I hate to cut you off, but we should really get to unloading." She set her glass on the table and stood.

"Oh, right. What a bother I can be." Gertrude turned to Austin whose expression flashed from intense to boyish. "It was nice to meet you, son. I do hope you'll come again."

His lips curled into a smile as he looked at Alice. "You can count on it."

Trent followed Ethan down the sidewalk, into his apartment complex, and up a steep row of stairs.

"Sorry, but there's no elevator."

In the dark stairwell, water dripped from large, yellow circles on the ceiling and pooled on the ground. "What floor did you say you lived on?"

"The ninth."

"Bet you don't go to the gym much." He grabbed the metal railing attached to the wall. "Thanks again for letting me stay here."

Ethan turned to him with a red-faced smile. "No biggie. It's not the Hilton, but it's better than the streets."

Or my car.

"Besides, someone gave me a couch to crash on when I was crawling my way out of addiction. Least I can do is pay it forward."

By the time they made it to the ninth floor, a sheet of sweat covered Trent's back and chest, and his lungs burned. The thick stench of mold wafting from the carpet didn't help. He swiped at his forehead with the back of his hand and followed Ethan down the hall to his apartment.

They entered a typical bachelor pad, minus the dirty clothes and empty food containers. Dingy white walls and hodge-podge furniture gave the apartment a thrift store feel. A row of pictures lined a small bookshelf tucked against a far wall. Trent walked over to them and picked up a picture of Ethan and a blond woman dressed in ski gear. Their wind-burned cheeks scrunched into smiles.

Ethan joined him. "That's my wife . . . ex-wife." He spoke slowly, like the words hurt coming out. "And those are my kids." He motioned to three 8-by-10 frames to the right. I haven't seen them in almost five years, but I keep praying." He crossed the living room and fell against the couch. Trent set the picture down and followed.

"Was it the drinking?"

"Among other things. Tracy held on as long as she could. Tried to get me to go to counseling." He raked his fingers through his hair. "But I was too stupid to pull my head out of the bottle."

An image of Alice flashed through Trent's mind. "They know you're sober?"

Ethan shrugged. "Not sure. I tried to tell them. Left messages. Until Tracy changed her number. Then I sent cards. They always came back marked "return to sender." I wouldn't be surprised if Micah, my little one, has forgotten all about me. He was so young when I left."

Would that be Trent? Living alone in a whitewashed dive with nothing to show for the past 19 years but a stack of photos on a thrift store bookshelf?

"So, what'd you think of the meeting?"

"Lot of crying and hugging."

Ethan laughed. "Yeah, that's how I felt at first, too. But now that I'm standing on the other side, I say, who cares? It comes down to me and the bottle and whether I'll have enough strength to stand. There's no shame in recovery."

Trent squirmed.

"Only shame is staying locked up in that self-induced prison." He stood. "You thirsty?"

Trent raised an eyebrow.

Ethan smiled. "For water." He rounded a Formica breakfast bar separating the living area from the kitchen.

Angry voices seeped through the walls and ceiling, accompanied by banging doors and stomping feet.

Ethan rolled his eyes. "Ah, the joys of paper-thin walls." Returning to the living room, he handed Trent a glass of water. "But don't worry, most of them knock off around 11:00. Unless it's payday. Then you might as well plan on an all-nighter, which is a bear when you got to be at work in the morning."

"Thanks for the warning."

Trent walked over to the sliding glass door leading to a small balcony and glanced at the adjacent apartment complex. Clothes were draped over rod iron railings and plants dotted numerous windowsills. A fat Siamese sat on top of a rusted fire escape ladder, his tail twitching in the hot summer air.

"You got a family?"

Trent swallowed down a lump in his throat. He shrugged.

"You talk to them much?"

He stared at his hand and rubbed his finger where his wedding band used to be. "No, not yet."

But now that he had a place to stay, he'd get himself together, get his job back, and convince Alice to come home.

Like that would happen. She'd moved on. Had a job, and the way she flirted with that man at the diner . . . Trent clenched his jaw and shoved the memory aside.

Ethan crossed the room and patted Trent's shoulder. "There's always hope, my man. Just take it one day at a time. Just one day at a time." His face went firm. "First thing we need to focus on is keeping you sober. And out of trouble." He returned to the couch and plopped down. Lacing his hands behind his head, he stretched his legs out in front of him. "And the best way to do that is to keep you busy. How would you like to rip up carpet for a change?"

"For fun or cash?"

"Cash. Paid by the day. I own a flooring company and am always looking for more men."

"Yeah, OK."

"Great. You can start first thing in the morning."

Trent shuffled back to the bookshelf and picked up the photo of Ethan and Tracy. He replayed Ethan's words in his mind. "There's always hope." He set it back down. "I got to go."

Ethan's forehead creased. "Where?"

"To see Alice."

Ethan sprang to his feet. "I don't think that's a good idea. Not yet. Give her time. Give yourself time."

Time for what? For her to fall in love with that man at the diner? To realize that she didn't need him anymore?

He shook his head. "It's been long enough."

Trent stomped across the room and threw open the door. He marched down the hall and narrow stairwell. Twenty minutes later, he turned onto the road leading to the diner. He checked the clock on his dash—4:30. Should he wait for Alice to get off work? He had no idea when that would be, but he couldn't just barge in. "Hello, Alice. I've missed you. Can I have a cup of coffee? By the way, can you come back? Our home's gone, and I'm crashing on a stranger's couch."

Yeah, that'd go over real well.

CHAPTER 41

Alice's feet and calves ached. A blister burned on the back of her heel. Pressing her palm into the small of her back, she grimaced. Boy was she looking forward to this two-day break. Working a six-day stretch was exhausting, not that she was complaining.

It'd been her choice to take extra shifts—to save a little more money. So far she'd tucked away $490. Austin's $20 tips helped, even if they did make her uncomfortable. She told herself he was just being nice, after witnessing her mental breakdown a week ago, but the intensity of his eyes said otherwise. And yet, it was nice to be noticed.

"Got any hot plans for your off days?" Melba grabbed a dishrag off the bus station and shot Alice a wink.

She pulled her purse out from under the counter. "Just more unpacking, cleaning, rearranging, that sort of thing."

Melba planted her hands on her hips and cocked her head. "You mean you and Mr. Curly aren't gonna hit the town?"

Alice blushed. "We're just friends."

"Guess you better tell him that, 'cause the way he's got his eye on you, I'd say he's hoping for more, if you know what I mean."

"I think you've misread him, Melba." She fished in her purse for her keys. "I'll see you on Thursday."

Alice hurried out of the restaurant before Melba could say anything else. The hot, muggy air outside engulfed her. She stood on the curb, blinking, as her eyes adjusted to the sun's intense rays.

Her van sat in the far corner of the lot. Her blistered feet protested as she made her way around station wagons, delivery vans, and compacts. She winced as a sharp pain shot up her right leg and thought longingly of her bathtub. A bubbly soak and a good night's sleep would do her good. After she checked on Gertrude.

A smile took hold as she unlocked her van door. Gertrude was good for her. Her sweet nature and silly jabber beat sitting alone. Plus, it was nice to feel needed. And Gertrude was as predictable as Washington rain. No surprises, no hidden agendas. Nothing but a pitcher of lemonade and fresh baked cookies.

Alice set her purse on the floor and slid into the driver's seat. Her tense muscles melted into the cushions as she leaned against the headrest. She inhaled, her smile widening as an image of Gertrude's porch rocker came to mind.

Cleaning and unpacking could wait.

She cranked the key in the ignition. The van sputtered and jerked. She sighed. Not today. She turned again, the tension returning to her shoulders. She tried three more times, the engine responding in gasps and wheezes. Slumping forward, she rested her forehead on the steering wheel. There went the $490 she'd worked so hard to save.

Someone tapped on her window, startling her.

She looked up to see Austin standing over her, smiling. She straightened, tucked her hair behind her ears, and lowered her window.

"I was getting gas when I saw you sitting in your van. Thought maybe you could use some help."

"Are you a mechanic?"

He leaned forward and rested his elbows on the door, his face less than five inches from hers. Alice swallowed as his cologne filled her lungs.

"How about I offer you a ride home until you can find someone to take a look at your vehicle?"

She massaged her forehead. What choice did she have? Turning her key a million times wouldn't do any good. At least she didn't need the car until Thursday. Actually, it'd be nice to be homebound for a couple days.

"I'd really appreciate it, thanks."

She gathered her things, locked her van then followed Austin to his truck.

He opened the door for her. She slid in.

"Now, let's see if I can remember how to get to your apartment." He turned on the radio. Hank Williams poured from the speakers.

She stifled a laugh. "I never would have pictured you a country-and-western fan."

Austin raised an eyebrow. "You calling me a city boy?" His eyes danced as he leaned back and adjusted an imaginary cowboy hat. "I'm what you'd call an urban cowboy." He made a tight U-turn, then headed toward the parking lot exit.

Chewing her bottom lip, Alice glanced at her van one last time.

"You in a hurry?"

A familiar car approached. She inhaled sharply. Trent sat in the driver's seat. He stared back at her, his dark eyes going from wide to defeated in an instant, as if the life had been sucked right out of them. Alice averted her gaze, a lump lodging in her throat. *Oh, Trent, what's become of you? How'd this happen?*

"You in a hurry?" Austin asked again.

"What do you mean?" She stammered, the image of Trent's sad eyes still haunting her.

"I'm starved. Mind if we stopped by a burger joint on the way?"

She slumped in her seat and stared out the window. "Sure. Whatever."

"Great, because I hate eating alone."

Ten minutes later, they pulled into a crumbling parking lot shared by a boxlike café with pale cream stucco and a gray mechanics shop. The sign dangling from the flat red roof read, "Elsie's Kitchen."

"Don't let the dingy windows and peeling paint fool you. This place has the best burgers around."

She studied his easy smile and teasing eyes. "Why didn't you get something back at the diner?"

His face hardened, the intensity in his eyes sending a shiver through her. His smile returned just as quickly. "Got so busy running around, getting gas, helping you, I guess I forgot about my growling stomach. Besides, I think there's a law about eating at the same place twice in one day."

He led her across the lot and held the door open for her. "Thought I'd shake it up a bit. Go from greasy pancakes to greasy burgers."

Once inside, she clutched her purse in front of her and looked around. This wasn't the drive-through window she expected. Long rectangular booths lined each wall, jagged tears revealing yellowed stuffing. Plastic red-and-white-checkered tablecloths covered the tables. Countertop 1950s jukeboxes sat between ketchup bottles and salt and pepper.

"You all right?"

Alice fingered her wedding ring. "I wasn't expecting . . ." *a date.*

No, this wasn't a date. He was just lonely and didn't want to eat alone. Besides, he was helping her out. It wasn't like she could dictate when he should take her home. And this sure beat a $20 cab fare.

"Is this all right? Because if you're short on time . . ."

"No. No, this is fine."

His smile returned. He grabbed a menu from the hostess stand, tossed a wink to the redheaded waitress then led Alice to a booth in the back.

"Ladies first." He motioned for Alice to sit.

Alice's stomach tightened as she slid across the smooth plastic seat. Austin sat next to her, lifted the menu, and chuckled.

He held it in the air. "Should've grabbed two, huh?" Holding the menu between them, he scooted closer. His leg brushed against hers, causing her breath to catch. "Mind if we share?"

She straightened and cupped her hands on her knees. "This will be fine."

"Found this place by accident heading home from work one day. The freeways were all backed up, so I thought I'd take a detour." He laughed. "I took a detour all right. An almost two-hour one. By the time I passed this joint, I was so starved it felt like my stomach was being ripped out. Their greasy burgers saved my life."

The waitress approached and placed two glasses of ice water in front of them. "What'll it be?"

Austin set the menu on the table. "I'll take a bacon cheeseburger, no mayo. Heavy on the onion." He glanced at Alice. "If you don't mind a little onion breath."

She jerked back, eyes wide. What did that mean?

"To drink?"

"Mmm, give me one of those giant root beer floats, with extra whip cream."

The waitress looked at Alice. "And for you?"

"Oh, I'm not hungry. Thank you anyways."

"Ah, come one." Austin made an exaggerated sad face. "You're not going to make me eat alone, are you? You have to get something."

Alice allowed a small smile. She really needed to relax—to quit riding the shirttails of her imagination. "All right. I'll take a float, too."

After the waitress left, Austin said, "Have you been able to find out any more about your house?"

She frowned. So this *was* a pity party thrown in her honor, then. "I've got an appointment with a lawyer next Monday—a free consultation. But I doubt there's much I can do at this point, not that I can afford, anyway."

Austin pulled his glass closer and stirred the ice with his straw. "I'm sorry to hear that."

She fiddled with the sugar packets. "Life goes on. It's probably my fault for not paying closer attention. I should've known something was wrong." Why was she telling him all this? "What about you? Where do you work?"

"I'm what they call a career coach."

"That sounds interesting."

"Not really. More like a glorified shrink, in many ways. Teach people to maximize their strengths and minimize their weaknesses."

They talked about the diner, the cost of gas, how they thought the Seahawks would do next season. It was almost like they were old friends, and it felt nice. By the time the waitress gave Austin the check, Alice chided herself for making such a big deal out of coming here.

Austin tossed $20 on the table then slid out of the booth. "You ready?"

She nodded and followed him out of the restaurant and to his truck. As usual, he held the door open for her. She climbed in and let him close it.

He got in and fastened his seatbelt. "You know, I have a friend who's a mechanic. I'll ask him to give your van a once over."

For free? Hopefully, though she didn't have the courage to ask. "That would be great, thanks." If the mechanic found something major, like a shot transmission, she'd be wiped out completely.

"No problem." Austin eased into the street, following the steady flow of traffic. The image of Trent's pained expression back in the diner parking lot remained imprinted in her mind, tearing open old wounds that had only begun to heal.

Was he sober?

She closed her eyes and rested her head against the warm glass. She didn't want to think about Trent or his addictions. She didn't have the energy. Not anymore. All she wanted to do was get home, draw up a nice hot bath, and forget about everything.

"You all right?"

She opened her eyes. "I'm just tired. It's been a long week."

Austin's face softened. "I can imagine."

They returned to small talk as he drove past Green Lake Park and the adjacent private golf course, and for that, Alice was grateful.

"Ever play?" he asked.

"Once. But after about ten pond shots and a few dead squirrels, I gave it up."

He let out a low whistle and turned down Alice's street. "Remind me never to take you golfing."

"As long as you wear safety goggles and a hard hat, you'll be fine."

Laughing, he pulled along the curb across from Gertrude's house.

Alice faced him. "Thanks. For everything."

She paused to watch a kitten chase a windblown leaf across the road. When she turned back to Austin, she halted at the intensity in his eyes. Before she could respond, or even decide how to, he cupped the back of her head and leaned forward, his breath hot against her face.

"Stop!" She pressed her palm into his chest and pushed him away. "What are you doing?" His eyes darkened. She held up her left hand. "I'm married."

The tendons in his jaw twitched and a dark shadow fell over his eyes. Just as quickly, his easy smile returned. He traced her cheek with his finger. "I'm sorry. I don't know what came over me. You're just so beautiful."

Fumbling for the door handle, she dashed out. She mumbled a final, "Thanks for the ride" over her shoulder, taking the steps two at a time. Gertrude met her at the door with a pitcher of lemonade and raised eyebrows.

"Your friend's not staying?"

"Not today." She inhaled three quick breaths and watched Austin's vehicle disappear down the street.

CHAPTER 42

Trent yawned, his eyes still heavy with sleep, as Ethan pulled into a circular drive lined with ferns and flowering dogwood trees. A slanting, hexagon-shaped house with a single windowpane stretching from floor to roof nestled between two western hemlocks.

Ethan parked and got out as the rest of his crew pulled up beside him in a white van.

He grabbed a clipboard off the dash and turned to Trent. "You can shadow today. Help carry things in, clean up the trash, stuff like that. But don't worry, I have a feeling you'll be laying flooring in no time."

Trent eyed his callus-free hands then watched the other men, muscular and dressed in faded T-shirts and ripped jeans, pile out of the van. Something told him this wouldn't be a walk in the park.

Ethan bounded up the front steps while his crew unloaded buckets, towels, and tools.

After a few chimes of the doorbell, a gray-haired man in a navy polo and plaid shorts answered.

"Good morning, Mr. Rice. You ready to have your floors gutted?"

"I'm past ready, son."

The man moved aside to let Ethan and the other guys, weighed down with tools, in. Trent set his load against the wall then watched as Ethan's crew made quick work of the carpet, slicing through its thick fibers and ripping it off the ground. Once they freed it from the tacks, they rolled it up and hauled it back to the van while others tore up the carpet pad.

Ethan tossed Trent a broom. "Sweep up all the staples and other junk."

He nodded and got to work. Anything to take his mind off Alice sitting in someone else's truck, as if headed on a date. Three days later, he still couldn't get the image of her and that man out of his head. It dominated his every thought. Who was that guy? How long had Alice been seeing him? Was that why she left? No, he knew why she left. His addictions drove her away. And yet, if it hadn't been for this man, would she have stuck it out?

"Hey, Trent. Wanna help me with this asphalt felt?" Ethan jerked his head toward a thick, black roll next to the wall.

"Sure." He needed the distraction. But despite the physical labor and hectic pace, the day dragged on. The temptation to numb his emotions with alcohol pulled at him, causing his hands to sweat. Gritting his teeth, he squeezed his eyes closed. Would sobriety ever get any easier?

At noon they took a break and the crew filed out onto the driveway. They sat on overturned buckets and toolboxes. Ethan produced a stack of cups and set them on the ground next to a jug of water. He grabbed one, filled it, then handed it to Trent.

"Thanks." Trent pulled a paper lunch bag from a nearby crate and sat against the retaining wall.

Ethan joined him. "How're you holding up?"

Trent shoved a handful of chips in his mouth. "It's a job."

Ethan studied him. "I can tell your mind's working on something. It hurts, I know."

He shrugged and took a gulp of water.

Ethan placed his hand on his shoulder. "Just give her time."

He huffed and shook his head.

"There's always hope, man. And hope never disappoints."

Trent wanted to believe him but some bridges were too far gone for repairing.

A couple of days after her encounter with Trent, with her van still sitting in the diner parking lot, Alice called Beth. "Hi. I'm sorry to bother you."

"You could never bother me. Is everything OK?"

"Yeah. Well, sort of." She took a deep breath. "Is Ed around?" Why was it so hard to ask for help? "My van's having problems. I know Ed's pretty mechanically minded. I was hoping maybe he could come take a look at it. I'd owe him big time."

"I'm sure he'd be happy to. Hold on." The phone clanked against something hard, followed by silence. Beth returned. "Where's it at?"

"The diner."

"We're on our way."

Beth and Ed showed up at Alice's apartment 30 minutes later. Beth wrapped her in a hug. "I've missed you."

"I've been meaning to phone you." Beth had called three times since Alice moved. She'd planned on calling her back, eventually. "I've been so busy, with work and moving and all." She indicated a stack of boxes lining the far wall.

"No biggie." Beth glanced over Alice's shoulder. "Your apartment's homey. And Gertrude seems like a real sweetie."

Alice laughed. "So you met Gertrude."

"And her lemonade." Ed rubbed his stomach. "You ready?"

"Just let me grab my purse." Alice darted to the kitchen and returned with her purse. She locked the door behind her then followed Beth and Ed to their car.

They paused to wave good-bye to Gertrude who stood on the porch, a glass of lemonade in hand. She waved as they drove away.

Beth swiveled to flash Alice a smile. "Love this neighborhood!"

"Yeah, I really lucked out, considering my budget." A boy in a baseball cap raced down the sidewalk on his bike.

"You know, you could have stayed with us. For as long as you needed."

"Oh, I know." Alice spoke fast. "But I wanted to get my own place, for the boys."

"I understand. Have you heard from them?"

She shook her head and faced the window. Beth reached back and squeezed her hand. "They'll come around. Just keep praying."

Or start praying. Why didn't Alice pray more? Because it hurt too badly, every prayer a reminder of how far she had fallen—how much she had failed. She was so tired, emotionally and physically. Waiting tables, tracking down financial records, calling creditors, unpacking—it was overwhelming.

Ed turned on the radio and contemporary Christian music poured from the speakers. He and Beth hummed along while Alice watched the houses blur together.

"What's your van doing?" Ed glanced at her in the rearview mirror. "Can you describe it for me?"

"Whenever I try to start it, it makes a *rrrruhrrreew* sound. But it never starts."

"Then it's not your transmission. That's a good thing. A new transmission, even a used one, would cost a pretty penny. It's not your battery, either." He switched lanes. "Could be an electrical problem—with the crank sensor, power relay. Might have a bad ignition coil." He turned left at the light.

"How much would that cost to replace?"

"At the auto repair shop? Could run you as much as $500."

Alice blinked. There went her savings.

"But I could do it for $100."

She smiled, relaxing against her seat back. "Thanks, Ed."

"Although, if something's wrong with your engine's computer, you're going to have to take it in."

"How long would something like that take to fix?"

"Depends on where you take it and how busy they are."

What if Ed couldn't fix her van? How would she get to work? And what about her appointment with the lawyer? She'd have to take a taxi.

Ed merged onto I-5 south and moved into the right lane behind a pickup loaded with furniture and boxes secured by bungee cords.

Beth reached back and touched Alice's knee. "Don't worry about it, sweetie. We'll help you out. Worst case scenario, you can borrow my car."

Ed looked at Beth with wide eyes. "Then what are you going to do?"

"I'll take yours. I'll drive you to work in the morning—"

"Every day? What about when I get an early shift?"

Beth shot Ed a warning glare. Gripping the steering wheel with both hands, he frowned and focused on the road. The tension in the vehicle made Alice squirm. No one spoke until he pulled into the diner parking lot.

He stopped next to Alice's van and cut the engine. "Here we are."

"How about you and I get ourselves one of those insanely large milkshakes you told me about while we wait for Ed to work his magic." Beth glanced at Ed. "You mind?"

Ed waved them off. "Anything to get you out of my hair."

Beth pushed her lips into a pout, threw her hair over her shoulder in mock irritation, and grabbed Alice by the elbow. "Wow, such love." She laughed and led her across the lot and into the diner.

Melba met them with a grin. "Couldn't get enough of this place, huh?"

"I don't know about that." Alice scanned the restaurant for empty tables, her hands clammy. She exhaled. Austin wasn't here. Good. She turned back to Melba. "My friend wanted to try one of your famous chocolate milk shakes."

"Oh, did she now?" Melba tucked her order pad in her waistband and grabbed two large glasses off the rack. "Extra whip cream?"

"Extra, extra." Beth shot Alice a wink.

"Better make that two," Alice said.

"How about three?" Beth said. "We can't go back empty-handed."

Alice led Beth to a corner booth in the back, and then settled into the smooth red cushions. She smiled as Beth slid next to her. She'd really missed her friend, more than she'd realized. Beth was the one person Alice could always count on, the one person who loved her without expectation or judgment. And it felt really good to see her again, to get in a little girl time, even if the circumstances were less than pleasant.

"So, tell me about this apartment of yours. How'd you find it?"

Alice told her about the Church of Sacred Reflections and Betty Frye, and was glad Beth didn't give her a guilt trip for trying another church. She seemed to understand Alice's need to start fresh, unnoticed.

"It's small, traditional. Mostly an older congregation, minus a handful of young families." She told her about Betty and her mile-a-minute storytelling.

Beth shook her head. "What a coincidence, huh?"

"What do you mean?"

"Of all the churches you could have gone to in the Seattle-Kirkland area, you picked the one that advertised a rental in the church bulletin. And of all the people you could have sat by, you sit next to the woman renting it out."

"Yeah, pretty crazy."

"You know, you're always welcome at Bible study. The girls miss you."

She toyed with her silverware.

Beth touched her hand. "Don't worry. They don't care. I mean, they care, but not in the way you're thinking. Their hearts go out to you."

Alice ran her finger along a scratch in the table. Luckily Melba returned before the silence became too unbearable, bringing three large milkshakes with her, one in a to-go cup. Two inches of whip cream mountained the tops.

She deposited the drinks then planted her hands on her hips. "So, what's up with you and Romeo? Where'd you two go the other day?"

Alice's face burned.

"What's this about?" Beth raised her eyebrows.

Alice shifted. "Oh, Melba's just teasing me."

"Listen to Miss Bashful over here." Melba cocked her head, the skin around her eyes crinkling. "Girl's got herself a sugar daddy if I ever saw one, the way he flashes that cash around. Gives her a $20 tip for a plate of pancakes. I swear that boy has your schedule memorized." Melba laughed, loudly, drawing attention to their table.

Beth straightened, the skin around her mouth and eyes stretching taut. "What's she talking about Alice?"

Alice thought about the day at the burger joint, the drive home, and how Austin had kissed her. And how badly she had wanted him to, if only to feel loved, wanted, beautiful.

She cleared her throat. "He's just trying to be nice. You know how some guys are, always looking for that damsel in distress."

Beth let the subject drop but Alice could tell by her stiff demeanor that she was upset. And that infuriated Alice. Who was Beth to judge? Alice hadn't done anything wrong. Besides, Trent walked out on her a long time ago.

The two ladies made a few attempts at casual conversation, but it was strained. Alice was relieved when Melba returned with the check.

Beth grabbed it. "This one's on me." She glanced out the window. "And it appears Ed is done."

Alice followed her line of vision. Ed stood propped against the front of her van, ankles crossed, arms folded. That meant one of two things: either he fixed the van or deemed it beyond repair. Hopefully, for her bank account's sake, it was the former.

Beth fished in her purse for her wallet, pulled out a $10 bill, then set it on the table. "Shall we?"

Alice stood and crossed her fingers. "Wish me luck."

"Oh, ye of little faith." Beth picked up Ed's milkshake and followed Alice out of the diner and to Alice's vehicle.

"So?" Beth handed Ed his drink, and he took a long slurp.

Alice picked at a nail. Ed's creased brow concerned her. "Do I need to call a mechanic?"

He smiled. "Nope." He wiped his hands on the front of his jeans. "It was a piece of cake. As easy as plugging in the spark plug wires. Which concerns me."

Alice frowned. "I don't get it."

"Spark plug wires don't just pop off. Someone had to unplug them."

"I still don't understand."

"Someone messed with your vehicle."

"That doesn't make sense. The hood release is inside the van."

"Maybe they used a Slim Jim."

She shook her head. "That doesn't make any sense. Why would someone do that?"

He shaded his eyes to scan the lot, studied a group of teenagers filing out of the adjacent convenience store. "You get a lot of hoodlums around here?"

"No more than anywhere else. Mostly middle-aged blue-collars." She ran her fingers through her hair, her mind flipping through the many faces she'd seen at the diner, pumping gas, in the parking lot. Some of them looked rough, with long beards and tattoos, but none of them paid her much mind. Except for old man Carl, but he drooled over anyone in a skirt. And no one loitered in the parking lot, at least not that she'd seen.

Alice gasped and brought her hand to her mouth.

"What is it?" Beth asked. "Do you remember something?"

"Trent! I saw Trent the day my van wouldn't start, pulling into the parking lot."

Beth shook her head. "No way. How did he find out where you work?"

"I don't know."

"You're wrong, Alice." Ed glanced around the lot again. "Trent may be a lot of things, but he isn't malicious. Never has been."

"Maybe you're right." But she wasn't convinced. Five years ago, she probably would have agreed with Ed, but now? Now she didn't know who Trent was anymore. He certainly wasn't the man she had married.

Austin? The thought jolted her, and she shivered.

CHAPTER 43

Trent hunched over the bar and stared into his Scotch glass. The ice cubes had melted to thin sheets, watering down the brown liquid. He picked up the glass, swished it, then set it down. Ethan's words, spoken at the Grace-filled Recovery meeting, swam in his mind.

"Christ came to set you free. Are you going to allow alcohol to imprison you?"

Trent massaged his forehead. What was he doing here? He'd come so far, and yet . . . what'd it matter? He'd lost Alice, his kids, his home. This was as rock bottom as it got.

Bringing the glass to his lips, he inhaled the sweet, caramel aroma. Sweat beaded on his forehead and upper lip.

Walk away. Just put the glass down and walk away.

He sat there, staring at his glass gripped in his sweaty hand, the other fisted in his lap.

Fifty bucks filled his pocket. Enough to drink himself into oblivion.

"The thief comes to steal and kill and destroy."

"Hey, there." A familiar voice made him jump. He tensed as Ethan settled onto an adjacent bar stool

Trent swallowed, his throat tight and scratchy. "How'd you find me?"

"I followed you."

The bartender approached. "What can I get you?"

Ethan glanced at Trent's Scotch, then at two college girls sipping martinis to his left. "I'll take an iced tea." He waited until the bartender walked away before turning back to Trent. "I knew where you were headed. When you came home that night, after finding Alice, I knew you'd lost hope. When men like you and me lose hope, the only place we know to go is the bottle."

Trent traced his finger along the rim of his glass.

"You're at a major fork here, heading one way or the other. And no one can take that step for you."

Trent watched the bartender fill a mug with beer, white foam frothing. The yeasty scent filled the air, mingling with the tang of fresh cut limes.

"Think long and hard before you take that drink, Trent."

"Think about what? How my wife's running around with another man? How my boys won't give me the time of day? Tell me, Ethan, where's the hope in that? You and all your cute little slogans, telling me to never give up hope, to have faith, to keep on keeping on. What has hope done for you lately? Besides collect dust on all those picture frames on your bookshelf?"

Ethan flinched and Trent knew he had hurt him, but he didn't care. All he cared about was finding a way to make his pain go away.

Ethan pushed his tea aside. "You're right. There aren't any guarantees. Even after you do everything you know to do to try to fix things, Alice still might not come back. And if she's the only reason you've got for staying sober, then you may as well take that drink." Ethan paused and lowered his voice. "But if you're tired of sleeping in your car, if you want something more out of life than a bag of food and a $20 gas card, then dig deep, find that tiny spark of life, and grab onto it with everything you've got."

Trent closed his eyes, breathed deep. He pushed the drink away. "Let's get outa here."

At work, Alice grabbed her purse from behind the hostess stand and faced Melba. "Guess I better go. I've got my meeting with that lawyer this afternoon."

Melba raised her eyebrows. "Oh. That's today?"

Alice nodded.

"You all right?"

"About to lose my lunch, but other than that, sure. I'm great."

Melba laughed and bumped her with her hip. "Girl! Don't be doing that! These are my good shoes."

Alice shook her head, chuckled, and headed toward the door. Nearly running into Austin. She jerked back, eyes wide.

"Hey." He offered that characteristic smile she once found charming but that now made her cringe.

"Hi." She dipped her head and stalked toward her car.

Austin matched her stride, chuckling. "Slow down, will you?"

She cast him a sideways glance, not sure whether to comply. If only to set him straight—let him know that she had zero romantic interest in him. She decided on the latter, and stopping abruptly, turned to face him. "Did you mess with my van?"

"What?" He half spoke half laughed the word, as if that were the most ridiculous thing he'd ever heard. His smile faded. "You mean did I have my guy come look at it?" He shook his head. "Not yet, but . . ." His brow wrinkled. "Is it here?"

She crossed her arms, her hands fisted. There was no way to know whether or not he told the truth, whether he or Trent, or someone else, for that matter—not that anyone else would have cause to do such a thing—had been the culprit. Regardless, she needed to set some firm boundaries with this guy. "I'm not interested, OK."

"You have another mechanic in mind?"

"Not in the car, Austin. In you. In anything romantic."

He stared at her for a long moment. The hard glint in his eyes pricked her skin. "I know, it's a tough time for you. I get that. I'll wait." He stepped closer, his gaze intensifying.

She backed up and clutched her purse in front of her. "No. I said I'm not interested. At all. Ever. Please, you need to leave me alone."

She turned and stepped toward her van but he grabbed her wrist. He leaned toward her, his breath hot on her face. "And I said I'll wait."

She yanked her arm, trying to break free, but he held fast, unblinking. Then, with that crooked, creepy smile, he released her.

She spun around and hurried to her van, her heart pounding, and jumped in. She immediately locked the doors and glanced back to find him still watching her. Shivering, she turned her key, praying the engine would start. The moment it revved to life, she threw the van in reverse and the van lurched back. Shifting to drive, she accelerated and screeched out of the lot.

That man knew where she lived. How could she have been so stupid?

Alice sat on the edge of a black leather captain's chair, stiff-backed, as Mr. Cojan sifted through her financial records. Her pulse still raced, her hands clammy. She told herself again and again she was blowing things way out of proportion. Lots of guys were stubborn, and cocky, thinking they could win a lady over given enough time.

For someone who'd spent most of her adult life trying to avoid drama, Alice sure had stepped in a mess of it.

"Thank you for bringing these in." Mr. Cojan, a tall man with beady eyes and brown slicked back hair, set Alice's financials down.

She nodded. It hadn't been easy, and she probably hadn't found everything, but hopefully Mr. Cojan could get a subpoena for the rest. Not that she wanted to know. The $178,000 she knew about now was more than she could handle.

"According to Washington law, marriage dissolution can be granted if one or both parties can establish, to the satisfaction of the court, that the marriage is irrevocably broken."

"I don't want to dissolve the marriage. I just want . . ." What? To get her finances in order. To free herself from the cancer Trent had become. But divorce?

Mr. Cojan leaned back and crossed his arms. "Perhaps I misunderstood. What is your desired outcome?"

She looked at her hands. Desired outcome? It was too late for that. "I want to clean up my credit."

He picked up the papers again. "Are these credit cards still in use?"

"I don't know."

"Are you in communication with Mr."—he glanced at the paper—"Goddard?"

"Not really. Is there some way I can separate myself from Trent's finances, without divorcing him?"

"You can file for a legal separation, which would provide for the distribution of all assets and debts. Issues related to child custody and support would also be arranged."

She swallowed.

Mr. Cojan leaned forward and propped his elbows on his desk. "And although this initial consultation is free, I will need a check for $1,500 if you wish to retain my counsel."

Alice blinked and brought her hand to her neck. "I don't have that kind of money."

"It's likely the courts will make Mr. Goddard reimburse you."

"He can't afford that."

"We'd ask the courts to garnish his wages."

Was Trent even employed?

"You said the courts would divide our debt. Is it always divided equally or will they take into account his gambling?"

"I'm sorry, but it doesn't work that way. At this point, you and Mr. Goddard are equally liable for all debt accrued during your marriage. Unless you can get Mr. Goddard to agree to different terms. Mediation really is your best option. Much more cost-effective."

"What do you mean by cost-effective?"

"That can vary, depending on the mediator fees and whether or not you hire an attorney to help with the process."

"If we mediate, do I need an attorney?"

"It is highly recommended. Legal counsel will ensure that your legal rights are protected and all necessary documents are filled out appropriately. Most mediators charge between $100 and $300 an hour. Our fees are $200 an hour."

Alice blinked. Two hundred dollars an hour? Along with the mediator's fees, she could afford about an hour's worth of mediation. "How long does something like that take?"

"That depends on how long it takes you and your husband to agree."

She squeezed her eyes shut and pinched the bridge of her nose. Every day she stayed married to Trent, her debt increased, and yet she didn't have the money to do anything about it. She opened her eyes, feeling sick. "Is this something I can do myself?"

He laced his fingers together. "It's not recommended."

"I understand, but can I?"

He didn't respond right away. "The Office of Civil and Legal Aid might be able to help you if you qualify. And you can check out the

Civil Help for Women Web site." He grabbed a pen, wrote something on a slip of paper then slid it across the desk.

Alice stared at the two URLs scrawled in large letters. "Thank you." She folded it in half and tucked it into her purse.

"You're welcome." He handed Alice's financial records back to her, checked his watch, and stood. "Anything else?"

"No, there is nothing else." Standing, she grabbed her purse and clutched it and the papers to her chest.

Mr. Cojan strode to the door and held it open. He handed her a business card.

"Thank you."

"If you decide to retain counsel, give us a call."

Alice nodded and turned away before he could see the tears brimming in her eyes. They blurred her vision as she hurried out of the office, down the hall, and past the receptionist. Luckily the lobby was empty and the elevator door opened quickly, but the minute it closed, her resolve shattered in deep-chested sobs.

She stepped out into a dark parking garage. Sucking in one shuddered breath after another, she hurried to her van, threw open the door, and fell against the seat.

A car to her right beeped and a man in a gray suit approached a blue Honda, keys in hand. He glanced at Alice. She looked away and rummaged in her purse for a pack of tissue.

Wiping her face and nose, she flipped open the visor and studied her reflection in the mirror. Mascara streaked her cheeks and her eyes were red and puffy. She searched her purse again, this time for face powder. A cream card tucked in the back pocket caught her attention. Her name was written across the front in large, flowing letters. She recognized the handwriting immediately. Beth. She tore open the envelope and pulled out the card.

A picture of two little girls swinging side by side stared back at her. Laughter filled their eyes and four tight braids were secured in matching purple ribbons. Three words were printed along the bottom in a child's handwriting: *More like sisters.*

She opened it and read the verses printed inside: Ecclesiastes 4:9−10, "Two people are better off than one, for they can help each other succeed. If one person falls, the other can reach out and help. But someone who falls alone is in real trouble" (NLT).

Below it Beth had written: "You don't have to do this alone."

Alice tucked the card back in the envelope and wiped her eyes. *Sweet Beth, what would I do without you?* Putting the van in reverse, she left the parking garage and headed east on Central Way. She arrived at Beth's 20 minutes later and was immediately ushered inside.

"Alice!" Beth wrapped her arms around Alice.

The kind gesture unleashed a fresh surge of tears.

Pulling away, Beth led Alice to the couch where she crumbled, face in her hands.

Beth dipped her head and rubbed Alice's back. "Oh, Heavenly Father, we ask for Your comfort and strength."

Alice closed her eyes as Beth's words flowed over her like a gentle wind, penetrating deep into her heart, echoing in her soul.

CHAPTER 44

Trent stood near the warehouse door, a throng of people in front of him. They huddled in packs of twos and threes, smiling, engaged in animated conversation. A few kept to themselves, tucked in back-row seats, shoulders hunched, eyes on the ground.

"You ready?" Ethan placed his hand on Trent's shoulder.

His stomach dropped. He shook his head. "I don't know."

Ethan nudged him forward. "Ah, it's not that bad." He scanned the crowd, nodded to a lady in a bright orange tank and ripped jean shorts, then turned back to Trent. "We've all been there. Well, all of us working toward sobriety, anyway. This is an important step in recovery, my man."

Trent shoved his hands in his pockets and let Ethan lead him to the front of the room. Without a word, he removed the microphone from the stand, handed it to Trent and left. Trent stood in front of the podium, dots of perspiration exploding across his forehead. A man with a long gray beard shot him an encouraging smile. Trent averted his gaze and focused on Ethan seated in the front row. Ethan nodded.

Trent swallowed and cleared his throat. The room quieted.

"I'm Trent and I'm . . ." He shifted, glanced up then back at the podium. "I'm an alcoholic. And a gambler."

"Hello Trent." Everyone spoke in unison.

"I come from a long line of drunks." His voice trembled. He stared at an Exit sign on the far wall to avoid making eye contact.

"Took my first drink in middle school. Vodka. Found it in the pantry. One of those big bottles you see at bars. I poured myself a big old glass, just like I'd seen my pop do." He snorted. "Spent the night hugging the toilet bowl. Old man wasn't too happy about that either. Not because of my puking, but because I wasted good liquor."

His temperature rose as the memory came rushing back. "For the next six years, Mom followed both of us around with rags and trash cans. Didn't matter what went on inside so long as the neighbors didn't know about it." His eyes stung. "She took her life five years ago."

He paused, took in a few deep breaths. "I blamed my father for her suicide, swore I'd never speak to him again. And I haven't." Sweat pooled in his palms. He wiped them on his pants. "Guess I became just like him, huh?"

He took a deep breath before continuing. "I met the girl of my dreams in college. Sweeter than cotton candy with beautiful blue eyes and the prettiest laugh. I ended up marrying her." He gripped the podium as memories of their early days together resurfaced. "We were doing great for a while. I had a good job, we had two boys. They're teenagers now." He shook his head. "My oldest boy's following in my footsteps. What a legacy, huh?"

His gaze swept over the crowd. A few listeners shifted in their seats, some of them looked away, but most of them nodded, expressions soft, compassionate.

"My wife finally had enough. She left me. My boys, too. I can't say that I blame them. I saw my wife with another man the other day." The muscles in his jaw twitched. "Sent me running straight for the bottle. Only this time, thanks to a friend, I didn't drink." He looked at Ethan.

"Way to go, man!" someone from the back called out. This was followed by a whoop.

He stepped back from the podium, not sure what to do next, feeling awkward, exposed, and yet, unburdened. It felt good to quit the hiding.

Everyone clapped, and someone gave another whoop. Ethan came to his side, Bible in hand. He set his Bible on the podium and clamped a hand on Trent's shoulder. "Thanks, Trent."

Applause continued as Trent returned to his seat. Everyone quieted when Ethan started to speak.

"We've all been there, right? When we feel like there's no hope and all we want to do is drown our pain in a bottle. That's why we need each other, to carry each other's burdens, to pull us up out of the gutter and bring us to higher ground.

"Some of you know all too well how Trent feels. You've lost your family, your job, your house, and it seems like nothing's ever going to change. Like the pain will last forever, but I'm here to tell you that that is a lie from the pit of hell."

He locked eyes with Trent. "It will get better. If you keep pushing forward, one day at a time, one hour at a time, one minute at a time. Because God is faithful." He flipped the pages in his Bible. "Jesus said in Matthew 11:28–29, 'Come to me, all you who are weary and burdened, and I will give you rest. Take my yoke upon you and learn from me, for I am gentle and humble in heart, and you will find rest for your souls.'" He looked up. "Are you tired of carrying this heavy burden alone? Then lay it down. Let's pray."

Trent bowed his head. *Oh, Lord Jesus, help me. Please help me, because I can't do this alone anymore.*

The librarian glanced up as Alice approached. "May I help you?"

"Can I use the Internet?"

"Absolutely." The woman handed Alice a pen and a clipboard. With a long, polished fingernail, she pointed to a computer station on the far wall. "You can use computer number five." The librarian gave Alice a notecard. "This is your username and password. Printing fees are ten cents per page. You pick them up here."

"Thank you." She crossed the room, settled into the rolling chair, clicked on the Internet browser icon, and waited for a search engine to pull up.

She pulled out the slip of paper the lawyer gave her and typed in the first web address. The Office of Civil Legal Aid website pulled up. She read the qualifications given. Did being $178,000 in debt qualify as low income? Only way to find out was to ask. Luckily a phone number was included at the bottom of the screen. She pulled a slip of paper from a desk organizer in the center of the table and jotted it down. After tucking it in her purse, she typed in the second URL, then searched through the site.

She skimmed various articles on divorce procedures, temporary support orders, and legal separation laws then clicked on the "online resources" icon. On the next page, a list of states pulled up. She clicked on Washington and navigated to the forms she wanted. Purchasing a Washington State Settlement and Separation Agreement was as easy as clicking the mouse.

She added the form to her "cart" then fished through her purse for her wallet. Except all her credit cards were maxed out. She sighed and dropped her wallet back in her purse. She needed to call Beth and risk having to listen to her friend lecture her on the sanctity of marriage. There weren't any other options.

"Alice, I'm surprised to see you here."

Misty's sugary voice arrested Alice's thoughts. Reacting quickly, she minimized the screen. Unfortunately, one look at Misty's raised eyebrows told her she hadn't moved fast enough.

"Is everything all right?"

Alice forced a smile. "Everything's great. Thanks." She glanced around the room hoping for an excuse to leave. Not finding any, she looked at the clock and pushed away from the computer. "Oh, my. I didn't realize how late it is. I need to go."

She dashed out before Misty could press her further. She didn't slow until she reached her car. Her stomach knotted, making her ill.

Might as well get this over with.

She phoned Beth.

"Alice, I've been meaning to call you. How are you?"

"I need a favor." She frowned, realizing she only called when she needed something.

"Is it your van again?"

"No." Alice scraped her teeth over her bottom lip. "I need to buy something online but I don't have a credit card."

Beth hesitated. "Sure. No problem. Come on over. You can use my computer."

Thirty minutes later Alice sat in Beth's living room, fighting a headache.

Beth crossed her arms. "I'm not helping you get a divorce."

"It's not a divorce, Beth. It's a separation."

"What's the difference?"

"The difference is that Trent and I will still be married, but he won't be able to drag my credit through the mud anymore. He owes a boatload of money! And as his wife, I am responsible for every penny. If we get separated, I'll only be responsible for half. And I won't have to pay a dime on any debt he racks up from that point on."

Beth stood and paced. She turned back to Alice. "I don't know. I understand how you feel—"

"Do you? How could you possibly understand how I feel?" Her voice quivered. "I need you to do this for me. Please."

Beth studied Alice, her eyes softening, and then threw her hands up. "All right. I don't agree with what you're doing, but I'll do it."

Alice leapt forward and wrapped her arms around her. "Thank you. I owe you one."

Beth pulled away. "I have a feeling I'm going to regret this." She sighed. "Come on."

Alice followed her down the hall, up the stairs, and to an office two doors down. She handed Beth the slip of paper Mr. Cojan gave her. Beth took it and plopped down in front of the computer and followed Alice's directions to the downloadable forms.

Beth swiveled her chair. "Do you even know where Trent's living?"

"He left an address on my voice mail."

Beth's eyes widened. "He called you?"

"Like a hundred times. Although not as much lately as he used to."

Beth wrinkled her brow, holding Alice's gaze, then turned her attention back to the screen. Five minutes later, she grabbed the forms from the printer and handed them over. "Don't say I never did anything for you."

"You're a life saver." Alice gave her a sideways hug. "I need one more favor."

Beth pulled back with a guarded expression.

"I need someone to serve them."

"No way, Alice Goddard. Absolutely not."

Alice sighed. Now what? Melba, maybe?

CHAPTER 45

A few days later, Alice sat on the wicker chair tucked beneath a weeping willow and watched as a hummingbird flitted from one rosebush to the next. The morning sun sifted through the branches, warming her shoulders and neck. She wrapped her hands around her coffee cup and inhaled the pine-scented, late summer air. Gertrude would be out soon, and the two of them would get to work, Gertrude supervising while Alice performed the manual labor of turning her quaint patio garden into the lush paradise it once was.

But for now, Alice relaxed, alone with the birds, her thoughts, and her Bible. She set her cup down and ran a hand along the smooth leather cover. A quickening pricked her soul, a longing.

She closed her eyes and let the words spill, unhindered, from her heart to her Heavenly Father. She had so much to be thankful for—her job, this apartment with its fragrant patio garden, for Beth and Ed, and Gertrude. If only Danny and Tim were here to share it all with her.

Footsteps crunched on the adjacent path. She turned, her breath catching. *Danny!*

A large duffel bag dangled from his shoulder. Gertrude shuffled along beside him, her face brightened by a wrinkled smile.

Alice sprang to her feet, her hand at her neck. He melted against her.

She pulled away to look him in the eye, cupping his face in her hands. "Oh, Danny. It's so good to see you."

"Well, I guess I'll leave you two to yourselves." Gertrude's eyes sparkled. With a wave, she hobbled off.

Danny clutched a lopsided duffel bag. Was he staying? She was too afraid to ask.

"I got your card." Danny observed the garden, glanced at the door leading to Alice's rental, then back to Alice. He raised his bag. "Where should I put this?"

She smiled. "Follow me."

She led Danny to her apartment, through the tiny living room, to a back bedroom filled with unopened boxes. "I know it's not much, but we can make it work, right?"

He grinned. "It's fine. Better than sleeping on Alex's floor." He reached over and picked up a football that had fallen out of a container and tossed it in the air.

"Want to go for a walk?"

"Sure." He dropped the ball back in the box.

The sun seemed even brighter as they made their way out of the apartment and along the gravel path leading to the front of the house. Daffodils and daisies danced in the gentle morning breeze, their cheery faces angled toward the rising sun. Gertrude sat on the porch nursing a glass of lemonade. She waved as Alice and Danny passed, her eyes nearly disappearing in a full-faced smile.

Alice glanced at her son from the corner of her eye, her heart overflowing with praise. *Thank You, Jesus. Thank You.*

They walked in silence for a while, the soft breeze blowing through Alice's hair and filling her nose with the scent of freshly cut grass and cedar mulch. Across the street, a couple sat on a porch swing. A brown haired little boy played with blocks at their feet. She remembered when her boys were that age, back when they clamored to be with her, even going so far as to toddle after her into the bathroom. But now...

Danny had come back. Hopefully in time, Timmy would as well.

Alice chuckled to herself as she watched the blocks tumble across the deck. She looped an arm through Danny's. "How've you been? Did you play soccer this summer?"

"No. Alex and I kick the ball around a bit, but that's about all."

"What about your brother?"

Danny frowned.

"Is he still staying at the Luttrells'?"

"For now, but he's talking about moving in with a friend from work."

"He got a job?"

"At Wendy's. He hates it, though. Says all the grease is making him break out."

Alice laughed, humored but saddened at the same time. She was glad to know Timmy was doing well, but oh, how she missed him. She needed to stop by, keep reaching out, for as long as it took.

A thousand questions surged to her tongue, but now wasn't the time. Instead, she turned her attention back to the pale blue sky in front of her and gave Danny's arm a squeeze.

"I'm glad you're here."

Childlike eyes met her own. "Me, too."

They continued in comfortable silence, the early autumn breeze fresh and crisp. A few cars passed by, along with an older man walking what appeared to be a labrador-poodle mix.

Alice stopped at the corner of North Bagely and 77th. "What do you say we head back now, see if my friend Gertrude has any fresh baked cookies to share?"

Danny grinned. "Sounds great."

On the way home, Danny talked about his classes, his favorite teachers, and those that drove him crazy. But from the sounds of it, he was doing well. Working hard and staying focused.

"Will I have to change schools?"

Alice gave him a sideways glance. "Living with me, you mean?"

He nodded.

"I don't think so. Not with you already being enrolled." As for next year, they'd deal with that when the time came.

"I made varsity football."

"Yeah? That's awesome!" She didn't have to ask about Tim. That boy lived and breathed the sport, and it showed. Most likely he was their starting quarterback. A nice way to end his high school career.

"We have our first game in two weeks."

"Nice. Where?"

"Bellevue." He scratched at his neck. "Want to come?"

She slung an arm over his shoulder and pulled him close, his elbow poking into her side. "Of course I do."

He went on to tell her about some of his most memorable practices, including one where linebacker Fritz Odenton had been so busy trying to look good for some freshman girls on the track team, he'd walked smack into a bunch of hurdles.

"He got all tangled up in them, just like in those cartoons."

Alice laughed, envisioning the deep red on the normally cocky teenager's face. "I guess that teaches him to keep his eyes on path, huh?"

"And off the girls."

Nearing Gertrude's, she stopped, her gaze zeroing in on a green pickup parked in the shade three houses down. That was Austin's vehicle. A shiver ran through her.

What was he doing here? And how long had he been there? She hugged her torso, watching, feeling him watch her.

"Mom?"

She turned to find Danny looking first at her then at Austin, then at her again. A crevice had formed between his drawn brows. Forcing a smile, she gave his arm a squeeze, not sure what to do or say.

Before she could decide, Austin stepped out of his vehicle and began walking toward them. The sun was to his back, causing an elongated shadow to extend in front of him. His stride long and quick, his boots made a clomping-scraping noise on the asphalt.

Reaching Alice, he shoved his hands in his pockets, and though he'd maintained his smile, the skin around his eyes remained taut. "Hello."

"Hey." She swallowed, feeling vulnerable. Exposed. Which was crazy. He'd probably stopped by to . . . to . . . what, exactly? Ask her out? He could do that at the diner. In fact, he'd done so twice since their previous . . . encounter, and she'd turned him down after each one. Based on the scowl he'd given her after the last time, she thought for sure he'd taken the hint.

"This must be your son." He turned to Danny and extended a hand. "I'm Austin. A friend of your mother's."

Alice didn't like the way he stressed the word friend. "Can I help you with something?"

His eyes narrowed before smoothing back into his stiff-smile expression. "I stopped by to see if I could take you out to lunch."

"I already ate."

"Dinner then. Both of you."

To Danny she said, "Give us a minute?"

His face hardened as he eyed Austin, appearing reluctant to leave.

"It's all right." She shooed him off. "I won't be long."

With another hard stare at Austin, Danny stepped away, lingering near the curb on the other side of the street.

Alice crossed her arms, feigning courage. How could she say this in a way that would leave absolutely no ambiguity? "I'm not interested, Austin. I need you to leave me alone."

His eyes flashed, and she held her breath, glad Danny remained close. Her thoughts zinged back to their conversation about Austin's wife, followed by remembered clips from reality crime shows. Was she being paranoid? No. The chill that ran up her spine and set the hairs on the back of her neck on edge said otherwise.

Sliding her hand behind her back, she reached for her phone in her back pocket, held it. Her heart drummed against her rib cage.

She stepped back, pulling her phone out so he could see it. "You need to leave, now."

"Want me to call the cops?" Danny called from across the street.

She swallowed, watched as Austin looked from her to Danny then back to her again. Then, with a smirk, he raised his hands, palms out, and backed away.

"Talk about overreacting." He shook his head and ambled back to his truck.

Breathing shallow, Alice held her ground, phone still in hand, until he got back into his vehicle, started the engine, and drove away.

Danny came to her side immediately. "You know that guy?"

She faced him with a forced smile. "He's just someone from work. One of the diners."

"I've seen him before. Hanging around."

"What do you mean? Hanging around where?"

"In his car, just sitting there. Like he was waiting for someone or something."

Or watching her house.

Trent crossed the living room to the sliding glass door and watched the traffic below. A thick blanket of clouds covered the Seattle skyline, making it appear much later than it was. A man in a black hoodie stood on the corner, head jerking back and forth, hands shoved in his pocket. Moments later a woman approached with long, scraggly hair that fell over her face and draped across her back in thick, matted clumps.

"You ready to go?"

He turned to see Ethan standing in the middle of the room with a guitar bag draped over his shoulder. A duffel stuffed with bagged lunches sat on the breakfast bar next to a 24-pack of water.

He shrugged. "I guess."

Cruising the streets on the outskirts of Pike Place Market for a bunch of homeless folks so that they could invite them to hang out down at Victor Steinbrueck Park wasn't his idea of a great time, but he didn't have anything better to do.

"Mind grabbing the grub?" Ethan hoisted the water with his free hand and balanced it against his hip.

"No problem."

Trent grabbed the food bag, sending an unappetizing mixture of bologna and tuna drifting to his nostrils. He followed Ethan out of the apartment, down the hall, and toward the stairwell. A lady in pink shorts and a floral blouse exited her apartment. She walked a few steps ahead, a chubby-cheeked boy clutching her hand.

Ethan paused to flash them both a smile. "Think it'll rain today?"

The woman bristled and twined her car keys between her fingers. "Maybe."

The kid stared at Ethan's guitar, his freckled face twitching on the verge of a smile. His bright blue eyes swept across Ethan's torn jeans. "You guys in a band?"

Ethan laughed. "In some ways."

The kid's eyes widened. "Cool! Where do you play?"

"On the corner of Western Avenue and Virginia." He looked at the woman. "You're welcome to join us."

The woman frowned and placed a protective arm around her son's shoulder. Ethan and Trent exchanged glances, Ethan's eyes holding a mischievous twinkle. Heat rose in Trent's cheeks. He stared at the ground, lips flattened. The woman picked up her pace and Trent slowed his, while Ethan lingered between them, clearly oblivious to their discomfort. Once they made it to street level, the woman put her hand on the back of the kid's head and pushed him toward a blue four-door parked along the curb.

As soon as they were out of earshot, Ethan grinned. "I'm thinking they're not coming."

Trent frowned and followed Ethan to his van. Tools and fast food wrappers cluttered the floor and passenger seat. Loosely rolled carpet and used carpet padding filled the back. He climbed in, careful not to step on the ketchup packets and hamburger wrappers piled on the floor.

Ethan slid behind the steering wheel. "And we're set."

"So, why don't you do church at the warehouse or something?"

"You ever heard the story about the paralytic?"

"Maybe. I don't remember."

"It's from Mark 2." Ethan eased onto the road. "Jesus was at this house in Capernaum, and when everyone heard about it, they packed the place. Like elbow to elbow. Next thing they knew, dirt started falling on their heads. They looked up to see four guys digging through the roof. Then, a man was lowered down on a mat."

He turned right and continued west. "The man's friends knew he couldn't get to Jesus on his own, so they helped him." They drove past a brick apartment complex with barred windows and took another right. "These men and women down at the market are crippled by alcoholism, drug abuse, prostitution, you name it. And they can't get to Jesus. It's our job to bring Jesus to them.

"Some of the fellas from work and a bunch of guys from our recovery meetings are going to meet us down at the market." He pulled behind a brown station wagon and continued to 3rd Street, where he made another left. "Pulling others out of the gutter helps them stay sober." His eyes intensified as he looked at Trent. "Reminds us why we're fighting this thing."

Trent grabbed his cell from his back pocket and checked his missed alerts. Alice hadn't called. Neither had the boys. He scrolled through his contacts until he found her number and hovered his finger over the call button. After offering a silent prayer, he returned his phone to his pocket.

Fifteen minutes later, Ethan pulled into a parking lot under the freeway that skirts the waterfront and grabbed his guitar.

He threw a bunch of water bottles into a plastic bag and stepped out. "You got the sandwiches?"

"Sure."

Ethan made a visual sweep of the lot then turned toward a man in a torn flannel shirt sitting against a cement pillar in the far corner. The man looked up, raised a hand, and nodded.

"Good ol' Kenneth. Never missed a worship service yet."

Trent moved the bag to his other shoulder and followed Ethan across the asphalt.

"Hey, there, buddy." Ethan wrapped Kenneth in a hug.

Trent stepped backward. The stench of body odor and urine was overpowering.

Ethan motioned to Trent. "Kenneth, this is my friend Trent."

Trent stepped forward and reached out his hand. Blackened fingers closed around his.

"Trent here's been coming to our recovery meetings. He's been sober eight weeks now, ain't that right?" Ethan slapped Trent on the back.

He looked at a torn backpack stuffed to overflowing on the curb. A half-eaten burger and a pile of squished fries that looked like they'd been dug out of a trash can lay on a soiled napkin.

"Good for you, bro." Kenneth grinned, revealing a row of black, broken teeth.

Trent grimaced as the man's warm, sour-smelling breath flooded his face. He angled his head to the side and forced a smile.

Ethan reached into his bag and pulled out a water bottle. He handed it to Kenneth. "You hungry? We got tuna and bologna."

The man licked his lips, a trail of saliva clinging to the corners of his mouth. "Ooh, eee, there ain't nothing like your tuna sandwiches. Thanks, my friend. Might as well save this for later." He wrapped the napkin around the burger and fries and tucked it into his backpack.

A woman with black hair tangled in thick clumps joined them.

Ethan grinned. "Hey there, Shilo."

She rubbed her shoulder, twitching as her dark eyes focused on the bag of waters.

"You clean?" Ethan handed her a bottle.

Averting his gaze, she grabbed it, unscrewed the top, gulped half of it down, and wiped her mouth.

Ethan studied her while she devoured a fingernail.

He nudged Trent. "Shall we go? The others will be waiting."

His face heated as the four of them made their way across the parking lot and down the sidewalk toward Steinbrueck Park, with it's tall cedar totem pole and bay views. A handful of locals lying on blankets reading, a couple of college-aged guys tossing a Frisbee, and a few foreigners with selfie sticks shared the park with the city's ever-present homeless population. Tourists in jeans and T-shirts wrinkled their noses and moved aside as Trent and his newfound "friends" approached.

Trent focused on the concrete in front of him and pretended not to notice the sideways glances. He wasn't sure what hurt more, to be associated with the homeless or his awareness of how similar he and Kenneth truly were. The only difference between them was that Ethan had offered him a place to stay and an invitation to a recovery meeting.

"Great!" Ethan said. "Joe brought his bongos."

Trent glanced up to see a man with long dreadlocks sitting cross-legged on the ground maybe 100 feet from the Tree of Life sculpture, which always looked more like a whale tail to Trent. Street folks had gathered around—a woman with thin hair, a man with a large black backpack, and an old man hunched over. Others sat or lay on the grass and benches.

Trent froze and stared at Cutters, across from the park, remembering the night he took Alice there. She'd been so incredibly beautiful that night, so . . . hopeful. She'd been trying so hard to save their marriage, asking him to go to a marriage conference, to counseling. To fight for their love. As he should have. If only he would have.

"So," Ethan set his guitar down by Joe, "what do you say we go fishing?"

"What?" Trent looked at the bay.

Ethan laughed. "Not that kind of fish. You and I are going to go catch us some men." He gazed toward the waterfront. "It's probably too late to head down by the grain pier. Those folks are probably packed up and gone by now." Early morning, one could often find a handful of men and women camped along the Elliott Bay bike trail. Some slept in makeshift tents, which were made from plastic tarps stretched over tree branches. Others slept on park benches or on the ground, a handful lucky enough to have blankets or sleeping bags.

"Grab the water," Ethan said.

He led Trent down the street toward Pike Place with its brick road, farmers market, and artisan stalls. Here, they wove around market shoppers and past the fish company, which was thronged by tourists watching the fishmongers toss massive fish. More tourists formed a long line outside of Beecher's Handmade Cheese, one of Trent's favorite Pike Place stores. One year he and Alice bought a gift basket for her parents—Flagship cheese paired with a fruit nut crostini. Then Trent had purchased a package for themselves, which they enjoyed that evening while watching the sun set on their back porch.

Oh, Alice, how I miss you.

Shaking the memories aside and the painful emotions they evoked, he followed Ethan up a steep hill, zigzagging through streets and alleys on their way to 3rd Avenue.

Half a block down a group of rough looking teenagers gathered on concrete stairs cutting between two buildings. A kid with brown, greasy hair and a goatee jumped up when they approached. He shoved a small cardboard box in front of them.

"Got any change?"

The rest of the teens straightened, watching Ethan and Trent closely.

"No, but I've got water." Ethan handed each of them a bottle. "And bologna." He gave Trent a jerk of his head. Trent distributed the sandwiches.

"Nasty!" A kid with earrings lining both ears threw his sandwich on the ground. The others looked at the sandwich, then at Ethan.

The kid with the goatee's grin only widened. "Yeah, I'm not a bologna man, either. How about tuna?"

All eyes turned back to the kid with the earrings. He frowned, grabbed his water, and unscrewed the lid. His Adam's apple bobbed up and down as he emptied the bottle.

Ethan took another step forward. "We're having a little praise jam down by the fishmonger's shop, if you're interested."

The kid snorted. "And why would we want to hang out with a bunch of religious fanatics? No thanks."

Ethan shrugged. "If you change your mind."

He and Trent continued to walk through the market streets, stopping to talk to the homeless along the way. Most of them declined Ethan's offer, a few came along, almost all of them took the food.

After 30 minutes of "fishing," Ethan glanced at his watch. "We'll need to head back soon." He stopped to watch a legless man sitting on a pile of newspapers turning soda can pop-tops into necklaces. "We got one more stop, then we'll head back."

Trent followed him down the street to a back alley where a man with thick wiry hair sat cross-legged with his back pressed against a brick wall. He clutched a bottle-shaped paper bag in his hand. A German shepherd lay panting beside him.

"Good morning, Reagan. You coming to our meeting today?" Ethan squatted to pour a puddle of water on the ground. The dog lapped it up.

"Nah." The man brought the paper bag to his mouth and took a long gulp. Drops of liquid seeped from his lips and dribbled onto his gray beard. Dark, empty eyes landed on Trent's.

He shivered and looked away as the memory of himself sleeping in his car, covered in dried sweat and filth, resurfaced. If it wasn't for the grace of God, this could be him. Even now, he barely held on. He reached into his back pocket and felt his wallet, with the picture of Alice tucked within.

Lord Jesus, have mercy. Don't let me end up like this, sleeping on the streets, alone.

CHAPTER 46

Trent's off day couldn't have come soon enough. It'd been a crazy-busy week of long days filled with hard labor. He'd pulled three 12-hour shifts since he and Ethan's little worship session down at Pike's Place. But no amount of work had been able to get Reagan's hollowed eyes out of Trent's mind, and the stark reminder that Trent was but one day away from becoming that man. Had been him, in fact.

Resting his leg on the coffee table, he reached for his toes. His hamstrings burned as tense muscles stretched.

Ethan laughed, plopping onto the couch across from him. "Tad sore, are we?"

"Laying carpet's much more demanding than staring at a computer all day."

But the growing wad in his wallet made it well worth it. At the rate things were going, he'd be able to pay Jay off in three months, and then he could start chipping away at his other debt. Maybe even call one of those debt consolidation companies. Once he did that, he'd show up at Alice's apartment with a bouquet of flowers and a ring and ask her to marry him all over again.

To think, he'd almost lost contact with her forever. If Ed hadn't told him where she was staying. Minus the diner. He could always find her there, along with Mr. Smooth Talker. Though he hadn't seen the guy in a while. Did that mean they'd broken up? The idea encouraged him.

"You think you'll get your job back?" Ethan leaned forward and rested his elbows on his knees. "You said your boss told you to take time off. That makes it sound like the job's still there, if you want it."

"I don't know. It's been so long. I'm sure they've found someone to replace me by now."

"You never know. Remember, there's always hope."

Trent frowned. "Do you really believe that? I mean, I see all those photos of your wife and kids." He motioned toward the bookshelf. "At what point do you give up? When do you quit praying for a miracle?"

Ethan stood and disappeared into his bedroom. He returned with a thick spiral notebook and tossed it onto the table. "Never." He locked eyes with Trent. "You never give up. You never stop praying."

Trent grabbed the notebook, flipped it open, and read the dates printed upon page after page.

> *December 5, 2010. Took my last drink today. Lord, help me be strong, for Tracy. Bring her back to me. Show me how to get her back.*

> *January 23, 2011. Tried to call Tracy today. I got her answering machine. Lord, please soften her heart. Help her and the boys to forgive me.*

> *June 13, 2011. Watched the boys play basketball. Prayed for them while I sat in the stands. And for Tracy. She looked so sad. I tried to talk to her after the game, but she wouldn't listen. Lord, take away her anger and heal our marriage.*

Trent read prayer after prayer. *September 9, 2012; February 15, 2013; Mother's Day 2014, Father's Day 2015.*

He closed the tablet and set it back on the coffee table. Years of prayers, years of hope. He wasn't sure he could hang on that long.

"Why'd you let me stay here?"

Ethan set his soda down. "When I saw you at the food bank that day, hair sticking up all over the place, bags under your eyes, dressed in slacks and a country club shirt, I knew you'd just hit bottom. I knew if you stayed there long, you'd give up. I had to help you to your feet before that happened."

Trent leaned his head against the cushions. He was discouraged, but not defeated. Not yet.

But he was close.

A knock sounded—probably someone from Grace-filled Recovery. Ethan stood, strode across the room, and opened the door.

"Can I help you?"

An older woman in cotton shorts and a baggy shirt that had a giant smiley face on the front stood in the hallway.

"Does Trent Goddard live here?"

He stood and crossed the room. Ethan moved aside.

"I'm Trent."

"This is for you." The woman handed him a manila envelope and left.

Trent's name was written in Alice's handwriting across the front. Ethan placed a hand on his back and guided him to the couch.

"Do you want me to open it?"

He shook his head. The room narrowed as his peripheral vision darkened. He tore off the corner of the envelope, slid his finger along the flap, and pulled out typed documents. The image of the official King County stamp stared back at him.

He dropped his head in his hands, the papers falling to the floor.

Ethan wrapped an arm around his shoulders, prayers of intercession pouring out, but Trent didn't listen. A million things raced through his mind, instantly halted by one driving thought. He wouldn't let her leave. No matter what it took, he had to get her back.

"I'm not going to let this happen."

Ethan's eyes widened. "Don't do anything stupid, man."

Tuesday morning, Alice tried to focus on her job, but she kept glancing out the diner windows.

"You all right?"

She jumped at Melba's voice and gave a nervous laugh. "Yeah. I'm sure I'm blowing this all out of proportion."

"Doesn't hurt to play it safe, though. Isn't that right, Frank?" She raised her voice to the cook.

"Huh?"

"I was saying, Alice is doing the right thing in how she's handling Mr. Pretty Boy."

"You know that's right. And I'm ready. Just waiting for a reason to practice my right hook."

Melba crossed her arms. "And add assault charges to your record? I don't think so. Besides, Mr. Wilson's got it handled."

Alice followed Melba's line of vision to the diner entrance where her boss stood, chest puffed out, eyes trained on the parking lot.

She smiled, touched at how protective and supportive everyone had been. Maybe too protective. "I doubt Austin will come within a hundred feet of this place, the way Mr. Wilson's manning the door."

"Oh." Melba's eyebrows shot up. "I'll tell him to hang back some." She darted off before Alice could say anything more, and soon, she and their boss were engaged in hushed conversation. A moment later, Mr. Wilson had moved his post to the first table, sitting stiff and awkward looking. It'd be hilarious, if Alice weren't so freaked out by it all.

Melba grabbed a carafe of coffee and an empty mug, and returned to their boss. She shot Alice a wink while she filled it.

The rest of the morning dragged by with Alice trying to act professional and polite, trying not to jump at every incoming customer, and Melba keeping Mr. Wilson's mug filled. Poor guy had to be floating and beyond ready for a bathroom break. But based on the jut of his jaw, he didn't plan on moving.

By 10:30 a.m. the last of the breakfast crowd had left, and only one table was occupied. "Guess I'll take my break now." She dropped a damp dishrag on the counter and started for the break room.

"Girl." Melba grabbed her by the wrist, and Alice's heart pinched.

She stared from Melba to the diner entrance with wide eyes. Austin. His eyes zeroed in on the diner door, his chin lifted. He paused, pulled on the front of his shirt, straightened his collar, and finger combed his hair. Then, with a slight, cocky smile, he entered, scanning the restaurant.

Alice jerked back and flattened herself against the hall wall. She looked at Melba, her pulse pounding in her eardrums. *What now?*

Melba faced her. "He drives a truck, right?"

Alice nodded, her legs trembling.

"What kind?"

"I don't know. A green Chevrol—no, a Dodge."

Melba gave a jerk of her head, spun around, and scampered out of the restaurant, her fleshy arms pumping something fierce. Peering around the corner, Alice remained where she was, watching her boss and stalker.

"What do you mean I can't come in here anymore?" A vein bulged along Austin's temple, his neck red and splotchy. "That's discrimination."

"She doesn't want to see you." Mr. Wilson moved so that he blocked Austin's way.

"What are you talking about?" Austin looked around. His gaze landed on Alice, and she shrank back, holding her breath.

"You best leave before I make you," Mr. Wilson said, his voice deep and gravely. "Do I need to call the cops?"

"For what? Wanting something to eat? This is crazy. I don't know what you did to get Alice spooked—" He raised his voice. "Alice? I want to talk—"

"I said out," Mr. Wilson bellowed. "Now."

No response.

The door chimed open then clanked shut, and murmurs filled the diner. Austin's voice wasn't among them, but even so, Alice remained where she was, her heart beating so fast, it hurt.

Heavy footsteps approached. She squealed when Mr. Wilson rounded the corner. When recognition dawned, she released a gush of air and, caving forward, covered her face with her hands.

He drew near and wrapped his arms around her in a fatherly embrace. "Shh. It's all right. He won't be bothering you anymore."

She hoped he was right. Her fear? That Mr. Wilson's actions had made Austin angry. And he knew where she lived.

Oh, Lord, Jesus, please help me.

What about Gertrude?

The door chimed open again, and heels clicked on the linoleum. Melba rounded the corner wearing a wide grin and waving her phone. "Girl, we got him now. Look what I got." She showed Alice.

"Oh, Melba!" His license plate. She'd taken a picture of his license plate!

Melba swiped her finger across the screen, revealing another picture. This one was of his truck followed by images of Austin, first a back view, then side, then front on as he marched out of the diner. He looked furious.

She shivered and ran her hands up and down the backs of her goose-pimpled arms.

"Gonna send this to the police now." She tapped her phone a few times then glanced up. "You still got that detective's name and number?"

Alice nodded, dazed. Numb. "I'll call him."

Melba raised a hand and shook her head. "I got this. You need to go chill out for a minute. Breathe."

"I know that's right." Frank let out a low whistle, eliciting a nervous laugh from Alice.

Mr. Wilson placed a strong hand on her back. "How about you get Melba the detective's card then take a five minute break."

She nodded, pressing a fisted hand to her mouth. "Thank you."

That afternoon, still shook up from it all, Alice met Beth at a quiet coffeehouse on the outskirts of Seattle. She folded her napkin, spread it flat, then folded it again. "Hopefully now the police can find him. Figure out who he is—I'm not even sure Austin's his real name."

Deep lines stretched across Beth's forehead. "So now what?"

She shrugged. "The King County Police said they'd launch an investigation to figure out who he is. They seem to be taking my concerns seriously, although I know I don't have a whole lot to go on. I mean, we were sort of friends for a while. He came in to the restaurant to eat, gave me a ride. Twice." Why had she ever gotten into his car in the first place? She should've known better.

"Do you think he's the one who messed with your van?"

Alice swallowed "Probably."

"So then what, you just wait?" Beth said. "Maybe you and Danny should come to our house."

Alice stared into her cup, watching the foam melt into the coffee. She shook her head. "I need to stay with Gertrude, and I really don't want to keep moving Danny around. He's just getting settled in. So long as we keep the door and windows locked, we should be good. Besides, I'm probably getting all worked up over nothing."

"He was watching your house, Alice."

"Or stopping by to ask me out."

Beth's gaze intensified. "You don't believe that for a second."

Alice sighed. "No, I don't." She wrapped both hands around her mug, inhaling the cinnamon-scented steam. "Best case scenario, he'll get the hint I'm not interested, and I won't hear from him again." She glanced at the time on her phone. "I better go. School will be letting out soon."

"You're going to see Tim?"

Alice nodded. She breathed deep and released it slowly in an attempt to settle her nervous stomach.

"Let's pray." Beth extended her hands, and Alice placed hers in them. Then, she bowed her head as Beth prayed. "Father, please go before Alice. Soften Tim's heart. Break through his hurt and help him to listen, really listen, to what Alice has to say. And please give her the words."

"Amen. Thanks, Beth."

"Love you, girl." She gave Alice a sideways hug.

Alice hugged her back, incredibly grateful to have such a special friend. She'd stuck by Alice through so much, even when Alice had continually pushed her away. Alice intended to show Tim—both her boys—that same kind of love.

"Everything's going to work out. I believe that with every fiber of my being."

"I hope you're right."

Walking to her car, she considered Beth's words—the conviction behind them—wishing she shared her unshakable faith. If only she'd gotten help, for her and Trent, before everything fell apart. But God had resurrected a dead man and turned a murderer into the world's greatest evangelist. Surely He could restore her relationship with her son.

And her husband? The question came unbidden, jolting her. Stirring her heart with hope, but she quickly squelched it. She'd made her decision the moment she packed her bags. And Trent had made his the moment he . . . what, slipped in to addiction?

How could she feel compassion and hatred toward him at the same time?

Regardless, she had other things to worry about, like reconnecting with Timmy.

By the time she reached the school, students were already spilling out of the building and streaming through the parking lot. Alice drove directly to the back, where the locker room opened to the football field. Then, after a quick prayer for guidance, she got out of her vehicle and strode across the lot. She lingered near the doorway, watching for Tim among the exiting football players.

Danny loped out drinking from a sports bottle. Upon seeing her, he sauntered over. "Hey." He frowned, as if waiting for bad news. "What's up?"

"I'm here to see Tim."

"Oh." He stared at her, his expression unreadable. Then he smiled. "Got to go. See you later."

"Come home hungry. I've got a batch of cheesy chili in the crockpot." One of his favorites.

"Nice." He rubbed his stomach and jogged off, catching up with a tall red head with man-sized shoulders.

Tim emerged not long after, talking with one of the assistant coaches. The coach saw her first, nodded a greeting, then nudged Tim. He scowled, and the coach nudged him again.

"Go on, boy. Show some respect."

Tim rolled his eyes and marched over, crossed his arms. "What?"

"I miss you."

He continued to look at her.

"I wish . . . Can we talk? Please. Just for a minute?"

He eyed her a moment longer, glanced behind him. "Whatever." He followed her to a raised brick barrier enclosing a tree, where the two sat.

She didn't know where to start, what to say. "I really messed up, and I'm sorry. I'm sorry I wasn't there for you. That I let things get as bad as they did. That wasn't fair."

He blinked and dropped his shoulders.

She placed her hand on his, relieved when he didn't pull away. "I love you, Tim. I'll always love you. I'll do whatever it takes to earn your trust again. To . . . to . . . to make things right."

Staring at the ground, he cracked his knuckles one finger at a time. And while he did, Alice prayed. And held her breath.

"Can we meet for dinner?" she said.

When he lifted his gaze, the hardness in his eyes replaced by vulnerability and pain, and it took all her self-control not to pull him close and hold him tight. But that'd only push him further away.

He nodded. "I'll call you."

She released the breath she'd been holding. "I'd like that."

Thank You, Jesus.

Though they still had a long way to go, and Tim had a lot of healing to come, it was a start.

That Saturday, Alice cleaned up after breakfast and checked the windows and door were locked. It'd become a new habit. As had making frequent scans of the street. So far, no signs of Austin.

She needed to check on Gertrude as well. Closing the blinds, she turned to watch her son. He sat on the couch, sifting through an opened box of photo albums.

"What do you got there?" She sat beside him, shoulder to shoulder, and spread his baby book between them. "Wow, I haven't looked at this in forever." Flipping it open, she giggled at a picture of Danny covered in chocolate cake. Thick globs of frosting clung to his hair and dark streaks covered his round belly.

"I bet you don't remember that party, do you?" It was his second birthday, and Alice and Trent went all out. Balloons everywhere, crepe paper strung all over the place. They'd even hired a juggling clown.

"Nope. But I do remember one with some sort of tunnel and a fat bear in a red T-shirt. He totally weirded me out. It was so confusing. I couldn't figure out what was going on."

Alice laughed. "I remember that one, too. We spent so much money." She ruffled his hair. "You spent the afternoon under the table. Didn't come out until the giant bear and his tickle tunnel left."

She turned the page to a picture of Tim and Danny playing in the sprinkler. Questions about Tim swelled to her tongue, but she held them back. Instead, she offered a silent prayer and flipped the page. The next picture pricked her heart. Trent sat on the loveseat with both boys in his arms. Danny stared up at him with rosy, smile-bunched cheeks while Tim leaned against Trent's chest.

She studied her son. The pain in his eyes magnified her own. It wasn't supposed to be like this. Forcing a smile, she snapped the album shut and stood. "What do you say we see about getting ourselves some of Gertrude's fresh squeezed lemonade?"

"I guess."

He followed her out the door and toward the gravel path.

"I bet she's got a couple of chocolate chip cookies for us." She rounded the corner and blinked. Trent. He stopped in mid-step and stood, eyes bloodshot with dark circles beneath them. He held papers in his hand. The court documents she'd asked Melba to deliver?

She took half a step backwards. "What are you doing here?"

"Don't do this, Alice." His voice trembled. "Give me another chance. I'm sober. I've stopped gambling."

"It's too late for that. After all you've done." Hands fisted, she shook her head. "It's over, Trent. I've got a new life now."

"We can work through this."

"I'm done playing that game. Held on to your empty promises for far too long, but not anymore."

She spun around, her gaze landing on a wide-eyed Danny.

"Sweetie—" She reached for him.

Hands raised in front of him, he shook her hand away and ran for the apartment.

Alice turned back to Trent. "I want you to leave. Now."

He dropped the documents on the ground. "I'm not signing, Alice."

She grabbed the papers and shoved them into his chest. "For once in your pathetic life, do the right thing." She spun around and marched off.

Trent collapsed onto the ground, the gravel cutting into his hands and knees as Alice walked away. His heart cried out to God, but the words wouldn't come.

He grabbed the court documents, struggled to stand, and swiped at his eyes.

It hurt to breathe. Alice's words replayed again and again like a slow-motion movie. His last glimmer of hope had been shattered. It was over. He'd lost her. His sweet Alice.

Memories flashed through his mind: of their wedding day, and how radiant she'd looked in her white gown. Of countless nights spent on the dance floor, him singing softly in her ear. Of her as a young mom, their boys nestled, one under each arm, her with a peaceful, contented smile. And then the day when he came home to find her and her things gone.

I've lost it all, everything that matters. Now what? Where do I go from here, Lord?

"The thief comes only to steal and kill and destroy; I have come that they might have life, and have it to the full . . . The thief comes to kill and destroy. To kill and destroy. To kill and destroy."

CHAPTER 47

Alice watched Danny eat his cereal with a heavy heart. Things had been strained since Trent's visit. She hated Trent for that. And she hated him even more for the way her heart squeezed when she thought of him and his promise to change.

He said he was done with the drinking and gambling. What if it were true? What if she believed him, and his sobriety didn't last?

She touched Danny's shoulder. "You want to go out for ice cream?"

He stirred his cereal. "Not really."

"It's a beautiful day. How about we go to Seward Park? I'll pack some jerky and granola."

"I don't feel like hiking."

She sat in the chair across from him. "I know this is hard on you, and I'm sorry."

He glared. "He said he's sober. Why won't you give him another chance?"

"Sweetie, it's not that simple." How could she help him comprehend addiction? Most likely he was thinking of Tim. How could she explain to him the difference between walking out on an alcoholic husband and turning your back on an alcoholic son?

Love always hopes. The words flowed through her mind softly, gently.

What are You saying, Lord?

To Danny, she said, "I know this is hard for you to understand, but your dad is sick."

He slammed his fist on the table, making her jump. "But he's better. You heard him!"

"I know what he said, Danny, but it—" *won't last. It never does.*

The phone rang. She snatched it up and glanced at Beth's number displayed on the screen. "Hello?"

"Is everything all right? You sound so . . . on edge."

Alice breathed deep and let it out slowly. "I'm fine. How are you?" She continued to watch Danny.

"I called to invite you to a prayer meeting. Well, not a meeting really, more like a prayer . . . experience."

"What do you mean?"

"I've got a bunch of stations set up at the church—music, candles. It'll be great. A time to be refreshed by the love of Christ."

She started to decline, then stopped. Maybe some time with Beth and the other Bible study girls would do her some good. She could use the support. "That sounds great. What time?"

"I'll pick you up in a few."

Ending the call, she turned to Danny. "I'm going to go to a prayer meeting with Beth. Will you be all right?"

He gave a one-shoulder shrug.

"I won't be long. And I'll have my cell phone." She froze and glanced out the window. "Lock the door after I leave, OK? Don't answer it, no matter what. And keep the pepper spray close by. You know where it is, right?" She'd purchased two canisters, one for home and one for her purse.

"Why? That guy from the other day?"

She nodded. "Yes. I doubt there'll be a problem, but it'll make me feel better to know you're locked in."

"Like a prison, huh?" He gave a crooked smile.

"Something like that." She ruffled his hair.

Twenty minutes later, Beth stood at her door with a plate of muffins, beaming.

"What's this?"

Beth pushed past her and set the food on the table in front of Danny. She nudged his shoulder. "Hey you."

He gave her a stale smile, then lowered his eyes again.

Beth faced Alice. "I'm gifting you with leftovers. I got so used to cooking for four, guess I overdid it."

Alice crossed her arms and pretended to be offended. "Are you saying I'm a pig?"

"Only when it comes to chocolate covered cherries and caramel corn." Laughing, she followed Alice out of the apartment.

They walked down the path side-by-side, waving to Gertrude as they passed the porch, then climbed into Beth's car.

"What's up with Danny?" Beth pulled into the street.

Alice tucked her hair behind her ears. "Trent stopped by yesterday."

"Oh." She paused. "Melba served him the papers?"

Alice nodded.

"How'd he take it?"

"Not well. Neither did Danny."

Beth's eyebrows shot up. "Danny was there?"

She nodded. "He saw it all." She sighed. "He doesn't understand. You know how kids are, always ready to forgive and forget. But it's not that easy."

"Have you tried?"

Alice tensed. "For 19 years. And until you've been knee deep in your husband's vomit or had loan sharks staking out your house, I'd suggest you keep your questions to yourself."

Beth frowned and turned her attention back to the road. Neither of them spoke for the rest of the drive. When they pulled into the church parking lot half an hour later, Alice wanted to storm down the street, as far away from Beth as possible. She probably would have if Gina, one of the Bible study girls, hadn't met them in the parking lot.

She ran to Alice and wrapped her in a hug, her thick, unruly hair smothering Alice and tickling her nose.

Alice wiggled free.

Pulling an arm's length away, Gina grabbed both of her hands. "It's so good to see you."

"You, too, Gina."

Beth started to unload boxes from the trunk and Alice put on her familiar plastic smile. "Let me help you."

Anything to avoid the 20 questions that were sure to come at any moment.

Beth raised an eyebrow and moved aside to allow Alice access to a basket of lotions. She picked one up, popped the lid, and inhaled the soft scent of lavender. She snapped it shut and offered Beth a smile, determined not to let their little squabble ruin her morning.

The three of them crossed the courtyard and carried their boxes into the Bible study room. Beth motioned for them to set everything on the counter, then shooed them away.

"Now go on. And if you see any of the other ladies out there, tell them to hold on a few minutes. I'll call you when I'm ready."

Alice and Gina exchanged glances then plodded back outside. They sat at a white table in the center of the courtyard.

"How've you been?" Gina asked. "Beth said you have an apartment in the Green Lake area."

Alice nodded. She tensed as she thought about Beth and her well-intended prayer requests. But then again, it had brought Danny home. Maybe in time, it'd do the same for Tim.

The rest of the ladies showed up and gathered around the plastic table, chatting about shoe sales and smoothie recipes. Apparently spinach was palatable when blended with kiwi.

"I can't wait to see what Beth has planned." A brunette Alice didn't recognize looked across the courtyard to the small metal door leading to the Bible study room. "Knowing her, we'll all leave with mascara streaking down our cheeks from bawling our eyes out."

Alice hoped not. Raccoon eyes weren't her thing.

"You got a lot to confess this week, Tessa?" Gina's eyes twinkled mischievously as she reached into her purse. She pulled out a tube of lipstick and applied a thick layer to her lips.

Beth poked her head out of the door and smiled. "All right, ladies, I'm ready."

They stood and made their way inside. The lights were dimmed and sweet smelling candles burned at various stations throughout the room. Praise music drifted from speakers on the counter.

Beth clasped her hands in front of her. "Instructions are provided at each station. And don't hurry. Use this time to connect with God."

Alice set her purse on the counter and walked over to a tall mirror. A verse was taped to the glass.

Jeremiah 31:3, "I have loved you with an everlasting love; I have drawn you with unfailing kindness."

Instructions were attached to the lace tablecloth. *Look at yourself in the mirror as you read the verse. Let God's love sweep over you. You are His child, created by His hand, created in love. You are His beloved, a precious treasure. He rejoices over you with singing. He will uphold you with His right hand.*

She closed her eyes and repeated the verse in her mind. The words penetrated her heart and settled deep in her soul.

She moved to the next station. Small wooden crosses lay in a basket lined with linen. A metal link of chains lay beside it next to pink

Post-it notes. A hammer rested on the chains and again, instructions were taped to table.

Jesus died to set us free from bondage. John 8:32 "Then you will know the truth and the truth will set you free." Ask God to show you what is holding you in bondage and keeping you from fully experiencing the victorious, abundant life of a believer saved by grace. Ask God to replace the lies that have invaded your mind with truth.

Thoughts swirled through her mind—of failure, old hurts, shattered dreams. Beneath them all, a glimmer of hope pressed forward as an old memory verse resurfaced. "I will go before you and will level the mountains; I will break down gates of bronze and cut through bars of iron" (Isaiah 45:2).

She closed her eyes. *Oh, Lord Jesus, I am so sorry. Instead of turning to You, I have forged my own way, pretending like I didn't hear Your voice. But I know Your voice. Oh, sweet Jesus, I know Your voice and I'm listening now.*

Alice moved to the next station. She gave a soft sob when she saw Beth on her knees, a towel folded by her side, a bowl of water in front of her.

Beth touched Alice's elbow and led her to a chair. Removing her shoes, Beth dipped Alice's feet into the water, running a soft rag over her skin. A Bible lay open to John 13 beside her. She began to read:

"It was just before the Passover Festival. Jesus knew that the hour had come for him to leave this world and go to the Father. Having loved his own who were in the world, he loved them to the end.

"The evening meal was in progress, and the devil had already prompted Judas, the son of Simon Iscariot, to betray Jesus. Jesus knew that the Father had put all things under his power, and that he had come from God and was returning to God; so he got up from the meal, took off his outer clothing, and wrapped a towel around his waist. After that, he poured water into a basin and began to wash his disciples' feet, drying them with the towel that was wrapped around him."

She closed the Bible and then looked Alice in the eye. "One by one, Jesus washed each of His disciples' feet. He scrubbed the dirt from Peter's toes, knowing that before the night was over, Peter would deny Him three times." She lifted Alice's foot and squeezed the washcloth over it. Sudsy drops caressed Alice's toes. "He kneeled in front of Thomas, already hearing his demand for proof after Christ's resurrection. Then came Judas."

A lump lodged in Alice's throat.

"Jesus took Judas's feet in His sinless hands, the bowl beneath turning a deep shade of brown as the filth dripped from them."

Alice closed her eyes as an image of her kneeling in front of Trent came to mind. *This hurts, Lord. This hurts so much.*

Memories, good and painful, surfaced: Trent sitting across from her in a restaurant, candlelight reflecting in his eyes. Of him slouched in his recliner, empty beer bottles at his feet, another in his hand. Of him running behind a young Danny who was just learning to ride his bike. And of him encasing her waist with his strong hands, leaning in close, and whispering lyrics of their favorite song in her ear, promising to love her forever.

As she'd promised him. Before the sickness of alcoholism grabbed hold of him.

"I have loved you with an everlasting love. I have drawn you with loving kindness." God's words poured over her.

"I will uphold you with my mighty right hand. Do not fear."

Grabbing her shoes, she ran out of the room, through the courtyard, and into the parking lot. Crumbling against the brick wall, she pulled her legs to her chest and buried her face in her knees.

CHAPTER 48

Trent turned on his side and pulled the pillow over his head. Ethan banged around in the kitchen getting ready for his weekly Pike Place worship service.

"I really think you should come."

Trent didn't respond. The refrigerator swooshed open followed by clattering as Ethan fished through the shelves. After a few more clanks and bangs, footsteps shuffled across the carpet. The recliner squeaked as Ethan plopped down across from him.

"Best way to crawl out of the mud is to help others. Nothing like seeing someone else passed out on a sheet of cardboard to keep a man sober."

Trent shoved the pillow aside and rolled over. He pushed himself to a sitting position. "I'm sober. What more do you want from me."

"You can't stay crashed on the couch forever."

Trent grabbed the remote and turned on the television. "I won't. I'll be at work come Monday."

"So that's your game plan, huh? You're going to go to work, come home, zone out to the television like a zombie until it's time to go to bed and do it all over again?"

Trent changed the channel.

Ethan stood with a huff. "If all you've got to live for is a nightly sitcom, your sobriety isn't going to last."

Trent's grip tightened around the remote. "I just need some space, that's all." A ludicrous statement, considering he was shacked out in Ethan's living room.

Ethan placed a hand on Trent's shoulder. "I understand how you're feeling. And I'll give you space. Just be careful how far you let yourself climb back into that pit, because once those negative thoughts start spiraling, it's near impossible to climb out."

Trent mumbled his assent and changed the channel again. Ethan was right, and in a week, or a month, or however long it took that jagged gash in his heart to heal, he'd listen. But right now he wanted to forget all about it. And if he couldn't lose himself in a bottle, the television was the next best thing.

"All right then." Ethan sighed. "I guess I better go." His footsteps retreated. "Don't hesitate to call."

"Don't worry, I won't do anything stupid."

An extended pause. "I'll see you in a few hours."

And then he left, leaving Trent to stare at the television screen and four blank walls.

Nothing was on. Nothing that could crowd out his thoughts and that hateful look Alice gave him when he'd shown up at her house. Her words mocked him, cutting deep. "It's over, Trent. I've got a new life now."

He tossed the remote onto the coffee table and stood. His muscles twitched as he paced the small apartment.

He glanced at his wallet sitting on the counter, his heart racing, hands clammy. His car keys lay a few inches away. Cash burned in his pocket, enough for a week's worth of drunken amnesia.

He squeezed his eyes shut and shook his head. *Don't do it. For once in your pathetic life, do the right thing.*

He marched into the kitchen, threw open the cupboards, and rummaged through cereal boxes and soup cans. He slammed the doors shut. Fresh coffee brewed in the pot. He poured himself a cup and crossed to the sliding glass door. Thick, gray clouds blanketed the sky, and laundry dangling from balcony railings flapped in the wind. He walked back to the coffee table where Ethan's journal lay tucked beneath a newspaper.

Nothing more than a collection of unanswered prayers. He grabbed it and flipped through the pages. Ethan waited five years for what? His wife wasn't coming back. Neither was Alice. And yet, each day the words beneath each entry were just as fervent as the day before.

What about now, five years later? Did Ethan still ask God to restore his marriage, or had he finally given up?

Trent turned to the last entry.

"Holy Father, Your tender mercy amazes me. Thank You for holding Trent up last night." Trent took in a quick breath. *"Thank You for bringing him here. I'm so glad I didn't take my life two years ago, when Tracy ended things for good, because I know, had I given in to the darkness, Trent wouldn't be here today. Help him get through this, Father. Give him something to live for."*

Trent closed the notebook and returned it to the table. A dull ache clogged his throat as he slid to his knees. "Oh Lord, what a mess I've made. I don't deserve Alice. I don't deserve to be a father. I'm sorry. So sorry. Please forgive me." As he pressed his forehead against tightly folded hands, he once again thought of Reagan.

Reagan needed him to stay sober. Kenneth needed him to stay sober. All of them down at Pike Street needed to see the top of the ladder. They needed to see someone who had made it to the other side.

"Help me, Lord. Help me stand up under this pain." He rose on shaky legs and plodded into the kitchen where the separation documents lay in a crumpled wad on the counter. He smoothed the sheets flat with a shaky hand.

After 19 years, it was over. And even though it didn't feel like it right now, God would carry him through this.

He remembered Ethan's words. *"There's always hope, man. In Christ, there's always hope. But you got to want it. You got to fight for it."*

He pressed his hands on the counter and squeezed his eyes shut. Was he a loser or a fighter?

Clenching his jaw, he stormed out, down the hall and stairwell and to his car. Revving his engine, he peeled away from the curb and sped toward the diner.

If that snake was there . . . Then what? Gripping the steering wheel with one hand, he slammed his other fist against it. He would not allow that sleaze to steal his wife.

Alice poured water into the coffee maker, pressed the brew button, and set the empty carafe on the burner. She swiped the sweat from her brow with the back of her hand and slumped against the counter. It'd been a crazy-busy morning, more than usual. But the tips were good. She'd made more in her first three hours than she normally made all day. And luckily, there'd been no sign of Austin. Hopefully that meant she was rid of him for good.

The side door opened, and Melba walked in, smelling like smoke. "You want to take your break now?"

Alice glanced through the dining room toward the windows and shivered, hugging herself. "I'm good."

"Mr. Curly still got you worried?"

"A little."

"Can't say that I blame you. Seems Mr. Wilson scared him off well enough, though."

Alice smiled at the memory of her red-faced boss, pointing to the door. "That he did."

"Well, least have a donut and rest your feet for a minute."

"I'll do that." She grabbed a glass of water then headed toward the break room, for a few moments of quiet. To think. And pray. Halfway there, her phone rang, and she glanced at the screen. A local number, but she didn't recognize it.

Her pulse increased. "Hello?"

"Mrs. Goddard?"

She swallowed. "Yes?"

"This is Detective Johnson. You'll be happy to know we've got your stalker in custody."

The air expelled from her lungs. "But how? I don't understand."

"Turns out you're not this guy's only victim. His name's Seth Arnold, and he's got a record. And a house full of . . . trophies."

She shivered. "You mean?"

"We're still investigating, but there's no doubt the guy's a predator."

"OK. Thank you. Thank you, Officer."

And to think, she'd been in his truck. Twice. She shivered and ran her hands along her goose-pimpled arms.

Trent's footsteps echoed, his pulse pounding against his eardrums as he crossed the lot. Hands fisted, his vision narrowed until everything in his peripheral turned a hazy gray.

He threw open the diner door and searched the area, the muscles in his hands and arms twitching. Alice turned to face him, wide-eyed.

Customers swiveled in their seats.

He crossed the dining room and stopped less than a foot in front of Alice.

She stepped back until she was pressed against the edge an empty table. "What are you doing here?"

"I can't let you go, Alice. I can't."

"You're making a scene." She scowled.

"I don't care. All I care about is you. I'm not letting you go. I'll do whatever it takes to prove that to you."

"Come outside and we'll talk."

Someone coughed and chair legs screeched against the floor.

Lord, please give me the words. Please help her give me one more chance. He followed Alice through the diner and out onto the sidewalk. The door closed behind him, and Alice whirled around. She crossed her arms and stared at him, her eyes searching his.

"Please. Hear me out." A tight band constricted around his chest, making it hard to breath. *Sweet Alice.* Man, he loved her. "I'm sorry. I'm so very sorry."

"That's supposed to suddenly make everything better?"

"No. Honestly, I don't know how to fix this, but I want to try."

"I don't know if I can."

"In Christ, there's always hope. You know that. He'll get us through this, if we'll just lean hard on Him." He swallowed. "I've changed. I'm sober, for good. I'm going to meetings. Let me show you. Give me another chance."

He reached for her hand and tugged her close. She stiffened and trembled slightly. "Nineteen years, Alice. Don't throw it all away without giving us one more chance." He lowered his mouth to her ear. "I love you so much it hurts. Always have." In a hushed tone, he started to sing. "Darling, if I were to lose you, you know I'd simply die."

He moved his hand to the small of her back, pressing her soft frame against his. His lips brushed her neck, and he inhaled the sweet vanilla of her shampoo. Pulling away, he looked into her eyes, brimming with tears. "What do you say? Can we give it another shot?"

A glimmer of hesitation flicked across her face.

"No more drinking." Still holding his hand to her back, he kissed her cheek.

She wiggled away. "And the gambling?"

"No more." He tried to draw her close again, but she resisted.

"And you'll get help."

"Absolutely. I'll do whatever it takes. Anything not to lose you." He held his breath, shooting up a silent, fervent prayer. Silence stretched between them. "So what do you say, my love? Will you go out with me this Friday?"

"We've got a long way to go, Trent."

"I know. We'll start slow. Like we're dating."

"We don't need steak dinners. We need counseling."

"I know. You're right. How about we do both?" He grabbed her hand, and, twining his fingers through hers, pulled it to his chest. "I promise to always make you my one and only, until the day I die. I will fight for your love, for our marriage, for our family, for as long as it takes." He searched her eyes, grabbing on to the love, the hope, he saw radiating from them. "What do you say? Will you go out with me this Friday?"

She laughed, and a tear slid down her cheek.

He wiped it away and then ran his thumb along her bottom lip. "Forever and a day, remember?"

She nodded as more tears fell. "I do remember." She studied his face, searched his eyes. "I missed you."

He threw his head back and laughed. "I missed you, too. I know I've told you a hundred times how much I love you. Now I'm going to prove it." Wrapping his arms around her, he drew her close in a breathless kiss.

New Hope® Publishers is a division of WMU®, an international organization that challenges Christian believers to understand and be radically involved in God's mission. For more information about WMU, go to wmu.com. More information about New Hope books may be found at NewHopePublishers.com. New Hope books may be purchased at your local bookstore.

Use the QR reader on your
smartphone to visit us online at
NewHopePublishers.com

If you've been blessed by this book, we would like to hear your story. The publisher and author welcome your comments and suggestions at: newhopereader@wmu.org.

Stories that inspire outreach!

Author Jennifer Slattery's collection of fiction novels include relevant plot lines and relatable characters that inspire readers to look for ways God turns great tragedies and failures into beautiful acts of love and grace. Perfect for book clubs, women's ministry groups, or even small groups, readers will not only be entertained by a moving story but transformed and challenged to be on mission with God!

 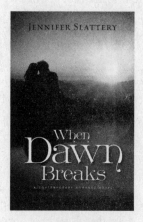 

Beyond I Do
JENNIFER SLATTERY
ISBN-13: 978-1-59669-417-0
$15.99

When Dawn Breaks
JENNIFER SLATTERY
ISBN-13: 978-1-59669-423-1
$15.99

Intertwined
JENNIFER SLATTERY
ISBN-13: 978-1-59669-443-9
$15.99

For information about our books and authors, visit NewHopePublishers.com. Experience sample chapters, author videos, interviews, and more!